MW00979947

HEMP

Nini Martino and Zack DiLiberto

iUniverse, Inc.
Bloomington

HEMP

Copyright © 2009 by Nini Martino and Zack DiLiberto

All rights reserved. No part of this book may be used or reproduced by any means, graphic, electronic, or mechanical, including photocopying, recording, taping or by any information storage retrieval system without the written permission of the publisher except in the case of brief quotations embodied in critical articles and reviews.

Certain characters in this work are historical figures, and certain events portrayed did take place. However, this is a work of fiction. All of the other characters, names, and events as well as all places, incidents, organizations, and dialogue in this novel are either the products of the author's imagination or are used fictitiously.If there are only a few historical figures or actual events in the novel, the disclaimer could name them: For example: "Edwin Stanton and Salmon Chase are historical figures..." or "The King and Queen of Burma were actually exiled by the British in 1885." The rest of the disclaimer would follow:However, this is a work of fiction. All of the other characters, names, and events as well as all places, incidents, organizations, and dialogue in this novel are either are the products of the author's imagination or are used fictitiously.

iUniverse books may be ordered through booksellers or by contacting:

iUniverse
1663 Liberty Drive
Bloomington, IN 47403
www.iuniverse.com
1-800-Authors (1-800-288-4677)

Because of the dynamic nature of the Internet, any Web addresses or links contained in this book may have changed since publication and may no longer be valid. The views expressed in this work are solely those of the author and do not necessarily reflect the views of the publisher, and the publisher hereby disclaims any responsibility for them.

Any people depicted in stock imagery provided by Thinkstock are models, and such images are being used for illustrative purposes only. Certain stock imagery © Thinkstock

ISBN: 978-1-4502-7360-2 (sc)
ISBN: 978-1-4502-7361-9 (ebook)

Printed in the United States of America

iUniverse rev. date: 1/7/2011

ACKNOWLEDGMENTS:

Many thanks to Chris Conrad, whose encyclopedic work, "Hemp, Lifeline to the Future," (Creative Xpressions Publications, Los Angeles, CA, 1994), first opened our eyes to the wonders of hemp and the shocking injustice of its prohibition.

Much love and gratitude also to our activist friends from coast to coast who encouraged and directed us in the writing of "The Hemp-man's Daughter," the screenplay on which this book is based.

1
The Hemp-Man's Daughter

Richmond, Virginia, Autumn, 1931

It was the eve of Kate Burnett's twenty-fifth birthday, and the last place she wanted to spend it was Temperance Hall. Kate was not a teetotaler, nor was she given to pretense. Here she was, nevertheless, at her daddy's request, inching her way through a horde of Prohibitionists; nodding and smiling sweetly to everyone who caught her eye, and feeling like a hypocrite.

"Stunning!" "Look at her!" "Prettier than her mama, I declare!" The women whispered, the men just gawked, as Miss Burnett came into view.

Although she was modestly dressed – skirted to her ankles, buttoned to her neck, and unadorned with makeup, it was difficult for Kate to pass unnoticed. Not only was she a classic beauty, with chiseled features, lush lips, golden hair, and blue eyes big as saucers, at a willowy seventy inches, she stood taller than the average man and a head above the women.

The rap of a gavel grew louder, and finally begat silence, as Kate took the seat next to her father, Noble Burnett. She answered his 'what took you so long?' look with a whispered, "Sorry, the parkin' lot was packed," and they turned their attention to the podium, where Noble's lady friend, June Stevens, was poised to speak.

"Thank you, ladies and gentlemen," June addressed the audience in a well-seasoned manner that befitted and accentuated her genteel appearance. "Thank you, and welcome to this very special event. My name is June Stevens – also known, I hear, as 'The Widow' Stevens." She paused and smiled, brow raised toward the titter from her cronies… "And I am treasurer of the Temperance League of Richmond. On behalf of the League, it is my utmost pleasure to introduce this evenin's speaker. Please join me in givin' a warm Southern welcome to the esteemed U.S. Commissioner of Alcohol Prohibition, noted lecturer, and advocate of temperance causes, Mister Harry J. Anslinger."

Anslinger, a medium-sized, balding, but otherwise non-descript man of thirty-nine, entered the hall from an anteroom, and took the podium to brisk applause. On his heels came underlings, federal agents Morse and Ryan, both in their late twenties, and outstanding if only for the differences in their appearance. Morse was tall, dark, 'pretty-boy' handsome, and perfectly groomed; Ryan, nicknamed "Wreck" by his fellows, was nearly a foot shorter than his partner, with messy, blonde hair, and an uncomely, impish face. The agents took "reserved" seats in the front row of the audience. Anslinger and June shook hands enthusiastically before she, too, hurried to her seat.

Acknowledging the applause for but a moment, Anslinger gestured for quiet. The audience complied, and he commenced to speak, thereby transforming his physical form, and, indeed, his entire persona, from the ordinary to the unforgettable. His face ablaze with passion, his eyes lit up like meteors darting about the room, Anslinger spoke in a deep, rich, booming baritone which carried the hundred-foot hall without a microphone. His style was unabashedly melodramatic, but his voice was operatic in quality, and his presentation was pithy and compelling. The audience was mesmerized!

"My Fellow Christians," he began, bowing deferentially to all, "time is of the essence, so I will be brief, and to the point. I bring you dire news from our nation's capital. The forces of corruption who would release the scourge of alcohol once again on our homes and streets are set to strike. These advocates of evil call themselves 'anti-Prohibitionists.' But make no mistake, Friends, what they seek is 'anti-decent,' 'anti-moral,' 'anti-law and order.' As God-fearing Christians and citizens of conscience, we are 'morally bound' to do whatever is necessary to stop them!"

The audience erupted into another round of applause. Noble joined in; but Kate rolled her eyes incredulously and fidgeted in her seat. He shot her a sideward glance; she returned her inimitable pout.

The whole idea of Prohibition did not sit well with Miss Burnett. To her mind, abstinence 'by choice' was one thing, abstinence 'by law' quite another. She deemed the latter to be un-American; and she eagerly anticipated the repeal of Prohibition, a repeal which the newspapers of the day, whether for or against, were calling "inevitable."

Anslinger defamed the anti-Prohibitionists, unremittingly, for another thirty minutes. At the same time, he assured his listeners that the situation, though dire, was not hopeless. All across the country, he said, members of the Temperance League and other "soldiers of righteousness" were "turning the tide of evil." He urged his audience to join in the crusade; to write to their newspapers, contact their congressmen, rouse their friends and families, and take to the streets in protest of the dreaded repeal.

"Balderdash!" Kate muttered under her breath, and tuned him out early on. She had little patience for the 'holier-than-thou.' Besides, she had more pleasant things to think about.

She lowered her eyes, slouched down in her seat, and reminisced about the night before – the silent yearnings, the tender looks that she and her new beau, Will Fairfield, had exchanged. Kate Burnett was falling in love, madly, irresistibly, in love, for the first time. And Will was falling for her. He had told her so on that last date. Her face flushed and her heart beat loudly as she recalled their steamy, good-night kisses; his words, the sweetest she had ever heard, turning over and over again in her mind:

"Delectable! ...Incredible! ...The most beautiful, lovable creature on earth, and she seems to be mine for the asking! I'm asking, Kate – sweet Kate, and I won't let you go!"

When Anslinger appeared to be winding down – not a moment too soon for Kate, she leaned toward her father's ear and spoke low, "I'll get the car; meet you out front."

Noble turned to her with a frown. "Aren't you going to say hello to June?" he whispered anxiously.

"You give her a hug for me, Daddy," Kate whispered back, "I'm afraid she'll ask how I liked her speaker!" With that, Kate made a dash for the exit; tailed, of course, by a crowd of curious eyes.

She pulled up in front of the building in her 1929 Model T Ford a few minutes later. Unhappily, she noted that federal agents Morse and Ryan were parked in the car ahead of her, apparently waiting for their boss. Kate's first thought was to move, to avoid further contact with Anslinger. But it was too late. The Temperance Leaguers, en masse, were already exiting the hall; and from her perch, Kate could see Anslinger walking full speed in the middle of the throng, with June Stevens and her father on either side of him!

As luck would have it, however, two ambitious, young reporters, toting cameras and notepads, appeared out of nowhere and sidetracked the speaker.

"Commissioner! Mr. Anslinger!" one of them shouted, taking the lead, holding out his press badge. "Remember us? Washington Times? Can we have a word, please? And a photo?"

Morse and Ryan were out of their car and ready to intervene in a flash. But Anslinger waved them off. He turned to the reporters, and kidded with them:

"I don't know, boys. My wife didn't like the photo you took of me last time; said it didn't do me justice!"

"You want the interview," he kept it up, ignoring the obvious discomfort of 'the boys,' "you gotta make me prettier! What do you say?"

The reporters didn't know what to say. They just smiled nervously, looking to each other for clues. Finally, the lead reporter blurted out, "Yes, Sir," and the other followed suit. Anslinger had a good laugh; but took their questions quite seriously.

Kate and Noble escorted June back to the hall during the interview. Upon returning to their car, they saw Anslinger and company piling into theirs, and they overheard the last of the questions and answers:

"One more 'quickie,' if you please, Sir," begged the reporter, holding the car door for the interviewee.

Anslinger took the seat next to his driver. "Shoot!" he said shortly, "and hurry it up!"

The reporter drew a deep breath, and was out with it: "Is it your position, 'for the record,' Mr. Commissioner, that the anti-Prohibitionists are *evil*?"

Anslinger stared down at him pensively for a moment. "They are the *servants of evil*," he stated with conviction. "You can quote me on that!"

"Servants of evil, indeed!" Kate grumbled, slamming her car door shut. "Who is he to judge?"

Noble remained silent and glum-faced while Kate started the car and took to the long, winding road which led to Katelyn Farm, their countryside home. It was a lovely Fall evening – mild and dry. They had just missed sunset, but the sky before them was billowing with clouds, all lit to glorious hues. The glow of twilight was bliss for Kate; it soothed her unfailingly, and heightened her sense of God's presence. She glanced over at Noble every minute or so, humming, smiling brightly, hoping he'd finally give in and smile back. When he didn't, she resorted to flattery.

Not that Kate thought her father was vain; she knew him as anything but. The slightest reference to his good looks, depending on who'd made mention, had always set him to laughing or blushing, if not escaping the scene.

"Did I tell you earlier how handsome you look in that dress shirt, Daddy?" she opened. Noble, half-smiling, caught her eye, and raised his hand to say "enough." But Kate could not resist:

"Elegantly handsome, I dare say! I noticed that the 'Widow Stevens' noticed too... Her eyes were all over you on our walk back to the hall... And did I tell you what Lucy Stevens told me her mother told her? The last time the subject of your handsomeness came up? Which it does quite often?" Kate rambled on, trying not to giggle, over Noble's repeated gestures to stop. "June said that mama was a very pretty woman, but that, apart from my height – which undoubtedly came from mama's side, she thinks that I inherited my finer features from you! She said that we have the same face, you and I; except, of course, that yours is older, and more masculine, and weathered from the sun... Oh, and she also told Lucy that she prefers the 'ruggedness' of your face to mine! I declare! June's words, exactly, accordin' to Lucy!"

Now she had Noble laughing, despite himself, and shaking his head in disbelief.

Kate Burnett adored her father. She thought of him as the kindest, most principled man on God's earth. She liked to quote her late mother as saying that Noble was "aptly named," "moral excellence personified," "the 'noblest' of men." To Kate's mind, Noble was also the humblest of men. Indeed, the trait Kate most appreciated in her father was his 'down-to-earth-ness.' His doting apprentice since childhood, and, of late, his full partner in their hemp farm, Kate had long assumed Noble's attunement to nature, and his deep, abiding love for their land and their crop.

On the other hand, she often differed with her father, quite openly, on political issues. She admired Noble's patriotism, and aspired to the same, but found him far too trusting of the powers that be, both local and national. He almost always, she almost never, gave a politician the benefit of the doubt; and in her opinion, those nods to local authorities had cost them dearly, with respect to their hemp business, in recent years.

A dark night fell about half-way into the hour-long ride back to their farm. Noble leaned over and asked Kate how she was doing, if she would like to trade places.

Actually, Kate was the more experienced driver-mechanic of the two. She'd been behind the wheel and under the hood of a tractor since the family purchased their first 'Model F' when she was twelve. Later, she went to college in Richmond for three years, and at the outset, her daddy bought her a new Model T of her own. No one, including Noble, knew the road between Richmond and their farmlands better than Kate did. Apart from that, she loved to drive. It made her feel like the thoroughly modern woman that she was!

"I'm doin' just fine, Daddy," she assured him, "thank you for askin'." Since Noble seemed willing to converse again, however, she took the opportunity to opine on the evening's events.

"Sorry to say, Daddy," she spoke in earnest, "but I'm not goin' to any more of those meetin's. I don't like hypocrites. And I don't want to be one."

Noble pondered her words at length.

"You think all those people are hypocrites?" he finally responded, pointing a thumb toward the site they'd left behind.

"Course not! You know I love the Stevens, and admire their work... I was referrin' to Mr. Anslinger."

"He seemed sincere enough to me."

7

"The man's a clever speaker," Kate returned, "I'll give him that. But he wins people over by frightenin' them and distortin' the truth. I don't like that. And I don't trust him. And..."

"Hold on a minute, Kate," Noble interrupted. "While you were daydreamin' back in that hall, I was actually listenin' to Mr. Anslinger. And I think you've got him all wrong. Man's tryin' to fix the problem at hand, Kate. I support him in that. Alcohol **is** a scourge – weakens people, body and soul. We don't need it. Better off without it... tobacco too, for that matter."

"*You've* got him wrong, Daddy – he *is* a hypocrite! The scourges he talks about depend on who he's talkin' to... Did you know he favors prohibitin' tobacco, federally, along with alcohol?"

Noble frowned, and shook his head "no."

"Certainly not!" Kate said assertively. "You don't mention *that* in the heart of Tobacco Land, even in Temperance Hall! It's just not fair, Daddy, to force your ways on people. If you think that alcohol and tobacco are evil, then by all means refrain from consumin' them. But who are you, or Mr. Anslinger, to decide for your neighbor? To make your preference his law? Prohibition is tyranny. That's why it isn't workin'. It's goin' to be repealed – everybody says so. And I, for one, will welcome that repeal with open arms!"

"All right, Kate," Noble nearly shouted. "I see your mind's made up. That's fine!" He lowered his tone. "I promise not to ask you to any more meetin's... after Saturday."

"Oh, no!" Kate moaned. "Tell me that Washington do is not this Saturday!"

"I'm afraid it is. We'll have a fine time, though. We're stayin' at your brother's instead of the hotel. Liddy said the baby is excited to see us."

"And I'm excited to see him – them," Kate said in truth. "But it slipped my mind, and Will and I were plannin' to spend the weekend in the country."

"Invite Will up to Washington. Bobby and Liddy can't wait to meet him; and they've got plenty of room."

Kate perked up. "Maybe I will, but only after that luncheon. I hate those fund-raisers, Daddy," she whined, "Can't I be excused?"

"Not this time, Kate. I paid a pretty penny for those tickets. Besides, we promised June… And Lucy's comin' – she's expectin' you."

"I suppose." Kate sighed. "And I suppose Mr. 'Mud'-slinger will be there as well!"

Noble smiled at her play on words, but avoided the question.

"Daddy?" she pressed him.

"Well, eh, yes, of course, he'll be there," Noble answered, and let out a chuckle.

"And why, pray tell, is that so funny?"

"Eh… well… it seems…" Noble stuttered, between chuckles, "Anslinger and the missus will be sittin' at our table!"

"No!" Kate shrieked dramatically, and then shared in the laughter.

Kate marked the next day as her happiest ever. She detailed it in a journal she had reserved for special occasions, a book which she treasured all the more as it was the last gift she had received from her late mother.

Only the high-points of her life – graduating from college, most notably, had been recorded in this journal during the pre-Will years; but the book was filling up rapidly – she could hardly keep pace with the high-points! – since she fell in love. Her unusually wordy, two-page entry, entitled, "My Cup Runneth Over," dated September 29, 1931, read:

Dear Diary, Oh, what a day! I turned twenty-five, and I love my life! I was up at first glimmer, and woke Daddy. We took our coffee outdoors, and watched in awe as the sun lit up the fields. Our crop is thriving – soaring, must have grown six inches while we slept!

We agreed to skip breakfast, save our appetite for brunch – wisely. Aunt Nettie spoiled me, as always, with an array of my favorites: roasted chicken, sweet peas, cornbread, and upside-down cake – scrumptious! June, Lucy and Aunt Beth came for the feast, bearing lovely presents – apparel and adornments. (I had intended to ask them to give to the poor instead, but daddy said it was a bad idea – "presumptuous, at best!") Both he and Will, however, cheerfully complied with my request. It made me feel better about having so much, while all around me there is hunger and misery.

Will arrived promptly at six, with a gift of home-grown roses from his greenhouse in Richmond – priceless! He looked incredibly handsome, in a suit and tie, and a crisp, white shirt that brought out the honey of his skin. He chatted with Daddy for a while, and then whisked me away to Fairfield Plantation, in his open-aired vehicle – or rather, I whisked him, taking the wheel at his suggestion. Such fun!

We dined alone, (except for the attendants), on the veranda of the mansion. The meal was delicious, but we barely ate or spoke, content to just gaze dreamily into each other's eyes. 'I think we're love-sick,' I proposed, to his amusement. Snuggling on a glider at night fall, we sipped coffee and cordials, and kissed and 'sweet-talked.' He must have said, 'I love you, Kate,' a thousand times – I happily lost count! I couldn't say it back at first somehow. The kisses and drink eventually went to my head. All I could think about by then was making love to him! He knew it, and without a doubt was tempted, but failed to take advantage, perfect gentleman that he is. 'That was one drink too many, Miss Temperance League!' he teased, and poured me another coffee, and took me home.

We sat in the convertible in front of the house, looking to the stars, listening to the night-noise; the dogs lying peacefully alongside. Suddenly, a shooting star arched across the sky, and another shot at once from the opposite direction; and to our utter amazement, their arches intertwined as they fell! And then they were gone. We were moved to tears – it was as if the Heavens had arranged the show just for us! Will held me close, and prayed out loud that our love would last forever.

'And I do love you, Will,' I finally owned, in whispers, against his chest. 'I love you so much, I was afraid to say it.' 'It was there in your kiss all along,' he replied. 'I'm the luckiest man in the world.'

Thank you, Mama, for this wonderful journal,
I know you're smiling down on me,
Goodnight.

Will returned to Katelyn Farm at daybreak the following morning. Kate and her two black labs were waiting for him on the pillared porch of the Burnett's plantation-style manor. They rushed to welcome him, dogs barking and jumping excitedly, as he pulled up close on the circular drive. He could barely exit the car, the lively hounds knocking him off balance, as they leapt in and out of the open-aired buggy.

"Hello, boys! …Easy does it! …Good boys!" he greeted them first, crouching down to their level, petting them vigorously, finally closing the car door behind him. "Yes, yes, I like you too. And you, too… good ol' boys."

Kate admired him from on high, her heart racing. She loved the looks of him, the intensity of his face, the way his deep set eyes, wide-set jaw, and straight, white teeth reflected the strength of his character, and the way his features contrasted with hers – his darkness with her fairness, his muscularity with her slenderness. She delighted in the fact that he was ten years her senior – a decade more experienced and worldly her Will! And she thought it a stroke of incredible luck that he was also two inches taller!

Will glanced up at her, caught her gawking, and flashed her a self-satisfied grin.

She bent down behind him, nuzzled his neck and shoulders. "Good mornin', Will Fairfield," she spoke softly in his ear, "I'm so happy you're here – as you've noticed! I fixed your coffee; it's in the kitchen."

Will raised himself up at once, and her, looking her over from head to toe. She was decked out in riding boots and britches – the first he'd seen her in pants, and a cropped, form-fitting jacket. Her lush, golden locks were half-tucked under a jockey's cap, the rest had sprung, and dangled unevenly about her adorable face. It was his turn to gawk.

"Good mornin', Will," she repeated, with a giggle.

"Good mornin', Katelyn," he finally came around. "May I call you Katelyn?"

"No, you may not! The name's 'Kate!'" she answered gaily, "But you may kiss me!"

She puckered her lavish lips toward his, eyes closed. Will kissed her, with relish, and let out a sigh.

"It's hard to believe how gorgeous you are so early in the mornin'!" he remarked. "And so cheerful," he added drolly, "it's a wonder anyone likes you!"

Kate laughed out loud – a deep, belly laugh, that had already become his favorite sound. It echoed again and again, as they walked, hand in hand, hounds trailing, to the kitchen to fetch the coffee, and to the barn to fetch her motorized carriage.

Will had come at her request for a tour of Katelyn Farm and paper mill. Although Fairfield Plantation, his family's countryside home, was situated, along with Katelyn, and several other hemp farms, in a county named Fairfield, after his great-grandfather, Will's knowledge of hemp was minimal. Kate was bent on fixing that. She wanted him to know every aspect of her crop – the wonders of it, the prevailing difficulties of growing and manufacturing its products. She wanted to be able to 'talk hemp' with Will, to get his input on major decisions; and, above all now, in the height of the Great Depression, she hoped to take advantage of his considerable influence as well.

Will was trained as a lawyer, but he worked, in-house, for his family's firm, Fairfield Tobacco. The Fairfields had been growing tobacco, initially in Virginia, and later also in Kentucky and the Carolinas, since the birth of the nation. Their company, headquartered in Richmond, was huge, its sales and distribution extending across the continent, and recently, beyond, into Europe. Moreover, owing a great deal to Fairfield's pacts with its competitors, tobacco had become 'king' in many regions of the South. Throughout the rural counties of Virginia, for instance, local politicians and businessmen of the day were either pro-tobacco, or they were out of favor.

First on Will's tour was a visit to the fodder plots, for an up-close view of a freshly sprouted hemp crop. He was awed by the sheer multitude of tiny, shield-like leaves, still shimmering with morning dew, and reaching for the sky. These baby greens, he now understood, were the stuff of the fragrant, verdant fields that had graced the distant landscapes of his boyhood.

As he and Kate returned to the main fields, she explained the whys and wherefores of sowing the various grades of hemp. Fiber-grade plants, like those towering before them, were grown close together, she said, to increase the length of their stalks. The all-important stalks contained the raw materials from which hemp rope, and paper, and such were manufactured. She noted that medicinal hemp – 'cannabis' – was grown for its leaves and flowers. And so those plants were sown far apart, to promote their bushiness.

Will asked if the Burnetts had ever grown medicinal hemp.

"Not for sale," she replied. "Not much money in it. But we've always kept a bush or two in the yard for medicinal purposes." She gestured toward the bushes behind the barn... "Didn't you?"

"I guess..." he responded, with a shrug. "I remember one of our nannies fixin' us a 'tea' when we were ailin'. 'Chamba,' she called it; sip or two cured all sorts of ills."

"That's it!" Kate said excitedly. "Cannabis! Aunt Nettie's cure-all for aches and pains; Doc Morgan's too. Put me to sleep, every time; woke up feelin' like new!"

The couple spent the early hours in the surrey, skirting the central fields of the farm's vast acreage, and on foot, taking in the sensory delights of the soon to be harvested crop. The weather – Indian-summer warmth, and a gentle breeze – remained idyllic throughout. Later, they rode horseback into the woodlands of the property, where Kate led him straightaway to her 'favorite place in the world,' a sprawling wild-flower meadow, set beneath the slopes of a hilly grove, and flanking a small – single acre, but deep, and lovely, spring-fed lake.

Will's eyes went misty as he gazed across the scene. The trees, against the blue horizon, were painted in full autumn color. As were the wildflowers – deep yellow stretches of black-eyed-susan, contrasting patches of white, daisy fleabane, and purplish-blue aster; the late morning sun emitting a golden glow over all. The intensity of its hues and abundance of birds and butterflies gave the place a surreal atmosphere; but even more stirring than its otherworldly beauty was a deep, abiding spiritual presence, that seemed to emanate from the earth itself. He turned to Kate:

"No wonder you're enamored with this place, Darlin'! … Talk about heaven?!" He tilted his head toward the hills, "You can almost hear the angels sing!"

Kate's face beamed. His reaction was precisely what she had hoped for. They dismounted, and led the horses to the water, Will carrying on, to her delight:

"And wouldn't that be the perfect spot – there, between the granddaddy oaks," he pointed to the hilltop before them, "to add another homestead? A little 'love nest,' perched above the meadow and the lake?"

"That's been my dream, Will, for years!" she exclaimed. "Exactly the way you pictured it!" She showered him with kisses, but backed away abruptly. Hands on her hips, head cocked, she spoke to him with a smile in her voice:

"Tell the truth now, Will Fairfield! My daddy told you 'bout my 'dream-house' on the hill; didn't he?"

"Not at all," Will kidded, "I read your mind!"

As they were about to re-mount, and take leave of 'little Eden,' Will had second thoughts.

"I *must* try the waters!" he announced shockingly. "That is, if you don't mind, Darlin'."

"My favorite place is yours," she happily replied. "And I shall join you," she added shockingly, "if you promise not to peek!"

"Promise!"

He stripped down naked, she to her under-garments, and they tiptoed – Will first, into the chilly, crystal-clear waters. Howling at the cold, giggling at their audaciousness, they swam and played, and briefly kissed; Will doing his best to keep his promise.

She, on the other hand, got a good look at his 'Greek-god' stature, on the way in and out, and made up her mind – twice, that she would, indeed, make love to this man, and soon!

Returning to the plough-lands at morning's end, the drippy twosome caught up with Joe Mays, the Burnett's foreman, whom Will had yet to meet. Joe, a strapping, six-foot, chocolate-skinned man of forty-three, was husband to Antoinette Mays, the Burnett's housekeeper, referred to affectionately by Kate as 'Aunt Nettie.'

Will and Joe took an instant liking to each other. Will had already met Nettie, and sampled her cooking. He told Joe, half-jokingly, that he would pay Nettie "good money" to come to Richmond on her day off and teach his housekeeper, Belle, how to cook. Will said that he, personally, would chauffer Nettie to and from.

Joe laughed it off, insisting that Nettie kept copies of her recipes on hand, solely for the purpose of sharing them.

"Just ask her, Mista Will. She won't say no," Joe promised. "And if Belle can read, she can read those recipes. Yes, Sir! My Nettie writes as good as she cooks!"

Joe offered to take Will through the paper mill for Kate. He knew the processes and machinery as well as she did. Having seen her burst into tears of late, at the mere mention of the mill, he also wanted to spare her having to discuss the mill's closure, and the lack of plans to reopen it any time soon.

With a nod from Will, Kate accepted Joe's offer. She urged the men not to dawdle, though, reminding Joe that Mike Anderson, the wholesaler, was coming for lunch at one o'clock, and that Mike was bringing good news. She wanted both Joe and Will to hear it first hand.

Kate returned to the house to help Nettie with preparations. The women greeted each other with their routine morning ritual – a lengthy hug, followed by a once-over to see how the other was doing, and then a short hug. They read each other well.

"You're lookin' mighty happy, Missy Kate, pleased to say," Nettie noted.

"Will's takin' an interest in the farm, Aunt Net," Kate explained, with a roll of her eyes and an exaggerated sigh of relief.

The two giggled, and chatted, and praised the Lord for their blessings as they chopped, and simmered, and stirred, and set a fine table.

Although Nettie had yet to turn forty, those who were close to her, regardless of age, revered her as an elder. They took their problems to Nettie, and found solutions. Nettie didn't say much; she mostly listened, and prayed for guidance. When her prayers were answered – usually within a day or two, she redefined the problem as the first step toward resolving it; and the rest came easy. It was her gift.

Nettie's appearance was also remarkable. She was a 'fine-looking' woman by most estimates, though curiously so. Her skin was black as night, and her hair was tightly coiled, but the rest of her features looked more Indian than Negroid. Her face was rounder and flatter, her nostrils less flared, her eyes more slanted than most Negroes. She was eye-catchingly slender and sinewy compared to her counterparts, as well, with a long, graceful neck, a proud stance, and an easy gait that gave her an air of serenity.

Her manner of dress, given her gender, age and race, was likewise unusual. She wore trousers to work on a regular basis. They were more suitable, and modest, she said, for the routine "rough and tumblin'" she did, both indoors and out. For fieldwork, she wore a smock-frock over the pants, for cooking, a chef's coat, for everything else, a bright-colored cotton blouse, and over that, a white, figure-eight-shaped apron, which featured a convenient pouch-pocket. The overall look was quite feminine, actually, as the apron and matching skull-cap had a ruffled border.

Mike arrived promptly for lunch, and Will shortly afterward. Kate sensed a tension between the two from the start. It worried her. She liked Mike, valued him as a friend, and as a business associate. She suspected that Mike was 'sweet' on her, because Noble had repeatedly said that it was so – "plain as day!" as Noble termed it.

Kate, however, was not sweet on Mike. She thought he was attractive, in a boyish sort of way. He had a pleasant personality, and a good head on his shoulders, but he lacked the charm and wit and sophistication that appealed to her. Beyond that, he was too fair, too lean, too short, *and* he hardly ever made her laugh.

Nettie prepared her 'famous' chicken gumbo for the main course. The recipe had been passed down, orally, from slave ancestors in New Orleans, and was finally set to paper by Nettie's mother, at the turn of the century. It had become 'famous,' Nettie advised the guests, with a wink to Kate, for putting the folks who ate it in a good mood. In keeping with the story, Will and Mike buddied-up to sing Nettie's praises in unison.

"Simply out of this world," voiced one. "Indescribably delicious!" agreed the other.

The cook was pleased, and ever so grateful. Even the weather had obliged her. She was able to serve the meal on the back terrace, overlooking the Burnetts' luxuriant crop. "Glorious day – praise the Lord!" she repeated, as she presented each course. And with her dessert, a sweet-custard pastry, which set the diners to ooh-ing and ah-ing, came thrilling news of the hemp-mobile! She and Joe sat in.

"The rumors I told you about Henry Ford, and his secret plans to 'grow' a car, are true, folks," Mike Anderson announced with gusto. "Hard to believe, I know," he made eye contact with his listeners, "but true. I have it from two dependable sources, one in Nebraska, the other in Michigan, where Ford's secret plants are located."

"I must've missed somethin'…" Will interrupted, his right brow cocked. "I know Ford's a genius, but what's this about *growin'* a car?"

"Vegetable-based plastics!" Mike proudly gave answer. "Entire chassis of his 'hemp-mobile' will be made of 'em. Amazing stuff – strong, durable, and tough as nails. Versatile as metal, but light in weight – big advantage in an automobile. Lucky for us," he looked to his hosts, "the finest of these new plastics are made of hemp."

"Of course," he went on matter-of-factly, "the hemp-mobile's engine will run on hemp-based fuel. But, here's the best news. Like I told you," he returned to the Burnetts, "Ford's been experimentin' with several 'growable' fuels. He's now decided that hemp's the one and only – cheapest, most efficient, grows like a weed in any climate. His experts say it produces *ten times* more bio-fuel per acre than corn, and it burns cleaner, makes it safer, less corrosive.

"It's official, then, my sources say, experimentin''s over. The 'corn-mobile' and the 'bio-mobile' are out, and hemp is in, all the way to mass-production!

"They're callin' hemp 'the future,' my friends!" He paused to relish the smiles of his listeners, beginning and ending with Kate. "Yes, indeed, 'the road to recovery!' So," he queried them, for emphasis, "what do you think Ford's growin', on thousands of acres, just down the road from his secret plants?"

"Hemp!" they all shouted, and laughed, and shook Mike's hand. Will got up and patted Mike on the back.

Kate made a brief entry in her special diary that night:

Hemp is the future! Praise the Lord! My prayers are answered!

Early the next morning, a Wednesday, Kate drove into Richmond, where she volunteered her services at Alan House, a soup kitchen, located in an old, formerly affluent residential district near the city's center. She, her best friend, Lucy Stevens, and June Stevens – Lucy's mother and Noble's sweetheart, had been volunteering weekly at Alan House since the onset of the Great Depression, two years prior.

The Stevens women were very well-to-do, the loss of Mr. Stevens a decade earlier notwithstanding. The women had inherited a fortune in real estate, which June, partnered recently with Lucy, had managed to grow, despite a collapsing U.S. economy. Amongst their vast remaining holdings were their upscale residence in Richmond and the elaborate country estate which bordered Katelyn Farm.

Gwendolyn Alan, a close friend of the Stevens family, had founded the Alan House Shelter in 1927, in her childhood home; and had been directing and funding the charity, almost single-handedly, ever since. 'Miz' Alan, as the volunteers called her, was a slim, silver-haired, 'old money' widow, with an aristocratic air that bordered on snobbery, and a visage so invariably strained that it concealed her former, legendary beauty, even when she laughed. She was said to be "ancient" – seventy-five, maybe eighty, but her exact age was a highly guarded secret. The Stevens liked to joke that not even God knew it!

Lucy Stevens, a petite and pixyish twenty-four year old, with an up-turned, freckled nose, and a winning smile, was pacing out in front of Alan House, when Kate arrived at eight-thirty. The autumn air was crisp that morning, but Lucy was uncloaked; wearing only her volunteer's 'uniform,' an apron, with the initial A, (for Alan House), embroidered on it; over a short-sleeved, navy-blue cotton frock.

"You'll catch your death out here," Kate shouted to her from the car, "and Miz Alan won't like it!"

Lucy laughed, and ran toward the automobile, rubbing her arms briskly against the cold. The two hadn't spoken to each other since Kate's birthday; and Lucy was excited to hear the latest about Will, whom she had yet, she regretted, to meet.

Once inside, Kate told her everything – practically, in giggles and whispers, as they helped to prepare the huge cauldrons of soup, and the endless batches of cornbread they served to the poor. The needy, the women noted sadly, were growing steadily in numbers each week, lining up earlier and earlier outside the building.

Unbeknownst to Kate, Will was also outside Alan House later that morn, awaiting the truckload of goods he had promised to donate on her behalf. Dressed casually in corduroy trousers, a heavy cotton shirt, and a felt fedora, Will leaned against his car, parked on the street near the open twin-gates to the premises, and warmed his face in the rising sun. As he watched the gathering, increasingly edgy crowd, his eyes kept returning to a sign in the window of the run-down, but still elegant and ivy-laced, stone mansion:

"Alan House Homeless Shelter/Soup Kitchen – No Vacancies. Hot Lunch Served Daily, 11:00 – 2:30. No Charge.

All God's Children Welcome. Donations Appreciated. **NO SMOKING INSIDE GATES!"**

The soup-kitchen door opened promptly at eleven, and the seating capacity – thirty-six, of the hundred or so in waiting were received. The door was no sooner shut, when two shabby, middle-aged ruffians began to argue, boisterously, over who was next in line.

Will's driver arrived simultaneously, in a large, conspicuously marked – company name in giant, red letters, above the image of a glamorous woman lighting a gentleman's cigarette – Fairfield Tobacco delivery truck. Will moved his car forward so that the driver could take his space; and then took off toward the crowd, shouting to his man that he'd be right back, he was going to "calm 'em down!"

The driver, a former heavy-weight boxer, who was also trained in security, had a look from his perch, and cringed. Fists were already flying!

"Maybe you shouldn't get into it, Boss?" he called after Will – too late.

Will, on the scene in an instant, managed to separate the brawlers, and moved in, face to face, with the one who had thrown the first punch.

"Say, Buddy," he spoke calmly, with authority. "No cause for fightin' here. Every one of ya is gettin' in – guaranteed! ... *Unless* someone calls the cops on ya'll – then you're outta luck! Don't want that! Let's take it easy, Bud... talk it out..."

The instigator, taken aback at first, dropped his guard, and began to nod, apparently relieved. But one of his pals suddenly bolted out of nowhere, and hit Will from behind; only to anger another onlooker, who jumped in to Will's defense. And then another took sides, and then another. Within seconds, Will's form was obscured beneath a pile of tumbling bodies and flailing limbs.

A minute into it, however, the sound of gunshot split the air, and halted the ruckus at once. Silence prevailed as a bloody-eyed Will emerged from the heap to the sight of his driver, standing – spread-legged and larger-than-life – on the hood of the truck, a smoking pistol, pointed toward the sky, in his hand.

"Let's break it up, folks," the driver took brisk command, motioning the trouble-makers away from the rest. "Before ya'll get shut outta lunch!"

No one chose to quibble with the big guy and his gun. The line was reassembled, with the now reserved brawlers to the back.

"Got somethin' for y'all," the driver softened his tone, and tucked away his pistol. "Bread n' blankets, folks – free! …Y'all heard me right! Free bread n' blankets, right 'n this here truck – 'nough for all of ya, courtesy of Fairfield Tobacco."

Most of the folks inside the House had screamed at the sound of gunfire, and either ducked, or ran for cover in the back room. Mrs. Alan rushed to the front room and took charge.

"Under the tables! Away from the windows!" she ordered the fearless, who quickly complied. She then hurried to the vestibule, and waited by the door, ears perked, for several minutes. At the absence of a second shot, she opened the door a crack, and peeked out.

Although their numbers had dwindled, the diners-in-waiting appeared to be calm.

Just outside the House gate, however, there stood a huge tobacco truck, from which two men were dispensing bread and blankets to the rest of the crowd.

"How dare they…" Mrs. Alan mouthed under her breath; but collected herself at once, and returned to the dining-room.

"All is well!" she assured her guests, directing them quietly back to their seats.

"Carry on!" she instructed her volunteers, and fetched a wrap, and marched outside, slamming the door behind her.

Kate ran to the window. Her jaw dropped at the sight of Fairfield's truck, and again at a glimpse of Will in the hold of the vehicle. She hastened to get Lucy in the back room.

"Come, Luce, quickly!" she whispered, leading her by the hand to the window. "That's Will, inside the truck," she pointed toward the street, "dolin' out bread. Can't see much of him, but that's him, in the hat, standin' over Miz Alan... Looks like he's talkin' to her!"

"Oh, dear!" Lucy exclaimed, and then lowered her voice: "I hope he doesn't tell her he's your beau. She hates tobacco worse than booze!"

Kate shook her head 'no.' "He promised not to mention me," she whispered. "Indeed, he said he was comin' tomorrow, when I wasn't here! I told him Miz Alan's husband was a smoker, and had died of consumption. He understood."

"Want to meet him, Luce?" she gently nudged her friend, gave her a happy face. "See for yourself what a charmer he is?"

"Not just now!" Lucy said emphatically. "But, wait! He's gettin' out of the truck, finally, into the light.... Took off his hat... Wish I had my binoculars!"

Nose against the window, Lucy focused in on Will, as he spoke with Mrs. Alan.

"A charmer, indeed," Lucy acknowledged, "just made Miz Alan laugh! And *very* handsome, Kate, from what I can see, apart from the big black eye!"

Kate had a closer look at Will, and gasped – his bloodied eye was visible from some forty feet away! Her first thought was to run to him. But he and Mrs. Alan took off suddenly toward his car, and reached it momentarily. Will climbed in, started up, and was gone, without a good-bye!

Mrs. Alan, frowning again, headed hastily back to the House.

"Not a word!" Lucy stressed, crossing her finger over her lips. Kate heaved a sigh, and repeated the gesture. They returned to their duties in the back kitchen.

A long, blaring whistle drew them out again shortly.

The source of the noise, a raggedy, innocent-faced, young waif, named Millie, was a regular at the soup kitchen, and first on the waiting list for residency. Millie, clearly overwhelmed by the thousand eyes upon her, stood wide-eyed and frozen in her tracks near the entry to the House.

"Mornin', Millie," one of the residents called out, "whatchya'll got there?"

Millie cleared her throat, smiled shyly, and summed up her nerve.

"What I got here," she spoke loudly, nodding to the volunteer, to Mrs. Alan, who failed to respond, and around the room, "a man's givin' out fer free! Just outside," she motioned toward the street, held up the goods, "free bread and blankets; 'tabacci' truck full of 'em."

Several diners got up immediately and headed for the door.

"No need ta rush," Millie recalled them, "man told me to tell ya'll. He's stayin' till after closin'. An' he's got plenty; 'nough fer all of ya, an' young'ns an' ol' folk at home."

A few of the diners rushed out anyway. Others went to the window to see for themselves.

The disgruntled Mrs. Alan stomped out of the room, climbed the back stairway to her office, and shut herself in with June, her volunteer bookkeeper.

It was after three o'clock before she descended. The diners had all gone; the CLOSED sign had been hung on the door. Kate, still in 'uniform,' and a few House residents were doing the last-minute tidying up, sweeping, arranging chairs, and such.

Mrs. Alan went to the window, and noted, with relief, that the tobacco truck had also disappeared. But then she spotted the boxes of bread and blankets, six of them, stacked near the entrance hall. She walked over, examined them briefly, and read the note on top. Brow furrowed, she returned to the window.

"Kate, Dear," she called for her remaining volunteer, straining to be pleasant.

"Yes, Ma'am," said Kate, hurrying to her.

"Is that your car, parked down the street, to the left?" asked Mrs. Alan, gesturing toward the vehicle.

"Yes, Ma'am."

"Would you mind doing me a favor?"

"Happy to."

Mrs. Alan hesitated, and let out a sigh, but finally voiced her request: "If Mr. Fairfield's driver fails to return for those boxes before you leave, would you drop them off at the Red Cross for me? I believe you pass the shelter on your way home?"

"I do," said Kate, "and I will. But we," she gestured toward the clean-up crew, "spoke to the driver when he left the boxes, just after closin'. He asked us kindly to distribute the goods tomorrow, to folk who hadn't received them today. Said he was deliverin' a separate load to Red Cross this afternoon."

Mrs. Alan rarely explained her decisions to anyone. She hated to. But she made an exception for Kate, of whom she was exceptionally fond:

"Yes, Dear. He left a note to that effect. However, I made it perfectly clear to Mr. Fairfield this mornin' that this is a House of Temperance, and that I could not, in good conscience, accept donations from a tobacco company!"

After making the delivery, Kate called in on Will at his home in Richmond. She had a standing invitation to visit him there on Wednesdays, after volunteering, or, in Will's words, "any time or day at all." She had never taken him up on it. He moved her so, emotionally and physically, that she'd been afraid to be alone with him so far from home. Passion over time had diminished her fear, but even if it hadn't, her desire to thank

Will personally, and to kiss his wounds, would have outweighed all on that day.

As she parked in front of his regal, two-story brownstone, she was happy to note that the car he'd been driving that morning – a high-end, and therefore uncommon, 1931 Packard – was in the carport. She took a deep breath, got out, rushed up the steps, and rapped on the door with the knocker.

Will's housekeeper, Belle, a rotund, fifty-ish black woman, with a large, shiny, bandana-framed face, answered.

"Hello, Miss Kate," said Belle, in a lilting voice that matched her appearance. "Do come in, please. Mista Will's expectin' you. Your friend, Miss Lucy, called to say you was comin'."

"Thank you, Belle. So nice to meet you."

Kate entered the foyer, and slowly removed her cardigan, while taking in the striking decor. Elegantly furnished and fitted, with parquet floors, and beamed, cathedral ceilings, the house was even more stunning inside than out. Its entrance hall resembled an art gallery; a magnificent, sky-lighted, winding staircase as a centerpiece; and what appeared to be 'priceless' sculptures, paintings, and hand-carved sideboards lining the walls.

"Yes, I had Miss Lucy call," Kate returned her attention to Belle, "as I stayed after hours at the House today, it bein' my turn. I couldn't go home, though, without seein' for myself that Mister Will was fine."

"Oh, he's fine, just fine, Miss Kate. Got him a black eye, nick on the brow – dried up already, thank the Lord. Been to the doc n' all; he said it looks bad, but it ain't. You'll see; I'll fetch him.... Oh, here he comes now!"

Will appeared in a silk smoking jacket as Belle disappeared with Kate's wrap.

"Welcome, at last, Angel Eyes!" he greeted her, with a silly bow, and the newest of the pet names he'd given her.

Kate stifled a laugh. His mockingly suave behavior combined with the dashing get-up made his purplish, puffy eye seem almost comical.

"Will, your eye..." she moaned sympathetically, gently caressing his face beneath the swelling. "It looks awful... Does it hurt?"

Will nodded 'yes,' and mouthed a silent "Ouch!"

"I'm so sorry," she whispered, "so sorry," kissing his face all around the wound.

Will loved the attention, but could not resist making light of the incident: "Lout who hit me got two black eyes!"

She smiled. She knew he was fine; his humor was intact.

He led her by the hand into the living room – as dazzling as the foyer, to a seat beside him on a sofa, with a picture-window view of a resplendent, walled garden. The extraordinary array of flowers, bursting with magenta, deep orange and golden hues; encircled a quaint, brick patio, canopied in blue, and an enormous, glass greenhouse.

"It's absolutely beautiful, Will!" she commented, rising, gesturing all around her, and outward to the heavens... "And a garden to take your breath away!"

"Thank you, Darlin'," he replied, drawing her smoothly back to his side. "I knew you'd love it. My parents found it. Their house in town is similar, a bit larger and fancier, though, just down the street."

"Why don't you stay, Kate?" he dropped the small talk, peered straight into her baby blues. "We'll dine on the patio tonight. Belle's got five of Aunt Nettie's recipes. She's just itchin' to try one on an unsuspectin' newcomer!"

Kate laughed, but shook her head 'no.'

"It's my eye, isn't it? You're repulsed by it?"

"Never!"

"But, seriously, Kate, you can sleep at my parents' if you like. They'd be delighted. We'll invite them to dinner; call your daddy while they're here. Let them talk to him, reassure him that there're 'grown-ups' lookin' out for you… What do you say?"

"I love you, Will," she spoke from her heart, "and I want to stay, but I can't, for a host of reasons. I came – for just a minute – to thank you, so much, for your generous donation. It was such a nice surprise for the poor folk; they were so pleased, so grateful."

"Not all of 'em," he quipped, winking the bad eye, to her grin. "And ol' 'Miz' Alan hated it!"

Kate sighed. "I'm so sorry 'bout that, too. I Hope she wasn't offensive… Was she?"

"Not at all," Will went on sardonically, "apart from sayin' that tobacco peddlers serve Satan!"

"No!"

"I jest," he owned, "but she did suggest that I could 'do more people more good' if I closed up shop!"

They shared a chuckle, reflecting on Mrs. Alan, the donation, the ironies of it all.

Kate told him the story of how she had come to love Gwendolyn Alan, and to overlook her quirks, and airs and intermittent rudeness:

"It was closin' time, one of my early days at Alan House. Lucy and I and Miz Alan had just locked up, when a family of four arrived out front. Bedraggled, really; the children in misfittin' hand-me-downs, toes stickin' out of the holes in their shoes. They looked dreadfully road-dusty. And weary, as if they'd come from miles. Turns out they had. The little boy – must have been nine or ten, and the girl, a bit younger, pressed their noses against the window, and stared up at us pitifully.

"Miz Alan said let them in. 'Hurry!' She put the pot back on to simmer, and thanked the Lord we had just enough to give them each a healthy meal.

"The father and mother apologized for arrivin' after hours; said they'd been on the road three days; on their way to a farm up-county. Kinfolk had sent them word there was work there, and a dry loft for sleepin'. They didn't wish to trouble us, but for a drink of water.

"Miz Alan insisted that they eat. 'No trouble at all.' She sent Lucy to the 'trunk room' as well, to look for shoes and clothes that might fit the children; and we wrapped them up some jerky for the road, and gave each a canteen of water. She and I carried on in the dinin'-room, where the family sat down to eat.

"The daddy and children must have been starvin', gulped down their bread and soup before the mama had eaten half of hers. The mama offered her remains to the daddy. But he declined. So, she passed the food to the boy, sittin' next to her; but he, too, shook his head 'no.' She put her arm around him, kissed him on the forehead, and nodded 'yes,' firmly; she was insistin' that he eat – no mistake!

"The boy just sat there for a moment, bewildered. But then he sort of smiled. He took a small bite of the bread and a sip of the soup, and passed the food to his sister, and nodded. The little girl did the same, a tiny bite, a tiny sip, and passed it to her daddy, and nodded...

"And so it went, around the table..." Kate's voice began to break up, "...the tiny bites... gettin' tinier, and tinier... None of them wished to take the last, Will..." She sniffled, and wiped her eyes.

Will, on the verge of tears himself, pretended to sob, to make her laugh.

She did laugh, and then carried on, emotionally:

"In the end, the mama savored the last crumb and droplet, slowly, and with relish – eyes closed; the rest of the family lookin' on, all smiles.

"Miz Alan and I had to leave the room, to keep from wailin' in front of them. She held her arms out to me in private, her face so warm and radiant – I'll never forget it, Will! Saintly, she appeared to me, truly. We hugged, and rocked, and wept on each other's shoulder.

"'That's why we're here, Kate,' she sighed, 'to learn about sharin' from those who have the least to share... No greater reward...'

"Well, I haven't missed my Wednesday 'reward' ever since. Even when I stayed in Washington, I did soup kitchen there with my sister-in-law, Liddy, who had had a similar 'do-gooder's callin',' as she described it."

Will, for once, was speechless; overwhelmed by his love for Kate. To him, she was the perfect woman – kindness, intelligence, endless charm and a sense of humor, wrapped up in an exquisite package. He wanted to ask her to marry him then and there, but all he could do was stare at her adoringly.

A grandfather clock in another room struck five. Kate jumped up, smoothed out her uniform, and moved toward the foyer, motioning for Will to come along. He did her bidding reluctantly, ringing a bell for her cloak at the door. She had a last look at his wound while they waited. "What did the doctor say?" she asked softly.

Will gazed at her seductively, but pitched her again with humor: "He said I'll be fine. But I shouldn't spend the night alone... I may need help!"

She rolled her eyes, giggled.

"Oh, and he wrote me a prescription for medicinal hemp! Got any?"

Kate melted. She wanted desperately to stay with him, to throw all caution to the wind. She initiated a passionate, open-mouthed kiss, pressing the contours of her body close to his, and moaning low.

That did it! He took her by the hand, led her back to the living room, to a telephone.

"Call your daddy, Kate," he whispered urgently. "Tell him you're spendin' the night in Richmond. At Lucy's, if need be – we'll get you there later!"

Kate was ringing the operator when Belle arrived with her cardigan.

"Oh, there you be, Miss Kate, Mista Will. I was lookin' for ya'll by the door."

Kate hung up the phone. In the moment it took to accept the wrap, and say thank you, she collected herself; and went home, sadly, after all.

Saturday came quickly. She and Noble left for Washington at dawn in her car. The weather en route was dreadful – dense fog in the early hours, followed by intermittent downpours. The sun finally peeped through as they approached the D.C. border, but they were already running late.

They made a brief stop at the home of Kate's brother, Bobby, who was pacing at the front window when they pulled up. He met them outside, and offered to drive them to the site of the fund-raiser – he knew a shortcut, could get them there in half an hour. They gratefully accepted, stole a minute or two in the guest quarters to freshen up, and took off at once for The Fountains Hotel, arriving precisely at noon, a bit harried, but on time.

The four-storied hotel was average in size, but exceptional in every other respect. Its exterior impeccably reproduced from an 'old world' masterpiece, the building was constructed in the early 1900's, by a team of architects and artisans from Florence, Italy. The interior had been fully refurbished and modernized every few years. It was located in Washington's elite business district, walking distance to many of the city's best restaurants, and a short drive from the Capitol. The Fountains took its name from the several working replicas of world-famous fountains on its grounds; most notably the miniature of the fabled Trevi fountain that trickled night and day in its lobby, enticing lovers and would-be lovers to toss a coin, make a wish, and see their wish come true!

Kate, on the arm of her daddy, made a grand entrance into the hotel. Adorned, albeit moderately, with makeup and jewelry, soaring over six feet, in high-heeled shoes, and a birthday gift from the Stevens – a long, clingy, honey-colored skirt, and matching scooped-neck blouse, she turned every head in the lobby, and discernibly reduced the din in the dining hall.

Noble, as usual, made light of it. "They think you're a starlet," he whispered her way, as they waited to be seated. "Take a bow, then!"

Kate faked a pout. "They might be gawkin' at you, Mr. Burnett – quite the prince charmin' in that three-piece suit!"

"I doubt it!" he laughed.

He laughed harder as Kate donned the cape she was carrying, and fastened it snugly about her neck.

Lucy spotted them from a distance, and came running.

"Kate! Mr. Burnett! What a relief! We heard about the storms on the road, thought you might get waylaid. But here you are – praise the Lord, safe, and on time!"

She and Noble traded compliments on their attire, and then she looked to Kate:

"My, my, Miss Burnett! Aren't you just lovely in your new birthday skirt!? ...And the new blouse? ... I presume? ...Under cover?"

Kate flashed her a knowing smile. The two were given to tease one another about Kate's inclination to hide her curves, and Lucy's to show hers off. It was Kate's turn:

"Why, thank you, Miss Stevens! And I must say you are pretty as a picture, and daring as 'the divorcee' herself in that outfit!"

Lucy laughed out loud. She was sporting a stylish suit, similar to one Norma Shearer had worn as 'the divorcee,' in a movie of the same title. The mid-calf hemline of the skirt was bold by Temperance standards, and the v-neck of the jacket plunged dramatically to the waistline. Beneath the jacket, moreover, Lucy was wearing a lacy, low-cut blouse, which propped up and accentuated her ample bosom.

June, also suited smartly, though modestly, in a pant-skirt, jacket and slouchy-hat, all done up in a pale, blue silk, the shade of her eyes, took a time out from officiating for the

Temperance League to greet the Burnetts. After exchanging hugs and pleasantries, she led them to the 'select' seating, surrounding the dance-floor, at the far end of the spacious, lavishly furnished room. Kate and Noble took their designated seats at a table, set opulently for six.

"Be right back, Sweethearts," June promised, planting a welcomed kiss on Noble's forehead, and motioning for Lucy to come along.

Noble rose, and eyed June longingly as her trim figure fluttered in and out of a maze of diners.

Kate observed her father with a happy heart. She thought the world of June Stevens, and hoped that June and Noble would be married one day soon.

Lucy Stevens hoped for the same; and often kidded with Kate about it:

"When's your daddy goin' to pop the question? Make us one big happy family?"

Lucy let it be known, however, that her "snooty little brother," Teddy, a freshman at Georgetown University, had reservations – mainly monetary – about such a union. Owing largely to the money-managing skills of Kate's brother, Bobby, the Burnetts were 'comfortable' financially, for the moment. But the Stevens were multi-millionaires; and, fond as he was of Noble, Teddy was uneasy about his mother marrying 'down' – especially then, in times of woe, with farms and businesses failing fast across the nation.

Noble, ironically, had like reservations. He loved June dearly, and intended to ask for her hand, but not until his enterprise was booming once again. The idea that June's children, or anyone else, might think that he would marry June for her money was abhorrent to him.

The décor of The Fountains' banquet hall was so outlandishly opulent that Kate felt ill at ease just being there. She counted fifty excessively decorated tables in the room, including a double-sized, extra-ornate head table, which was set up front, perpendicular to the rest, twenty feet or so from where Kate sat, and squarely in her view. Each of the tables was laden with polished silver – trays, serving dishes, cutlery and even water goblets, the finest bone china, embroidered Irish linens, and elaborate arrangements of fresh flowers, petite pastries, appetizers, and ripened fruit.

Background music – barely audible above the din – was provided by not one, but two, pianists, a man and a woman, dressed in glittery, formal attire, performing on twin Steinway baby-grands, which were set on a flower-decked stage, adjacent to the huge, empty dance floor.

It all seemed so wasteful to Kate, shamefully – cruelly – wasteful, in light of what she'd seen, in and around the Capital, that morning: mile-long breadlines, in the pouring rain; makeshift tent-and-cardboard cities, overflowing with the haggard, and disheveled down-and-out – many of them sign-carrying Veterans of World War I; and the procession of street-people, from all walks, of all ages, rummaging for food in the giant garbage bins, just outside the service doors of 'well-to-do' haunts.

Noble caught her pout upon returning to his seat.

"Nice place, hmm?" he offered with a grin.

She giggled slightly, at her own transparency.

"Well," she reflected, "like Aunt Net always says, 'riches and luxury don't bring ya happiness, darlin', countin' your blessin's does.'"

"I'm the one who taught her that," said Noble, deadpan; and got another giggle.

The pianists took a break, and the hotel's M.C. took the podium on the dance floor at a quarter past noon. He quieted the audience and called for all to be seated, pausing at length between brief announcements:

"Lunch will be served momentarily, ladies and gentlemen… There will be no speeches… Not even little ones… Thank you… Thank you."

Upon getting a signal, he then turned the proceedings over to his boss:

"Moving right along, folks, it is my great privilege to introduce your host, proprietor of this splendid hotel, and sponsor of this momentous event, the distinguished Congressman from the great State of New Jersey, **Representative William Hagar.**"

Hagar was a very impressive figure from afar. He was tall, athletically built, and appeared in public only in swanky, custom-made suits. At the age of forty-eight, he still had a full head of thick, pitch-black hair. As dictated by fashion, he wore his hair slicked down, and his mustache pencil-thin. His face, in profile, was fine – well-proportioned, straight nose, strong chin.

Up close and to the front, however, there was something very unsettling about the Congressman's façade. It wasn't just his crooked, thin-lipped smile, or his habit of avoiding eye contact with friend and foe alike, the man had the look and the air of a gangster. Virtually everyone noticed it, and talked about it, in whispers. His popularity amongst his constituents – he had won two, fiercely-contested terms in the House by a landslide – was thus a mystery to most of his fellows.

The audience applauded and cheered as Hagar rose from his seat at the head table, took a bow, and hurried to the podium. He thanked his guests, welcomed them to The Fountains, and repeated, with the crooked smile:

"There will be no speeches!"

As the cheers subsided, he wise-cracked, "And there will be no booze!"

But the snicker, predominantly male, from the audience fizzled.

"In all seriousness, though," he continued apologetically, "I want to thank you, again, ladies and gentlemen, for coming – many of you over great distances and storm-ridden roads – to support this righteous and worthy cause. I am also happy to inform you that every penny of the proceeds from this event are being used to fund a massive campaign, already underway, to derail the anti-Prohibitionists and their movement, and expose them for who they are..." he paused for effect, "the *servants of evil!*"

Mr. And Mrs. Harry Anslinger had entered the dining room in time to catch Hagar's last remark. Mr. leaned toward Mrs., and snarled, voice low,

"Son-of-a-bitch stole my line!"

Hagar closed as waiters began to file in with carts of food.

"Your lunch, ladies and gentlemen," he nodded toward the activity, "is arriving. Reverend Painter, from our First Presbyterian Church, will say grace. Enjoy yourselves, friends. And God bless."

June caught sight of the Anslingers, and rushed to get them after grace.

Mrs. Anslinger was a petite woman in her late thirties, as plain-featured as her husband, and plainly-dressed, for a woman of her means, in a bland, cotton dinner-frock and an unremarkable skull cap. She was, nevertheless, remarkably pleasant, soft-spoken, and bright. Upon taking her assigned seat, next to Kate, who liked her at once, the two struck up a chat.

Behind the Mrs. came Mr. Anslinger, who said hello to Lucy, and then addressed Noble:

"Mr. Burnett," he held out his hand, "I believe we met last week, in Richmond?"

Noble rose and shook his hand. "We did, indeed, Mr. Anslinger. I enjoyed your speech."

Since Kate was busy conversing, June waited to introduce her, making small talk with Anslinger as they took their seats – June across from Noble, Anslinger facing his wife:

"Did I tell you, Harry, that the Burnetts own an enormous farm – some eight hundred acres, just down the road from my place in the country?"

Anslinger turned to Noble with a wrinkled brow. "Hmm," he spoke disappointedly, "I suppose you grow tobacco, then, Mr. Burnett?"

Noble held his head high. "We grow hemp. Family farm, five generations, 1799."

Anslinger lit up. "You don't say!? A 'hemp-man,' alive and well in the middle of tobacco-land! Good for you, Mr. Burnett! Hemp's a wonderful crop – American tradition!"

"That it is," Noble smiled and nodded, "that it is."

Kate looked up at the mention of hemp.

Anslinger caught her eye, stood, offered his hand, and introduced himself:

"Harry Anslinger. Pleased to meet you, Miss. I take it you're the hemp-man's daughter!"

2

The Conspiracy

Kate found it oddly gratifying that hemp, rather than Prohibition, became the main topic at Anslinger's table during the meal. Indeed, the Commissioner's wife herself inspired a lively round of hemp-talk when she pulled a tiny Bible out of her purse and passed it around.

"It was my grandma's," she announced proudly, "printed on hemp-paper. It's sixty years old now, but practically new, as you can see."

Everyone had a look at it, and agreed.

"It's lovely," Kate commented on her turn. "I inherited a miniature as well, not quite as old, but made from paper produced at our own mill."

Kate went on to give a little discourse on the benefits of using hemp, rather than trees, as the raw material for paper:

"As every archivist knows," she proposed, "hempen paper has no equal. It lasts for centuries, without deterioratin'. That's why it's used for Bibles, like Mrs. Anslinger's, and for government documents, and such. Unfortunately, though, ordinary paper-goods, like magazines and newspapers, are made from tree pulp today; which is why they turn yellow, and crack and crumble, in no time."

Kate paused to allow her listeners their say on the "very poor quality" of the paper of the day; and then carried on:

"A more serious problem with regular paper is that it takes harsh chemicals to process it. This is good, I'm told, for the chemical companies; but deadly for our rivers and streams. Toxic chemicals, by the ton, are bein' dumped into waterways at mill-sites all across the country. At the least, they leave a terrible stench, and kill the fish... Lord knows what they do to folks downstream who drink from those waters, or even wade in them!

"Hemp fiber, by nature, is easier to 'cook,' as we call it, and so we are able to process it by kinder means."

"What about the cost, though, Kate?" Mrs. Anslinger asked. "Is tree-paper cheaper to make; and so preferred over hemp?"

"You wouldn't know it by current demand, Mrs. Anslinger, but hemp-paper is actually cheaper to make – or would be, mass-produced. Hemp yields *four times* more pulp per acre than trees – accordin' to the Department of Agriculture, which is actively promotin' hemp production. They say it takes *twenty years* to ready a tree for processin'; whereas a hemp crop is ready in three to four months! The Department also warns, in a recent bulletin, that uncontrolled loggin' is destroyin' our forests faster than they're bein' replaced."

The women at the table were looking quite concerned, and once again Mrs. Anslinger spoke up:

"That doesn't make sense, Kate! If hemp is better, and cheaper to process, why in the world are we cutting down trees to make paper?"

"I'm afraid it makes sense to 'Big Business,' Ma'am. And price-wise, I must admit, to the consumer. The loggin' industry's huge today, so are its allies in paper. Mass-production and distribution, for more than a decade, has kept their unit price low. And they've cornered the market, simple as that! Hemp farmers and millers are mostly small operators – can't compete, certainly not in hard times like these."

"Might as well get used to it," Noble chimed in, "'Big' is here to stay. Not just in paper, in general. Like you say, started in long before the Depression. Lucky for us," he nodded toward Kate, "hemp's a versatile plant – always be a market for it."

"I hope so," Kate said dully… "It's not the *big* that worries me, it's the *dirty*! Loggin' interests have already bought out several of the more competitive hemp mills out west, and shut them down! Even worse, I hear, they've bought up a patent on new machinery that would make hemp processin' faster and cheaper. And," she paused dramatically, "they're sittin' on it!"

Commissioner Anslinger's jaw dropped. He had followed Kate intently, initially because he was impressed with her knowledge, especially in light of her beauty. But in the end, he was deeply disturbed by the anti-hemp conspiracy she had described.

"Now that's a shame, Miss," he interjected; his wife, June and Lucy echoing the same.

"Downright un-American!" he went on, huffily. "There ought to be a law against such unfair practices."

"Perhaps not a 'law,' Mr. Anslinger," Kate responded, "but our wholesaler has suggested that we form an 'association,' to protect the common interests of growers, manufacturers and consumers. They've already done so in Kentucky, he says, and today, as a result, many of the rules and practices there favor hemp-folk. Whereas in Virginia, as we Virginians know," she looked to her fellows, "tobacco gets all the favors."

Coincidentally, June was secretly negotiating to sell off the bulk of her farmland in Virginia to tobacco. Fairfield Tobacco, had, in fact, made her an offer.

"Speaking of hemp," she promptly reversed the subject, "I believe the flags here in the capital are made of hemp as well."

Noble confirmed that they were, and had been since colonial times. There was a period, he noted, when "all of officialdom," began switching to flags made of cotton, which was cheaper. But the switch was short-lived. Hemp soon proved to be the superior flag material; stronger, more lustrous, more resistant to extremes in temperature, mildew, rot, and so on, and thus, in the long run, more economical.

"Well, my compliments, Mr. Burnett, Miss Burnett," Anslinger summed up the anecdotes of the day, "the finest bibles and the finest flags – you can't beat that!"

When it appeared that most everyone in the hall had finished eating, the Anslingers excused themselves to "make the rounds." They visited the head table first.

As Kate scanned the faces at that table, she found one of them vaguely familiar. Cupping her hand discreetly about her mouth, she leaned forward toward Lucy, caught her attention, and spoke softly:

"Don't look now, Luce, but who's that white-haired gent, with the big mustache, seated next to our host?"

Lucy knew everyone who was anyone in the Temperance Movement, especially the politicians, for and against. She'd been attending fund-raisers and lectures with her mother for more than a decade. She took her time, got several good looks, and whispered back:

"That's Andrew Mellon, soon to be *former* Secretary of the Treasury – U.S.!"

She glanced over her shoulder, saw that her mother and Noble were engrossed in each other, and returned to her friend:

"Rumor has it his head's about to roll," she gestured towards Mellon, ran her finger across her neck, stuck out her tongue, and faked a gag.

Kate grinned. But she remembered now, seeing Mellon's picture in the paper, and beneath it a favorable caption. "Isn't he the philanthropist?" she asked.

"Indeed," Lucy replied, "which is why he's lasted so long! Been in office since 'Teapot Dome.' Got away with that one, barely a slap on the wrist! ...Dirty deals 're catchin' up with him, though – finally! ...The rest of those men are his pals in 'Big

Business.' Tycoons, all of 'em; big supporters of Temperance, too."

On Kate's obvious interest, Lucy elaborated:

"The one at this end – forgot his name, is a chief at Gulf Oil, (which Mellon just about owns!)…"

"He looks like Wallace Beery," Kate put in, "doesn't he?"

Lucy nodded, "Even more so up close; same round, beady eyes, high forehead, exact same hair, puffed up, like a rooster!" She laughed; and so did Kate.

"And this guy works for Mellon?" Kate asked in amazement. "The Secretary of the Treasury *owns* Gulf Oil?"

"Well, not exactly," Lucy clarified, "it's a corporation now. But he's well-invested, and well-connected. The Mellons were bankers, initially, in Pittsburg. Then they got into oil, which became 'Big Oil,' while Mellon headed the Treasury, if you get my drift?" She winked at Kate, Kate winked back, and they giggled again.

"Anyway," Lucy continued with the 'who's who' in whispers, "the pretty lady in pink is the oil man's wife – Sanford, that's his name, yes, I'm sure of it. And across from Mrs. Sanford is one of *the* Du Ponts; Du Pont Chemicals, and his wife, the red-head; raised more money for Temperance than my mama! … Opposite Mellon – recognize him?"

"I do," said Kate, "but I can't quite place him."

"Newspaper chain…" Lucy offered a hint, "California, New York, Chicago, etcetera."

"Hearst?"

"Yep, the notorious William, Randolph!"

"Hearst and Du Pont," Kate mumbled under her breath, "sittin' up front, with Mellon and Hagar!"

Lucy paused for an explanation, but as none was offered, carried on:

"The other lady, cozyin' up with the Anslingers, is Mellon's sister. Or maybe sister-*in-law*? They're all related somehow… Mrs. Anslinger is Mellon's niece, as I recall."

Kate's eyes widened once again. "You don't say!" she mouthed silently. But, sure enough, as the informality between the Mellons and the Anslingers indicated, and June later confirmed, Secretary Mellon and Mrs. Anslinger were uncle and niece.

An hour into the three hour event, the M.C. returned to the podium to announce that dessert would be served, in the banquet hall and on the terrace adjacent to the lobby, in fifteen minutes. After dessert, at three o'clock, and again at nine, a sneak preview of an upcoming movie, entitled, 'Grand Hotel' – "by sheer coincidence," the M.C. noted wryly, would be showing in the hotel's theater. Neither were to be missed, the announcer advised, as the hotel's new pastry chef was "world class," and the film had received "rave critical reviews."

Having sampled the new chef's "divine" petite pastries, the Burnetts and the Stevens conspired to further indulge. The latter, however, had work to do first.

"If you'll excuse us," June asked kindly, "we've got a few more donors to thank, and dollars to collect. Shouldn't take us but a bit. Meet ya'll outdoors, 'bout fifteen minutes."

Noble and Kate replied, "Of course," Noble rising politely as the women took leave. When they were gone, Kate moved up a seat, next to her father.

"Daddy, see the two men chattin' at this end of that table?" She gestured towards Hearst and Du Pont.

Noble nodded.

"They're the ones wreckin' our paper market!"

"All by themselves?" he teased.

"Practically! The one to the left – the poser? Looks like he could be Hagar's brother? Partner in crime?"

"I see him, Kate! What about him?"

"That's William Randolf Hearst, the king of sensationalism! The shorter one – Mister Ordinary?" She shook her head. "He's a 'big-shot' too! Lucy said he's a Du Pont, Lammont, I believe. They make that no-good yellowin' newspaper Hearst puts out.

43

Hearst also provides the timber – owns *millions* of acres of trees; which is why he's anti-hemp!"

"Sounds legal to me," Noble dismissed her finger-pointing. "And what does it matter if newspaper yellows?"

"Seriously, Daddy! These men are dirty players. They hate competition!"

"Me too!"

"Like I said earlier, they're buying up hemp mills, just to shut them down."

"I didn't want to say so earlier, but you don't know that for a fact, Kate!"

"I do!"

"Don't!"

"Do!"

"Who said so? Anderson?"

"Yes!" Kate insisted. "It's his business to know."

Noble had the last word: "Anderson would say anything to impress you, Kate. Now, that's a fact! …Let's go get dessert!"

As they walked through the lobby to the terrace, Kate spotted another familiar face, one she was acquainted with personally.

"Isn't that BJ Jackson?" she tugged at Noble's sleeve, slowed him down. "Back there," she gestured behind them to the right, "in the tan, waitin' for the elevator?"

Noble looked twice over his shoulder at Jackson's backside. "Haven't seen him in years," he hedged. "Same wild hair! … Must be him!"

They stopped at Kate's urging, turned, and watched, as Jackson entered the elevator, and did an about-face.

"It's him!" they said in unison.

Kate waved excitedly, but BJ never raised his eyes. The cage-door slid shut, and up he went.

"Oh well, too late," Kate muttered disappointedly.

She had to laugh, though, as she and Noble carried on.

"I knew it was him! Not another soul in this world looks like BJ!"

Jackson, thirty-three years of age, was a big – six foot, burly man, with a swarthy complexion, and a mop of dark brown, very curly, very unruly hair. His facial features – eyes, ears, nose, mouth, teeth – all of them, were oversized, and gave him a curious, caricature-like appearance. The eyes – smoky brown irises with amber-speckled centers, thick, black lashes, and distinctly arched brows – were most outstanding. Women often described them as 'deep,' or 'mysterious,' and folks in general said they 'saw right through you."

"Wonder what he's doin' here," Kate thought aloud. "He's certainly not the Temperance type!"

"No, but he is the 'political type,'" Noble pointed out, "and there're plenty of politicians here."

"True," Kate said pensively. "I heard about his political ties, from Liddy, as well. She also told me that BJ had gotten engaged this summer. But had broken it off. Bitterly.

"Maybe I should introduce him to… Well, maybe not…"

"To whom?" Noble asked sternly, as if he didn't know.

"No one in particular," Kate played along. "Was just a fleetin' thought, Daddy, already passed from my mind!"

"Good! That's *very* good, Kate! I know my 'June-bug.' And she would *not* have been happy if your 'no one in particular' took up with the likes of BJ Jackson!"

Kate laughed. "You're right, as usual, Daddy. I promise to leave the match-makin' to someone better at it!"

Her gracious response aside, Noble's disregard for Jackson had always baffled Kate. It was so uncharacteristic of Noble. And Kate really liked BJ. She hadn't seen him in some years, but she remembered him as warm, friendly, smart, and extremely entertaining.

The remembrances were mutual, indeed, complicated, on Jackson's part, by a lusty infatuation with Kate. Although he hadn't given the slightest indication, he had spotted her in the lobby of The Fountains before she'd spotted him. With all the fuss she stirred, she was hard to miss. Had she been alone, he would have chased her down in a heartbeat, his urgent business on the fourth floor notwithstanding.

Jackson and Kate's brother, Bobby, were best friends and roommates in college, and were employed by the same D.C. firm – BJ as a lawyer, Bobby as an accountant – for a year or so after they graduated. Bobby later married BJ's cousin, Liddy Bouvier; BJ serving as 'best man' at the wedding. Jackson never married, however, and though he was based in Washington, his work kept him routinely out of town. He and Bobby still thought of each other as "close," but apart from teary-eyed hugging and reminiscing at the random wedding or funeral, the two hadn't socialized in years.

As he rode the elevator to the top of the hotel, Jackson recalled his first meeting with Kate. The occasion was the engagement party for Kate's brother and Jackson's cousin, whom Jackson had introduced. Kate was only seventeen at the time, but, much to her father's chagrin, she looked twenty-five; and she was already opinionated and outspoken, particularly on women's issues. Beyond that, she had the grit to walk right up to a stranger of the opposite gender – one of several who were ogling her, shamelessly, from across the room, and strike up a conversation:

"You must be BJ Jackson. No one else hereabouts fits the description."

"You're too kind, Miss Burnett," he responded at once, "but there are a number of tall, dark, outrageously handsome men at this party – just look around!"

Kate threw her head back, and laughed heartily.

He gave her a 'sad dog' face, and then laughed with her.

'This is going to be fun,' he thought. 'She's as easy to laugh as she is beautiful.' He carried on humorously, and, to the dismay of many, monopolized her attention, with a few token breaks, well into the evening.

"So, what do you think of our darling, Liddy?" he asked her for openers, having heard that Liddy had become her new mentor.

"I'm in awe of her, truly," Kate owned, "and I'm delighted that she's soon to be 'our' darlin' Liddy too."

BJ smiled. "Bobby's a lucky man," he affirmed. "He owes me!"

Kate cocked her head, and studied BJ curiously.

He cocked his head, and stared back at her; causing her to blush.

"So sorry!" "My fault!" their apologies overlapped.

"I didn't mean to stare," Kate went on to explain. "It's just that Liddy told me that you and she were like 'brother and sister' growin' up. I was tryin' to picture it, but I declare, there's not a shred of resemblance between you!"

"Not a shred," he agreed. "Lucky for Liddy she inherited our mothers' good looks, whilst I took after my father, who, like hers, is dark and hirsute, with a bulbous nose!"

Kate didn't know whether to laugh or be shocked; but BJ led with a chuckle, and she followed.

"Speaking of cousin Liddy," he got back on track, "did she tell you that she was a 'tomboy' and a 'terror' growing up?"

"She did, actually," Kate said gaily, clearly pleased to be in the know.

"With an *unholy* adventuresome spirit?"

"Yes, yes, she mentioned that, too."

"And that she got me into trouble continuously with her 'dares' and 'double dares'? Until I finally put my foot down one day, at the age of thirteen. 'No, Liddy!'

said I. 'Dare me if you must, but I will *not* join the Suffragette movement!'"

"She mourns your rejection to this day," said Kate, in giggles. "She told me so not long ago, when she asked *me* to join. I obliged her, of course – no dares necessary! Joinin' was a privilege and a dream come true for me."

"Oh, no!" BJ moaned dramatically. "No, no, no! You're too beautiful to be a Suffragette, Kate. And why bother? You can get anything you want from any man simply by batting your eyelashes!"

Kate stopped giggling, and looked at him agape.

"Why, BJ Jackson," she quickly collected herself, "I believe you're tryin' to get a rise out of me, and I am not goin' to let that happen. Now, I know you like to 'stir things up' – Liddy warned me 'bout that, and I did see it comin' – but what she failed to disclose was the extent of your 'crassness,' to which, I admit, I am totally unaccustomed, and ask you kindly to curtail!"

BJ burst out laughing. Her intensity and determination, together with the run-on sentences cracked him up. He had to have more.

"Besides," he went on, trying to keep a straight face, "we've already given you women the vote. What more could you possibly want, oh beautiful Suffragette? You think you can run the country?"

Kate glared at him, eyes narrowed. She understood, of course, that he was playing with her, but she wasn't going to let him win.

"In the first place," she said calmly, "nobody 'gave' women anything. We've had to fight, and plot, and picket, and plead for every right we've gained; not to mention the beatings, the imprisonment, the scorn of our own families, and even death! And, yes, I think that women – certain women – might run the country better than certain men, the latter includin' several persons currently in power!'"

Kate's face reddened as BJ continued to chuckle, but once again, she gathered herself:

"On a brighter note, Liddy also informed me that your mama, like mine, led many a Suffragette march in her day. I'd be much obliged, Mr. Jackson, if you'd thank her for me, and assure her that her darin' and sacrifice are very much appreciated by the women of my generation."

"You can thank her yourself," replied BJ between chuckles, "she's right over there, in the blue."

Kate gave him a nod and a smile as she backed away towards his mother. "Nice talkin' to you, Mr. BJ Jackson," she added, and batted her eyelashes at him.

BJ was still reveling in the memory of their repartee, as he reached the top floor at The Fountains. Following the elevator-operator's directions, he carried on down the posh corridor to the end, and knocked on the door of 'The Oriental,' penthouse suite number four, of seven; so named for its exquisite, hand-crafted, Chinese furniture, with inlaid artwork.

Fellow lawyer and former collaborator, Tom Worth, answered promptly. Worth, a baby-faced, red-headed, slight of stature, thirty-eight year old, looked more like a fledgling college student than the slick and savvy, long-term Washington insider that he was.

He and Jackson greeted each other warmly, albeit using surnames:

"Jackson – right on time, as usual! Nice to see you, my friend."

"You too, Worth. It's been a while. Damn! Don't you age, Worth? You look ten years younger than me, instead of older!"

Worth laughed. "I'm 'five' years older, not 'ten,' and well you know it, Buddy! But I've got troubles," he gestured toward his receding, graying hairline. "It's going fast, Jackson. I'll be looking like your 'grandpaw' soon if this keeps up!"

Jackson grinned. "So, how're you doing, Bud, really?" he asked in earnest.

"Not bad... Can't complain. Happy to be staying afloat these days – damned Depression, dragging on, half the country in the poor-house! ...Take a seat, my friend. I'll pour us a drink. Forget all about it. What's your pleasure?"

Jackson checked his watch as if it mattered – he wasn't about to refuse the drink.

"It's a little early," he said with a smirk, "but it's Saturday. I'll take a bourbon, straight, if you've got it."

"Got it."

Worth unlocked the loaded liquor cabinet beneath the so-called 'breakfast' bar which separated the kitchenette from the sitting room of the suite. He poured two bourbons, joined Jackson at the coffee table, handed him a drink.

Jackson said thanks, and stared pensively at the libation... "Won't be long, counselor," he smiled at Worth, nodded at the drink, "we'll be doing this legally again."

"Any day now," Worth concurred. "Someone should break the news to the crowd downstairs!"

They chuckled a bit.

"What a farce," Jackson denounced the fund-raiser, "– bootleggers and Anti-Saloon Leaguers, united for the cause!"

"Hypocrisy ad nauseam!" Worth agreed fully. "Which reminds me," he glanced at his pocket watch, "I need to bring you up to date on the hemp problem, before we get with the 'big boys.' I've already spoken to your 'client' – he's not happy."

Jackson shook his head disgustedly. "Wish he was still 'your' client, counselor – thanks a lot!"

Worth gave him a toothy grin, opened his briefcase, pulled out a folder, and handed it over.

Jackson looked bewildered as he scanned the set of photos inside.

Worth filled him in: "Henry Ford's hemp fields – Nebraska, U.S.A. He's already built the so-called 'hemp-mobile,' and taken it for a run!"

"Shit!" Jackson voiced his frustration, "It never ends!"

"Could get shittier. But we've got a plan – Hagar and I set it up. Mellon is in, unless you have some objection. And Hearst is in.

"Gotta tell you up front, Bud," he whispered, as though there were spies about, "I'm not thrilled to be beholden to Hearst – he's a petty, unpredictable, eccentric son-of-a-bitch!"

"I heard that's his good side!"

"Yeah. But I think we need him, Jackson. I wanted to get your take on that, and the rest, before we convene."

"I'm all ears, counselor. Pour me another drink, will ya?"

An hour later, in a small conference room on the same floor of the hotel, Mellon, Hearst, Sanford, and Du Pont, each looking serious, and business-like, in the same drab suits and ties they wore to lunch, were seated around a large, mahogany board table, with Mellon at the head. The curtains were drawn, the room unlit, except for the shaded lamp hanging low over the table, which cast a menacing shadow on the faces of the men.

There was a knock on the door. It opened, and in walked Jackson and Worth; who were dressed informally, suit-less, tie-less and hat-less, as usual; but fashionably, in light-colored sport-coats and dark, tweed, wide-legged trousers.

"Ah, the lawyers," said Mellon, obviously pleased to see them. "Where would we be without them?"

"In jail!" Worth quipped, getting a good laugh from all, except Hearst.

Mellon carried on as the laughter subsided. "You gentlemen're all acquainted, I presume? ...From one or the other of our previous rendezvous?"

Everyone smiled, and nodded or said 'yes.'

The lawyers took vacant seats on either side of Mellon; and he commenced, in a humorless tone:

"Gentlemen, we've got to get a hold on this hemp problem. It's getting worse. The rumors we talked about are no longer rumors. I met last night with an *eye witness*, says he, personally, test-drove a motor-car – a Ford – that runs on hemp-oil!

"The good news was the car wasn't up to standard. Ford wasn't satisfied. But they're back on the job, with new incentives, as we speak. My man couldn't get me a picture of the vehicle – it's all under cover; cameras and reporters 'off limits' at the plant. What he did get were photos of the goddamn hemp fields! Ford's growing tens of thousands of acres of this 'fuel,' out in the corn-belt somewhere."

"Jesus!" said Sanford, nearly jumping out of his seat. "This is disastrous!"

Mellon raised his palm toward the oil-man and spoke firmly:

"No, not yet, it isn't! And it won't be, my friend, if we use our heads. We've got some time – the next test-run isn't scheduled till March of next year. With a little luck, the car could fail again, and again, Ford being the die-hard perfectionist that he is.

"Obviously, we can't leave it to luck. The risks are too great at this point. We've known for some time that hemp is a growing threat to our interests, varied as they are. But this is 'huge,'" he shook his head emphatically, "not to be ignored! If and when this car takes off – pardon the goddamn pun, it's going to hurt us. Could very well ruin us, the lot of us! If we go down, it'll finish the economy. Forget about a recovery! We can't let that happen, to us, or to our countrymen."

"Amen," muttered Sanford; the rest expressing their accord.

"However," Mellon continued, smiling smugly, to the relief of his listeners, "we happen to have an ace in the hole, thanks to Mr. Hearst ..." He nodded to the newspaper magnate.

"Thanks to 'investigative reporting,'" Hearst corrected him, "uncovers the hidden story. Most Americans never heard of this, but the leaves and buds of the hemp plant contain a narcotic. Mexicans know all about it. Some Negroes, too. The Mexicans dry it, and smoke it. And get hooked on it! Makes 'em crazier and more violent than they already are.

"We've been running stories in California, a few in Chicago, and elsewhere, about murders and other crimes committed by these crazies under the influence of hemp – 'marijuana,' we call it; Mexican slang word for it."

He looked back to Mellon, who laid out the plot:

"Here's how we use this 'marijuana thing' to fix our problem: We step up the marijuana stories in the papers, nation-wide. Get the entire country aware of the menace, and the fact that it's growing.

"We also get my nephew, Harry Anslinger, on the case. I've set up a Bureau of Narcotics at the Treasury, and I just made Harry chief. The man's got a passion for prohibition. And he's got a following – clever speaker, gotta hand it to him. He and his people are going to need a mission, once the repeal goes into effect. And let's face it, gentlemen, barring an act of God, there's no stopping this repeal!

"So, we make Harry happy. We give him a new mission: Go get marijuana, and that means hemp, under government control!"

Sanford wasn't buying it: "How the hell do you *control* hemp, Andrew? It's grown all over the country – all sorts of uses. You can't take away people's livelihoods!"

"No, but you can 'persuade' them to grow something else," Worth interjected. "You can tax hemp, and license growers. Make hemp expensive and impractical to farm, which, in turn, will curb production, of hemp *and* marijuana. Good for us. Good for the public. Everybody wins!"

"Except the farmers!" Sanford argued. "We're in the worst depression *ever,* for Christ's sake!"

"It's the lesser of two evils," Jackson maintained, "and I think we can make it happen. There is a catch, though, and this is crucial. We've got to keep the whole thing under cover. We can't let it out that hemp and marijuana are one in the same. At least not now, in the midst of an economic crisis. We'd have the farmers and the manufacturers up in arms! Like you say, hemp is everywhere – a lot of uses. And it's cheap to grow; for the time being."

"As I told Mr. Hearst," Worth put in, "we need to build a stronger case against this drug as well. Now, before the news that marijuana is hemp gets around. What we've got so far is weak; mostly hearsay and conjecture.

"Also, as any doctor will tell you, medicinal hemp, cannabis, is a *sedative*, and a *pain reliever*. It puts you to sleep, friends; makes you feel *better*. Damned effective, too! I've tried it! But it doesn't work as a violence argument. Unfortunately. All it 'kills' is our case!"

"As I told *you*, Worth," Hearst responded testily, "nobody *smokes* medicinal hemp! They take it in tinctures, infusions – has nothing to do with our case!"

"Maybe so," Worth rebutted, "but we can't be guessing…"

"Gentlemen, gentlemen," Mellon interrupted, motioning for quiet, "Let's not worry about the case right now. Let's leave that to Harry. He'll make us a stand-up case, I promise you. Besides, we've got no beef with cannabis. Let them grow all the medicine they want – tax free!"

"I'm in," Du Pont declared, "at least for a 'wait and see.' … Unless someone has a better idea?" He looked around. No one responded.

"I'm in, too," said Sanford, insipidly, "something's got to be done."

"It's unanimous, then," Mellon summed it up. "Bill Hagar gave his blessing this morning; the lawyers – the best in the business," he motioned to Jackson and Worth, "are at our service. It's been a pleasure, gentlemen. We'll meet in three month's time, barring an emergency. Meanwhile, you can reach me at my home or D.C. office, or through Jackson here, or

Worth, with any new information or suggestions. You're all on my 'A' list, which means they put you through to me, night or day – don't let 'em tell you otherwise..."

Jackson indicated that he wished to speak, and Mellon gave him a nod.

"Just a quick reminder," said the lawyer. "Let us not forget that we're under cover! What we talked about today is *not* to be repeated, gentlemen, even to your wives. Word gets around! The fewer people who know about the hemp-mobile, and above all, the hemp-marijuana connection, the better our chance of accomplishing our mission. I can't think of a reason to alert anyone to this trivia anyway... Unless one of you has a hemp-man in the family?" He eyed the men, with a grin. " ...Eh?"

Hearst's expression went from bored to indignant; the rest answered laughingly in the negative.

Worth tapped his pen assertively to get the men's attention:

"Also on the marijuana – a final word: With all this hair-raising publicity on the drug, there's bound to be a lot of small talk about it. And that's good! Let them talk! Could get slippery, though, if you join in.

"So here's our rule of thumb – simple, fail-safe: No matter who says what about it, or asks you what about it, *never* use the words 'marijuana' and 'hemp' in the same conversation! You can't go wrong..."

Hearst, who had made it clear to Mellon and Du Pont from the outset that he would not be taking direction on this matter from anyone, and certainly not from anyone's "bossy underlings," looked like he was about to hit the ceiling.

Mellon caught it, and rose suddenly from his chair. "All right, then! That'll do it!" he cut Worth off mid-sentence; the well-compensated lawyer taking the slight quite in stride.

"Meeting adjourned, gentlemen!" Mellon went on, glancing at his watch. "That's under fifteen minutes – 'quick and painless,' the way we like 'em! Back to your wives for now, my friends!"

Everyone stood, and gathered their notes and briefcases.

"I heard, by the way," Mellon spoke in a hushed tone, as he led the conspirators out, "the movie they're running downstairs is excellent. And women love it! They've added two more screenings at my request. So, have a look, gents! Treat the missus! Might as well get something here for our money!"

Kate and Lucy had a passion for the movies, and had planned to see "Grand Hotel" at the three o'clock showing. June had used her pull to get them the best seats in the house. Reluctant as Kate was to miss a sneak preview, however, she asked to be excused, apologetically, at the last minute. She needed to spend the time with her family, and help prepare for Will's arrival.

"Don't be sorry, 'Sweet-pea,'" said Lucy to Kate. "I'd do the same, were I in your shoes. And, oh," she went on in good humor, "how I wish I were in your shoes!"

Kate thanked Lucy, and hugged her. "You're the best friend – ever, and I love you dearly!" she proclaimed.

She and Noble called for Bobby to come get them right after dessert.

Bobby's son, Davey, an adorable, precocious, three year old towhead, came running outside to greet them as they pulled into the driveway. The boy's elderly, black nanny, struggling to keep up with him, called out after him:

"Masta Davey, Masta Davey… Slow down, now, 'chile.' No need ta rush – they's comin' in!"

"Stop! Bobby! Please!" Kate cried out, upon sight of Davey, and leapt nimbly out of the car as it came to a halt. She bent down, hoisted the child into her arms, held him up to the sky, back to her breast, and up again, whirling him around, kissing his belly, giggling with him, telling him she loved him – absolutely adored him, and was "over the moon" to see him again.

Bobby's wife, Liddy, rushed out to join the welcoming party. She and Kate had become bosom-buddies over the years. The two shared a common bond, each having suffered the loss of their mother while still in their teens. Liddy, who was seven years Kate's senior, the first female in her family to be college educated, to drive a car, and to oversee the family business, the latter whilst blooming as an equal rights activist, and a devoted wife and mother, had also become Kate's role model. Kate sojourned with Bobby and Liddy for a month each summer after they were married, and moved in to assist and comfort them during the weeks before and after Davey was born.

Like Kate, Liddy was a pretty-faced, blue-eyed, tall, slender blonde, albeit to a lesser extent in each particular. The two were often mistaken for sisters, and had great fun pretending to be.

Bobby, paradoxically, bore little resemblance to his sister. No 'fair-boy' he, his complexion was ruddy and nearly always suntanned; his eyes and hair were chestnut brown. At five foot ten, he wasn't especially tall for a man, and his muscle-bound stature made him look shorter. His ears protruded slightly beyond the rough-hewn angles of his face, yet his was a face with eye-appeal, by all accounts.

Bobby's smile, though, was the charmer – giant-sized, and sunny, with just enough of the rascal in it to lend him the 'leading man' look. And how he loved to show it off, along with his pearly whites. It lit up his face, crinkling it boyishly, and reducing his guesstimated age by a decade. He was thirty-three.

"We've got presents for ya'll," Kate announced jubilantly upon entering the foyer of her brother's grand domicile. "I'll be right back!" She passed Davey on to Noble, and started up the winding stairway to the guest room she'd been assigned to that morning.

"Wait! Kate," Liddy called after her, "in all the excitement, I nearly forgot…"

Kate turned around, her face aglow with anticipation. "He called?"

Liddy smiled and cheerily confirmed, "He did – around lunch-time. He was already in the area, meeting with an associate. Said he'd be here 'bout six… We chatted for a while; he sounds wonderful!"

"He *is* wonderful, Liddy! I just know you're goin' to love him!"

The women began to rub their arms vigorously, suddenly aware of autumn's nip in the air; and then hurried off again.

"We'll be in the living room," Liddy shouted over her shoulder, "got a fire going."

Bobby and Liddy were the first to admit it: they'd been "incredibly lucky!" After seven years of marriage, they were more in love than ever, and had been blessed with a happy, healthy child. Despite the interminable economic depression, they were earning plenty of money – Bobby, amazingly, as an investment advisor! His steadfast clients – not one of them having lost their shirt in the crash of '29 – referred to him, reverently, as 'Boy Wonder.' Liddy, also known for her brilliant business mind, was second in command after her father, in the latter's D.C.-based trucking firm, and was duly credited with keeping the firm in the black through the ongoing crisis.

To top it all off, the couple resided in, and, for the most part, worked out of, their 'dream-home.' The house was situated on five hilly acres, in a countrified residential area in northern Virginia, a few minutes by car from the D.C. border. Originally a classic, two-story colonial manor, a pair of giant wings had been added to the main house to render it an enormous U-shaped mansion. The top floors of the wings were composed of guest suites, and 'his' and 'her' offices. As these rooms were designed to accommodate business as well as personal guests, they were accessible from both indoors and out. The ground floors of the wings contained quarters for live-in staff on one side, and on the other, garages and an expansive play/work room.

The lush, picturesque courtyard between the wings was another of Kate's favorite places in the world. An amazing variety of small trees, shrubs, and exotic flowers thrived within the walls of the fertile yard, which also provided a perfect balance of exposure to, and shelter from, the elements. There was always a heady fragrance in the air, and something magnificent to gaze upon in awe.

What Kate loved most about the space, though, was its interplay of natural and man-made design. Bobby had taken to building with the natural stones of the area, and had become quite the artist. His quaint stone walls were the groundwork of the courtyard; they formed seating arrangements, and flowerbeds, and lined the sloping lane to the cherry orchard below. The views from nearly every room in the house were spectacular. Moreover, as Bobby had re-routed the creek on the property into a stony bed that wound along the open end of the yard, under a bridge, and down, by the lane to the orchard, the sound of rushing water was everywhere!

"I had a peek at the new addition, 'Stone-man,'" Kate announced, upon rejoining the clan at fireside.

"It's gorgeous!" she referred to the tiered, stone fountain that Bobby had built in the center of the courtyard. "And the sound of tricklin' water," she spoke dramatically, "blends brilliantly, 'symphonically,' with the rushin' of the creek – pure genius!"

Bobby gave her the big smile.

"Runs in the family," he returned the compliment, alluding to Kate's considerable musical talent.

She muttered something about being "out of practice," and then kissed her brother on the cheek, and handed him a brightly wrapped parcel.

"From Daddy and me – a thank you, for havin' us," she clarified, and passed another parcel to Liddy.

Holding on to the third parcel, she took a seat on a footstool next to Davey, who was sitting, cross-legged, on a cushion on the floor.

"Is the big one mine, Auntie?" Davey asked her hopefully, holding out his hands. Everyone had to laugh, although Liddy promptly reminded the child to mind his manners. Kate sat on the floor with Davey while he opened his package. He had a good idea of what was in it. Kate and Noble had given him a hand-carved train and track set for Christmas, and had promised him the station that went with it for his birthday.

"Exthellent!" Davey shouted, as he lifted the colorful model out of the box. But on second thought, he asked fretfully, "Won't you be coming to my party, Auntie? Granpy?"

Kate assured the boy that they'd return in a fortnight for his birthday, with another present. "We wouldn't miss it for the world," Noble agreed.

Davey gave them each a hug, and then rushed off to his playroom with the new toy. He turned, though, half-way out the door. "Stop in, any time!" he offered, and left them chuckling.

Bobby felt compelled to echo, "Exthellent!" at the sight of his gift – a beautifully crafted, fine stone-chisel, designed for sculpting, rather than splitting, stone.

"Guess ya'll think I've built enough walls, hmm, Daddy, Sis?" he kidded with them.

Noble took it seriously, "Well, we figured that given your creative 'genius,' as Kate put it, and the way you have with stone, you might be as clever with the fine work as the rough."

"And, you just might like it!" Kate added.

"I just might!" Bobby agreed, wielding the tool like a sculptor, on an imaginary bust. "To tell you the truth, I've been thinkin' about doin' this for a long time. Ya'll read my mind! Thank you so much!"

Liddy, not to be outdone, hollered, "Exthellent, indeed!" upon opening her present. It was a black, felt, cloche hat, with a large, white satin dove stitched along the rim – very art-deco, and 'very' Liddy.

Kate noted that she had purchased the piece, presented as 'wearable art,' at an estate auction, in Richmond; the proceeds of which were going to various charities, including Alan House, and a women's rights organization.

"How perfect!" Liddy exclaimed, donning the hat, and parading about, to hoots and whistles from her audience.

The doorbell rang at five-thirty. Kate, with Davey on her heels, scurried ahead of the houseman to answer it.

Will stood in the doorway, grinning broadly, looking handsomer than ever, despite the remnant bruise under his eye. He held a huge bouquet in one hand, an overnighter in the other, his forearms supporting a stack of presents, leaning precariously against his chest.

"Hello, Angel Eyes!" he greeted Kate, bending forward to kiss her, toppling the presents, rescued handily by the houseman; much to the amusement of Davey.

Will stepped into the foyer, and observed the laughing child with delight. Crouching down to his level, he said to him: "You must be Davey. Pleased to meet you; I'm…"

Davey, unaccustomed to eyeing strangers up close, sped off toward his parents and Noble, who were standing by in the living room, waiting to greet Will. Once the grownups had hugged and shook hands, however, Davey decided that Will was not so scary after all, and approached him, hand extended:

"Pleased to meet you, 'Uncle' Will," he said clearly and endearingly, in his sweet, high-pitched voice.

Liddy said, "Oops!" and looked to Will, who was already saddling the child on his arm. "Hope you don't mind, Will," she spoke honestly. "It was either 'Mr. Will,' or 'Uncle Will,' and I thought…"

"Please, don't apologize, Liddy. I'm flattered." said Will. "And, you've given me an idea!" He winked at Kate.

She blushed.

Noble and Bobby started to chuckle; the boy caught the giggles, and then Will, and finally the women. And so it went, well into the night, a time for laughter, contagious and unsuppressed.

The evening meal was served early, to give Davey an extra hour with his guests. And how he amused them; the three-year-old reporting, with his cute, little lisp, that he was soon to be seven; that he wanted to grow hemp, like his Granpy, when he grew up; and that he hoped to take a sleep-over at the hemp-farm – soon, when he turned seven!

His mother kept rolling her eyes, and finally told him that he was being silly; to which the child replied with a giggle: "Yes, I am silly, but I'm also funny!" And the crowd cracked up again.

At eight o'clock promptly, the boy's nanny whisked him away for a bath and bed. The guests were invited to tuck him in a while later. In his prayers, Davey thanked God for his 'Granpy,' Auntie Kate, and 'Uncle' Will; the latter moving Kate and nearly Will to tears. Noble jokingly offered them his hanky as they returned to the dining room. Will, of course, had fun with it, sniveling and snorting in the cloth, and passing it back.

Bobby had set out bottles of brandy and various liqueurs while they were gone.

"Hope ya'll don't mind?" he looked to his father, skipped Kate, and then to Will. "Albeit slightly ahead of the repeal?"

"Don't mind if I do!" Kate lifted a glass, to her brother's grin.

"Help yourself," replied Noble. "I'll take a coffee, though, Liddy, if I may?"

"Certainly," said Liddy, and rang a bell for the housekeeper.

"To tell you the truth," Will responded, "after my experience today, I'm thinkin' about abstainin' till that Amendment's overturned."

With all eyes upon him, Will went on to explain that he and his associate had witnessed a raid in the private club they'd lunched in that day. He described the incident as "shocking," and "harrowing," with armed federal agents, backed by police, busting down the door, ordering everyone on the floor, firing warning shots; people running and screaming chaotically, trays and glass flying.

"Were you drinkin'?" Kate asked him worriedly.

"I was," he owned, "and scared – I'd never been in a raid before! Luckily, my associate had. 'Hit the floor,' he said, 'and don't make a peep!' It seems they never arrest the obedient boozers, and only rarely the mouthy ones. Too many boozers; not enough policemen, or jail cells.

"The Feds arrested the owners, though – on the spot. Handcuffed 'em, and hauled 'em in – for violatin' the Volstead Act; the owners complainin' all the while that they'd paid off the police, 'like always'! It was absurd! Bizarre!"

He looked to Kate: "Seems your pal, Anslinger, was behind it. Cops told us afterwards he's been on a rampage, arrestin' suppliers, fast as he can, before the repeal comes in. Jails are burstin' with small-time owners and runners. Nobody gets to the boss-men – smart lawyers, crooked judges, bribes, kickbacks… Anslinger knows it, but turns a blind eye. Police here hate him, call him 'the fanatic.'"

"'The fanatic' was with us," Noble offered. "He and the missus, sittin' right at our table."

"I heard," Will replied, "but his agents were at that club today, Noble, wreaking havoc." Again he looked to Kate:

"Remember tellin' me 'bout Anslinger's 'sidekicks'? One was tall, dark, neat as a pin? The other short, blonde, scruffy? 'Unlikely twosome'?"

Kate nodded yeses in rapid succession.

"It was them!" he declared. "Must've been! Unless they've got twins workin' for the Feds!"

Kate sighed. "Just when I was startin' to like Mud-slinger!"

"He did seem unusually 'thoughtful' today – even 'humble' at times," Noble went along. "And his wife is nice as can be! But it sounds to me like power's gone to Mr. Anslinger's head.

What he's doin' with the police, first off, is wrong. Makin' life more difficult for the honest cops; lettin' the crooked ones get away with 'murder,' long as they do his dirty work – it's just plain wrong!"

"Well put, Daddy!" Bobby remarked. "You'd think he'd know better, given the general mood of the country. Even folks who think alcohol's 'evil' are callin' Prohibition 'the greater evil.' They've had enough of the crime and violence it spawned."

"Not to mention the *billions* of dollars to criminal coffers at our expense!" Will put in. "And corruption in government, all the way to the top."

Noble could see where the conversation was going – where he, in fact, had led it. It troubled him to even think that the American government could be corrupt; that its system of checks and balances could fail to weed out the faulty policies and the bad seeds. He believed in the 'American Way.' For the same reason, he could not sit by, idly, and smile, while his loved ones broke the law.

Noble and his wife had abstained from taking liquor from the day Prohibition went into effect. They had done so, despite the infringement on their personal pleasures, to teach their children respect for the law. It was clear to him now that their sacrifice had been in vain.

He downed his coffee quickly, and excused himself; giving Kate and Liddy a good-night peck on the cheek, and for Bobby and Will a pat on the shoulder. He needed a good night's rest, he explained, as he planned to drive Kate's car home at daybreak, alone. There was still some post-harvest work to be done at 'Katelyn,' he said; it was 'calling' him. Also, he wished to allow the "love birds" to travel together, and take their time.

Kate and Will offered to 'caravan' behind him; but Noble wouldn't hear of it. He kissed the girls again, and went to his room.

"On second thought," Will piped up, when the elder was out of earshot, "to Hades with Anslinger! This 'love bird' will take a brandy after all, Bobby, if I may."

Bobby laughed, and poured Will a drink. He, Kate and Liddy took seconds, and the foursome had a fine time, trading life-stories, cheering "exthellent," chuckling, and having yet another, into the midnight hours.

At four-thirty that morning, Kate made an entry into her journal, entitled, "Engaged, and 'After-glowing'!" It read:

"Dear Diary,

Can you imagine? I'm to be Mrs. Will Fairfield! My 'Dream Man' proposed, spur of the moment, in the hallway of the guest wing in Bobby's home! Got down on his knee – right there, said he just couldn't wait! But he promised to buy me a ring, and ask for Daddy's blessing, straightaway. I, of course, replied, 'Yes – yes, my darling!' and we kissed, and wept for joy, the two of us.

And then he made love to me, for the longest time. He has the 'ladies first' approach that Liddy laughingly told me to pray for, and to encourage – the one that she insisted, 'in all seriousness,' makes 'all the difference' for a woman. Lord, she was right!

No wonder all the fuss about it! Such a mystical, magical thing, this coming together body and soul – I dare say, life-altering! The fluttering and tingling, from my belly to my toes, will surely fade. But I, Kate Lynette Burnett, shall never be the same!

My darling sleeps contently by my side now, in the green guest bedroom, just down the hall from the blue, to which he was assigned. I must wake him soon, alas, and send him off, lest we be discovered, intertwined, in the morn. I refuse to feel a whit of remorse for consummating an act of pure love, but Lord knows Daddy would see things differently! And Liddy

*would feel awful for having sent the 'love birds,' intoxicated as
we were, to the same wing!*
    P.S.: Don't worry, Mama, we took all precautions!
    With love,
    Your own, happy girl,
    K."

Will kept his promises, Noble gave his consent, and the
twosome formally celebrated their betrothal the following
weekend. Will's parents threw them a huge engagement party,
a hundred plus guests, in the banquet room of a charming hotel
near their office building in downtown Richmond. The hors
d'oeuvres of all sorts were delectable, the champagne flowed
freely (albeit undercover) throughout the evening, and a five-
piece dance-band played superbly, by request, everything from
the proper foxtrot to the zany Charleston. Young and old, led by
the fiancées, danced away into the wee hours. The consensus
among the guests as they finally took to their complimentary
rooms, was that the affair had been "marvelous," "smashing,"
"fabulous," and words to that effect.

The engagement, however, was tumultuous, from day one
after the party, and the wedding was postponed and called off,
again and again. As Will's work would soon be taking him
abroad for lengthy periods, the couple had originally planned
to wed in a year's time, in the autumn of 1932. The more
Will thought about leaving Kate behind, though, the more he
dreaded it.

He decided to have her accompany him to Europe instead,
assuming that once the proper arrangements were made, she'd
be delighted to go. Will's brother, James, and his family were
living in London; and Will was certain that they and Kate would
get along famously. James' wife, Tess, who, by coincidence,
was an alumnus of Westhampton College, Kate's Alma Mater,
wrote to Kate personally, offering her the guest suite in their
home, for the entire year, or any portion thereof. In the letter,
Tess described London-town as "fascinating" – a "must see"

for the educated woman; and depicted the suite Kate would be occupying as "charming and refurbished," with a bird's-eye view of a classic English garden.

The American tobacco industry, as of late fall, 1931, had yet to be affected by the great economic depressions at home or abroad. Indeed, more Americans than ever were smoking, and more Europeans were smoking American. The tougher the times, it seemed, the greater the need for a few pastime pleasures.

Nevertheless, Fairfield Tobacco was not taking chances. Like its competitors, it was establishing new markets in the Old World, to offset the effects of the Depression Era slump that could very well be looming at home. In England, under James Fairfield's supervision, the company's "Kings Blend" and "Knights Blend" – loose tobacco sold in bright red tins or pouches – had already become top sellers. Fairfield's packaged, pre-rolled cigarettes were also outselling the European, and most American brands.

James intended to accomplish the same in the countries on the Continent, beginning with France and Germany. It was agreed that James would head the operations once they were up and running; and Will, who, in addition to his expertise in international law, was fluent in French, and got by in German, would oversee the deal-making. By the time he and Kate were engaged, Will had completed the contract work in Richmond. But his family was expecting him to be in Europe for the closings; and Will felt he had no choice but to go.

Much to his dismay, however, Kate felt she had no choice but to stay. How, she asked him, could she leave Noble to fend for himself for a year, in the throes of the worst economic disaster ever, with the price of hemp plummeting, and competition from Big Business growing stiffer. She and Noble were partners; he'd come to rely on her over time, especially in the two years since 'Uncle' Ben, his brother, and previous life-long partner, had passed away.

As a compromise, Kate agreed to accompany Will to England, after harvest, for six weeks. Will was less than satisfied with her concession, though; and prior to arranging their passage on the ocean liner, presented her with a "better idea:"

"I want to marry you now, Kate – tonight, tomorrow, as soon as we can," he told her excitedly, over dinner one evening at their favorite restaurant in Richmond. "This way, we can be together, all year, back and forth. Who could deny us our togetherness, as newlyweds?"

A look of despair came over Kate's face.

He hesitated, brow knit, for a moment, but quickly recovered.

"Don't worry, Darlin'," he sought to ease her mind, "we can keep it a secret, if you like – except for our parents... And, of course, we'll carry on with the 'fancy' weddin', as planned, upon our return."

Kate had all she could do to keep from crying – the more he said, the worse she felt. She could not imagine what he was thinking! She'd been under the impression that Will 'knew' her, deep, in the center of her heart, and that he therefore understood that she could not, in good conscience, ignore her obligations, just because something more exciting came up. It struck her now that he had misunderstood her, and she him, from the beginning. Still, she loved him with all her heart, and the last thing she wanted was to hurt his feelings. She took a deep breath, and rolled her eyes towards the Heavens in a silent prayer.

"It's wonderful to know, Darlin', that you want to marry me instantly," she spoke in a sweet, empathetic tone. "And I'm inclined to say, yes, let's do it! But I'm afraid that it would make our separation even more painful. I cannot spend the comin' year in Europe, Will, married or single. Your work is callin' you there, and I know how important it is to you – and to us, to our future.

"But try to understand, Darlin', that for now, my work is *here*, and just as important to me. I must see Daddy through these hard times, for his sake, and for mine. I love that farm, Will; and I won't have it fail on my watch!"

Her good intentions notwithstanding, Will was crushed by Kate's response. And stunned. And annoyed. Any of the women he'd been involved with formerly would have jumped at the chance to elope with him – the sooner, the better, of that he was certain. Indeed, it was his failure to propose, or to even consider marriage that had brought his previous relationships – all of them – to dismal endings. But here was Kate, the only one he ever wanted, putting him off; perfectly willing to send him off to Europe, alone, for months at a time; not the least bit concerned that he might get lonely, or tempted to stray.

He stared at her, silently, for a few seconds, running his thumb and middle fingers along his jaw-line, from beneath his ears to the point of his chin. He was beginning to see an underlying selfish streak in Kate. He wondered if it had been there all along; if, under the spell of her beauty as he was, he had missed it. He was also beginning to resent that hemp-farm of hers, to which, it seemed to him, she was obsessively attached. It occurred to him that trying to change her mind about the elopement, even if he succeeded, would only make matters worse; but he found himself trying anyway:

"What if the hard times continue, Kate? For years? Or decades? Which could very well keep me in Europe throughout? Would you postpone our marriage indefinitely?"

"I wouldn't postpone it *at all*, Will! Not one day! We agreed on second Saturday next October; and I shall be ready, come rain or come shine, by mid-September, I promise you!"

He was not at all comforted. Now, he felt that she was measuring her words, and twisting his, to manipulate the situation. She was selfish *and* manipulative; it was finally coming out!

'Better now than after the marriage,' he thought. But where was that sweet girl he'd fallen madly in love with? And what happened to her unbridled passion for him?

"Will, Darlin', talk to me, please," she pled with him. "I love you so… Please say you understand."

He shook his head. "I don't understand, Kate. I don't know what you mean by 'love.' For me, loving someone means wanting to be with that person – not next October, but now, in this very minute, and every minute, forever after."

Kate's face hardened. "I see," she spoke sarcastically. "What you're saying, then, is that if you loved me, and I couldn't go to Europe, that you would shirk your obligations to family and business, and stay put here in Richmond, so that you could 'be' with me!"

"I would not have asked you, Kate, if I thought you 'couldn't' go. The truth is you could, if you wanted to – your daddy would never stand in the way of our happiness!"

"No, he would not; and neither would your parents. But this has nothin' to do with them. It's all about you and me, Will. And the truth, as I see it, is that I love you as you love me. I want us to be together as much as you do. I'm not willin' to shirk my responsibilities to make it happen. But neither are you!"

"The difference is, I admire that quality in you, while you begrudge it in me!"

'Manipulator!' he wanted to scream at her. 'Selfish, scheming, manipulator!' But he said nothing. He just glared at her. Then he got up from the table, found the waiter, paid the check, and returned.

"If you don't mind, Kate," he said stiffly, "we'll skip dessert for tonight. I need to get home. Do some thinkin'."

"Of course," she replied, jumping to her feet, smoothing out her skirt, collecting her handbag and her thoughts.

"And while you're at it, Will," she said snidely, before taking a first step toward the exit, "ask yourself how you came by your double standard."

"Double standard?" he heard himself asking, and regretting, at once.

She glanced over one shoulder, and then the other. People on either side were beginning to stare.

"Yes," she whispered, looking at him tensely, "one set of rules for men, another for women, an insidious feature of our culture... But I can't imagine how you came by it."

Before he could respond, she gestured toward the exit with her head, and strutted out.

It was almost as if she had commanded him to follow; and he had half a mind to sit back down and order dessert! But the gentleman in him overruled it. He tagged along behind her, fuming.

It had turned dark and drizzly outside while they were dining. Kate stayed put under the portico of the building, assuming that Will would run to fetch the car.

He came face to face with her instead, his jaw tight, the anger in his eyes flickering with the glimmer of restaurant lights.

It broke her heart to see him distressed. He was always so carefree in her presence – easy to laugh, quick with the joke. He made nonsense of the world, and encouraged her to do the same; and how she loved it!

She started to apologize, but he interrupted, lashing out at her in a condescending tone:

"If there's a 'double standard,' it's in *your* world, Kate, not mine! And I won't have you pinnin' it on me! I remember tellin' you, but you seem to have forgotten: My mother and father worked side by side in the office since I was an infant. She's as clever in business as he is, and everyone at Fairfield, includin' him, knows it! How would I come by a double standard?"

"You're not payin' attention, Will!" she snapped back. "That was my point, precisely: how could you, of all people, trivialize a woman's work? My work? You know how important the farm is to me, especially now – I've told you time and again. Yet, here you are, askin' me to drop what I'm doin', as if it were nothin', *for a year*, so that I could tag along with you to Europe, while you carry on with your 'all-important' work. And I should be fine with it – or rather thrilled with it, because we'd get married now, instead of later. As if I were some sort of 'gold-digger,' who just can't wait to get a man of means to the altar!

"How would you feel if I said, 'yes, Darlin',' let's tie the knot tonight. And tomorrow, off to England for six weeks. You'll help James as much as you can, and then return to the States with me, until after harvest. And back and forth, and so on, together – always!"

"Don't be ridiculous! There're millions of dollars at stake in these deals – I have to be there!"

"Money isn't everything, Will. I believe that my work is vital, not just for me, but for the country. Hemp is one of the most useful plants on earth. And becomin' more so. There are a lot of prominent people, Henry Ford among them – as you may recall, who see it as the road to recovery! I doubt that anyone, anywhere, includin' a Fairfield, would suggest that tobacco…"

"What's so important about you bein' at the farm all winter?" he interrupted again, no apology.

"Daddy and I are helpin' Mike Anderson set up a Hemp Association in Virginia – sorely needed."

"Anderson?"

"Yes! …Mike, our wholesaler."

"I know who he is, Kate… And I don't like him!"

"Well, that's unfortunate, Darlin', but what does it have to do…"

He turned away from her, left her standing there, sentence hanging, and went to get the car; and spoke not a word on the short ride – minutes which seemed like hours to Kate – back to his home. She wept quietly throughout.

The sky had cleared, and the stars were out, as they pulled into his carport. He noticed the trail of tears on her face in the moonlight, but he was not moved.

"I need a bit of solitude, Kate," he said firmly, "but I won't have you drivin' back to the farm, in the dark, alone. My houseman will be happy to take you home in one of my cars, or in yours, if you prefer. He'll stay at the Plantation, get someone to drive him back in the mornin', and deliver your car if you choose to leave it."

"Thank you, but *no*," she replied, straight away. "I'll stay with Luce. She's just a couple of minutes from here. I'll take my car – no need to worry."

"She's home? You're sure?"

"Quite sure. But even if she's not, and June is not, the housekeeper will let me in – I've done it before; don't worry."

"Fine. Good-night."

"Good-night."

They got out of his car at once, and she climbed into hers, which was parked alongside. He raised his hand and waved, so sadly; and she waved back. Then she exhaled heavily, closed her eyes, leaned her forehead to the steering wheel, and begged the 'powers that be' for help – "Lord, Mama, Somebody, *please*, tell me what to do!"

She was moved to get out of the car, and run to him.

He opened his arms to her, instinctively.

"We had our first fight, Will, and I'm so sorry," she whispered tearfully against his shoulder. "I'm sorry if what I said hurt you. It was not my intention – could never be. I only meant to be honest – to tell you how I truly feel… How else can we be close, Will? We must speak our hearts, and sometimes our fears. But I want you to know that my love for you is strong – unshakable, and so it will always be."

"I'm sorry too," he responded from his heart. "And I do love you, Kate… But we're so different… Perhaps too different to make a go of it."

It was clear to her that he needed to be alone. She wished him good-night again, without a kiss, and returned to her car. He waited and watched as she started up, turned on her lights, and drove away – direction Lucy's.

A few minutes later, she was parked in the beautifully illuminated, tree-lined driveway of the Stevens' mansion. It appeared that Lucy was home, as her new beau's Studebaker Roadster was parked in front of one of the garages.

Lucy and her beau, Jonathan Ledger, had met at Kate and Will's engagement party, and had fallen madly in love by night's end – one of the happier outcomes of that event. Jonathan, the son of the Fairfield Seniors' dearest friends, Daniel and Harriet Ledger, had grown up thinking of Will as his older, much to be revered and emulated, cousin.

Kate opened her windows, and sat there for a long while, staring at Jonathan's car, listening to the sigh of the wind, wondering what to do, and what Lucy and Jon were up to, if they were alone. She noticed the lights were on in Lucy's bedroom, but suddenly they were out! Kate decided that she couldn't stay. The thought of intruding on the couple was dreadful enough; and then to have to explain why she was there – to re-live the grief. She just couldn't face it, any of it!

She needed sanctuary – her room, her faithful dogs at her side. She turned her car around, and headed for home; and made it, in exactly an hour, without incident.

"Almost as if I had 'floated' home!" she thought haughtily, as she pulled into the old barn, which served as a garage for her car and Noble's. She got out of the car, greeted her frisky, frolicking welcoming party, grabbed a bag in each hand, and plodded toward the house; her attention returning to Will, their myriad differences.

"What makes him think," the Suffragette within her pondered, "that I'm less capable of driving in the dark than he is? Or his houseman is!?" She burst out laughing, then, at her own haughtiness.

It wasn't so funny the next day, however. Unable to reach Will in the morning, at home or at the office, she left a message with his housekeeper and his secretary: "Returned   to Katelyn, safe and sound. Please call soon."

Her bidding was not to be done. On his way to the office that morning, Will went to look for her at Lucy's, and discovered that she hadn't spent the night there. He was furious.

Lucy telephoned Kate the minute he left.

"You're in trouble, Sweet-pea!" she said mournfully. "He described what you did as 'deliberately disrespectful' – a 'slap in the face!' *Nothin'* I said made him feel better... He jumped up and headed for the door when I tried to make light of it. I ran after him, gave him a hug, and said, 'Sorry, Will.' He hugged me back, but couldn't speak, on the verge of tears as he was – probably a good sign, that!"

"I hope so," Kate murmured pitifully.

Lucy sighed, and groaned, "Dear me," but then brightened up:

"So, tell me, Miss Burnett, do you feel the need to be alone today? ...Or would you prefer a shoulder to cry on? And someone to giggle with, in between?"

3
The Fanatic

Katelyn Farm, Late Fall, 1933

The day was unseasonably cold and windy, but the sky was the bluest of blues, and the sun shone brightly. Kate, at her desk in the living-room, looked up from her work and out the bay window to her rose-garden. The last of the late-bloomers – wildly vivid pinks, all seven, were soaking up the sun, standing proud against the wind. She gave them a smile of approval; and they smiled back. There was a hearth-fire going inside; her dogs sprawled out on the carpet in front of it. The feeling was pure contentment.

She had just completed the accounting for the farm, post-harvest, and confirmed that she and Noble were in the black again, albeit slightly, for the fourth tallying-up since the onset of the Great Depression. All was well with the Burnetts. Their harvest had been ample, their machinery was up to date, their bills were paid; their workers well-paid. None had been laid off since the paper-mill closed, back in '31; and even the mill-hands were making ends meet, with part-time work on the farm, and part-time, down the road, at the Fairfield Plantation.

Noble and June Stevens were happily betrothed, but had yet to set their wedding date; and were "very tempted," as Noble put it, "to shun tradition, and elope!" Kate and Will, on the contrary, had set yet another wedding date – their third, second Saturday of October, 1934. The couple laughingly agreed, though, that should this date be scrubbed, they, too, would skip the pomp and circumstance, and go see a justice of the peace when the mood struck!

The grandfather clock in the entry hall announced the five o'clock hour, and Kate began to straighten up her desk – hurriedly, but delightedly. She had packing to do. Will was coming home, via New York, the next evening. She was meeting him in the city – taking the train in from Richmond. They were spending two nights on the town, furthermore, and staying at the Waldorf Astoria – Kate's favorite indulgence, one she allowed herself, guiltlessly, on occasion, frugal as she was in between.

In keeping with the terms of their reunion, Will would be staying home for the holidays; after which he and Kate would travel to Europe together, and remain through early spring. She'd return home for the growing season; and he would follow, as soon as possible. And so they'd come and go, until such time – three or four years by Will's latest estimate – as Fairfield's European branches were up and running efficiently.

The new arrangement worked brilliantly for Kate, in part because it worked for Will as well. He was back to his lighthearted, 'joke-a-minute' self again; and she thanked God for it daily. The period preceding their coming to terms included the toughest days she'd known since her mother died. Indeed, even as she prepared for Will's homecoming, the thought of how close they'd come to an irreversible split gave her the shudders.

It had been two years, almost to the day, that Will had left for Europe without her; an extreme over-reaction, in Kate's view, as their one and only tiff had been relatively minor; no notably nasty words spoken, no particularly grievous deeds done. Nevertheless, Will had stayed in Europe through the holidays, Kate's bleakest Christmas ever, and on and on, for six months. He had failed to respond to her letters, moreover

– three, four, sometimes five dispatches a week, for weeks on end:

Five months into the unbearable silence, and on the brink of becoming physically ill, Kate finally took Nettie's advice, and tried a new approach. She wired Will, and gave him notice that she would be sending him "love," in the form of prayers and visualizations, instead of letters, from then on.

Will wired her back the following day:

My Darling Kate, Thank you for your letters, and your love. Please carry on. My first reply, and attempt to explain, is en route. Returning home May 10th, via New York. Meet me there, Darling, please. I love you, Will.

Kate literally jumped for joy – five feet into the air – upon reading the message! And then she dashed into the newly-sprouted hemp-fields, and danced and twirled, between the rows of green; and from there, ran full speed into the meadow, shouting to the wildflowers, "He loves me still! ...I knew it! ...He loves me still!"

That evening, she copied the telegram, verbatim, into her special diary. It was her first entry since Will had left, as she preferred to log only happy thoughts and events, in keeping with the instructive inscription on the journal's opening page:

Darling Daughter:
To record one's life is to give it meaning and direction...
To record one's blessings is to see them grow...
Happy growing! All My Love, Mama.

Will's first letter not only made the cut, it heightened Kate's awareness of her personal power, and changed her, dramatically. She had long viewed her life as an extraordinary story, brimming with extraordinary characters and situations; and she fancied the idea – an uncommon life is what she wanted, no question. At the same time, she believed that such a life was her "destiny," as determined by God. Upon reading Will's letter, however, it struck her, immediately, that her love for this man and her intention to be with him had overcome every obstacle and every fear between them. It wasn't just her destiny at work here, she was sure of it, it was her will. She was, in fact, *co-authoring* her uncommon life with God!

Adding to the wonder and beauty of it all, it appeared that Will, with the help of the world's most extraordinary housekeeper, was coming to a similar awareness. His letter read:

I never doubted my love for you, Kate. Nor yours for me. But I feared that my need to be with you was greater, and that it put me at a disadvantage in our relationship. I attributed your rejection of my elopement offer, and everything else we quarreled about, to that imbalance.

I didn't know what to do about it. So I did nothing, apart from sulking. Once here, I buried myself in work, let your unopened letters accumulate, and tried, though I failed, miserably, to keep them, and you, out of my mind.

But then your wire came, and the thought that you might 'write me off' brought me to my senses! I read the entire stack of your letters that day, and lo and behold, the sweet love I thought I'd lost forever was there, on every page, in your words and expressions, in your tone and vulnerability. I knew that it was real! And all of my fears seemed suddenly foolish.

I've changed, Kate. I accept that we have differences, and I am prepared to work them out, or live with them. But I'm not prepared to live without your love!

Forgive me, Darling! Let me make it up to you! Let us shelter each other with love again. No harm can come to us then, of this I am certain!

All My Love, Will

P.S.: Thank you also for the tidbits of 'Aunt' Nettie's wisdom. Her comments on love were comforting. I strung a few together in an affirmation, and repeat it whenever fear threatens: 'Love is the answer, the only solution, the power divine. Born of the Spirit, love cannot fail, nor can fear, in any form, prevail in its presence.' (She's really quite gifted, you know. We must get her to reconsider a book, help heal the world!)

Prior to Will's departure, he and Noble, as a team, had tried to convince Nettie that she should write a book, compiled from the countless notes she had taken over the decades. Her thoughts and solutions were exceptionally "healing and uplifting" they told her, and were she to make them available in book form – a "how-to," or the trendier, "book of affirmations," she could help a lot of people. They offered to see to the publishing for her.

Nettie's response was a gracious, "thank you, but no!" The thoughts and solutions were not *hers*, she said. They came from the Spiritual world, many from scripture. All she did was to ask for guidance, and then look, listen, and deliver it. She made it clear to the men as well that God didn't speak to her, *in particular*. His word, love and light were everywhere, available to everyone, from within and without. Not everyone had developed her knack of "seein' and listenin'," she acknowledged. But many had, and some, most certainly, had also been called to writing. She had not. Absolutely not!

The men were disappointed, and looked to Kate to talk some sense into Nettie.

Kate laughed out loud at the suggestion. "You would have *me* talk sense into her? Sorry, my Dears, you're on your own!"

To Kate's mind, Nettie was one of those rare individuals who was doing precisely what she was meant to do, "answering her calling." The proof, for Kate, was that Nettie loved her life – every aspect of it, and her work, as a housekeeper and as a healer. In promoting the well-being of those around her, moreover, this granddaughter of slaves spent many of her waking hours in a meditative state, and, thus, had come to know personal peace. Not only did Nettie have more common sense than any person Kate knew, she was happier! Even so, given her family history, Nettie had good reason to keep a low profile:

When Nettie was a young girl, in Louisiana, her brother was kidnapped, and murdered by an enraged lynch-mob. He was fifteen years old; and had committed no crime, other than being noticeable – he was very tall, very bright, and some said "uppity." Despite the vociferous protests of the plantation owners the family worked for, the authorities made little effort to see that justice was done. The case was pronounced "unsolved," and abandoned within a month.

Nettie's parents and grandmother, devastated and dispirited, resolved to protect the rest of their clan. They took a loan from their kindly employer, bought a mule, packed it up; and with their girls, Nettie, eight years old, and her sister, twelve; headed north, to safer ground. As luck would have it, they ran out of money in Fairfield County, Virginia, at harvest time, and found work reaping hemp for Noble's father. Within a few weeks, they knew that their course had been guided, their long journey ended, they were "home."

Owing to the magnanimity of Will's grandparents, both the poor-white and Negro communities of Fairfield County had decent, albeit segregated, housing, and well-equipped, well-staffed school-houses. As the Negroes' access to white churches was restricted, they were also provided with their own little 'house of God,' and a traveling pastor. Nettie received a good education. She became an avid reader, and according to her teachers, an able writer. The moment her talents drew attention, however, she ceased to display them. When she was twelve, her pastor approached her and asked if she'd like to write a monthly bulletin for the congregation. Nettie fell apart, and ran from him, sobbing. The "fear of uppity," as she and her sister had dubbed it, in an attempt to make light of it, haunted her still.

Nettie completed her schooling that year, went to work for Noble and his wife, and following her pastor's advice, began to pray and meditate; initially, three times a day, and gradually, throughout the day, while tending to chores. "Goin' within," as she labeled her practice, became her salvation. She conquered her fears in short time, and began teaching others to do the same; privately, though, so as not to rekindle the fear in her elders.

Coincidentally, just after Will and Noble had spoken to her, Nettie was prompted by a group of church-women, after service one Sunday, to reconsider writing. She opened her heart to Kate about it, on the following day at the farm:

"They say I'm not practicin' what I preach, Missy. I tell them not to be afraid, but, seems to them, I'm afraid, afraid of spreadin' my own good word. They spoke kindly to me 'bout it, but they were serious. Said my solutions helped them, why not everybody. I should write 'em down, pass 'em around – at least among the coloreds!" She exhaled audibly. "Trouble is, Missy, my folks are still scared, not for us grownups anymore, but for my boys, n' my sister's boys." She shook her head. "Can hardly blame 'em!"

"Hardly," Kate agreed sadly. But then her face lit up. "I believe *I've* got a solution this time, Aunt Net," she declared, "I'll be right back!" She left Nettie sitting at the kitchen table, raced up the stairs to her sanctuary, and returned with a stack of five thin books. Taking a seat across from Nettie, she sorted out the books, placed three in a pile between them, and put the others aside.

Nettie looked to her with questioning eyes. "Books?"

"Books!" Kate repeated with a smile. "Liddy phoned me, a couple weeks ago, said I *must* get a hold of these books, writers of this 'new thought movement.' Some of them started a kind of church! She said she thinks they're sayin' almost exactly what you're sayin'. And she was right!

"I've read these," she slid the three closer to Nettie, "They're yours now." She pointed to the one on top: "Try this first – amazin'! Florence Scovel Shinn. Everything you talk about is in these books: 'God is Love and Life – in you and me, and all of us. What we think, and say, and "see" shapes our lives' – all that. They even talk about 'the here and now.' You're not alone, Aunt Nettie. These are your brothers and sisters, white as they are, I'm sure of it! And if you don't want to write, you don't have to; they're doin' it for you!"

"Praise the Lord!" said Nettie, with much emotion. "And thank you, 'Missy!'" They got up, hugged, and cried a few happy tears on each other's shoulder.

Kate and Will's first reunion in New York was blissful, and wild. Will's secretary had pre-arranged their entire stay – limo service to and from the port, and to Bergdorf-Goodman for a day of shopping, three nights in a luxury hotel, theater tickets and restaurant reservations. The couple had other ideas, however:

They gave the tickets to the elevator-operator, cancelled the reservations, and notified room service – they'd be dining in, for the duration! Kate had come with three bottles of champagne. They chilled the wine, popped a cork, toasted their reunion, dined, chitchatted, made love, and laughed till their faces hurt, all night long. Then they napped, caught the sunrise over the city from their balcony, napped again, and started anew.

Neither of them had ever felt as happy or fulfilled, and they told each other so. Their love-making was also increasingly satisfying, as Kate shook off her inhibitions. Will took great pride in leaving her breathless, and moaning in ecstasy after each session. "Welcome to the Waldorf, Miss Burnett!" he'd quip, "Anything else I can do for ya?" And she'd giggle.

The end came too soon – any end would have been too soon for Kate. The Waldorf Astoria, premier haunt of the rich and the famous, of all places, had become her 'place' in New York; room service at the Waldorf, her restaurant of choice!

She wasn't pleased to get a peek at the bill, though, at check-out.

"Good Lord!" she whispered to Will, "For three nights? It's scandalous!"

"On the contrary," Will had fun with it. "I'm thrilled, Darlin'. This is the least I've *ever* spent in New York! Saved thousands on the shoppin' alone... I think we should move in!"

She laughed again; and all the way home.

There was more turmoil to come, however, the worst of it just around the bend. Kate had sensed it, caught a troubled look in Will's eyes once and again, during the train ride back to Richmond. Schooled as she was by her housekeeper, "not to worry 'bout that which might not happen," she had put it out of her mind. But there it was, one sunny afternoon, a few days before they were to leave for England:

She and Will were at his home in Richmond, going over their packing lists. They had just finished lunch out on the terrace, when out of nowhere, Will confessed, humbly and sorrowfully, that he had had a brief affair – an "intimate liaison" he called it – with a woman in France, during his last stay. He described his feelings for this woman as a "fleeting physical attraction," and swore that he never loved her, or pretended to love her.

He felt compelled to "come clean" about it, he said, because he and Kate had become best friends, as well as fiancés. Close as they were, he saw no space for lies or deceit between them. The guilt, he submitted, would have "festered," and caused more pain in the long run, than a repentant confession in the short.

"More pain for *you*, maybe!" Kate shrieked at him, as she jumped up from her seat, and began to pace, "but *I* would've been none the wiser! ...Why? ...Why did you have to tell me?" she cried out bitterly, giant tears falling, her face contorted with anguish. "Why couldn't you keep your dirty, little secret to yourself?"

"I'm so sorry, Kate," Will kept repeating, and stuttering, as he walked alongside her. "So very sorry, I suppose I should've... or shouldn't of... I... I was goin' to, but... "

Kate covered her ears, and turned her back to him. She could not bear to hear another word. She was overwhelmed with shock, and grief, and anger. She wanted to run, and hide from him. But there was no escaping the vision he had already planted in her head. Wherever she looked, there they were:

Will, and this horrid little French woman, with large breasts and loud makeup, rollicking, naked, in bed, and speaking French!

Oblivious to the depths of her despair, Will walked around her, to where she could see him, and carried on: "What I did was wrong, and foolish. But surely not unforgivable, Darlin'? For I am truly sorry... Listen to your heart, Kate, please, and..."

"No!" she screamed. "I hate you, Will Fairfield! I hate you for what you did, and I hate you even more for tellin' me! ...How could you?

"God help me, *please!*" she lowered her voice to a tearful, quivering whisper. "It makes my skin crawl to think about it..." She returned to her seat, rested her elbows on the table, hid her face in her hands, and prayed in silence.

Will sat across from her, and apologized, yet again, for 'sharing' the burden of his guilt, and tried desperately to explain. He said that he hadn't intended to tell her initially, for fear that it would make matters worse – turn "a regretful, but insignificant act" into a full-blown disaster – precisely what had happened! Ironically, though, he noted, it was Kate's recurrent comments on the "perils of deceit" that had led him to reconsider. He started to quote her on one such comment, "A lie of omission is still ..."

Kate looked up at him, red-eyed, and cut him off: "Don't you dare! This is *your* doin', Will. I'll take none of the blame this time. Not one iota!

"Good God, I can't believe this is happenin'," she went on despondently, her voice breaking up again. "It's ruined – you've ruined it! ...It can never be the same!" She saw the tears welling in his eyes, and eased up on him a bit: "I know you didn't intend to, Will. But it's done. Ruined. I'm sorry.

She removed the diamond ring from her finger, and set it on the table.

"Consider us dis-engaged," she said somberly. "No weddin' for us, Will. I thought I knew you, but I don't." She got up with a groan, and stood, hunched over, as if shouldering the weight of the world, and then trudged inside to collect her things.

He heard her at the front door a few minutes later, ran to meet her, reached for one of the bags she was carrying; but she frowned at him, and tightened her grip on the bag.

"I see you're in a state, Darlin'," he spoke calmly and sincerely, "and if you're not up to drivin' all that way, I…"

Standing straight now, she glared at him, eyes narrowed, jaw clenched, and all but hissed!

He got the message! "You hate me now – I understand. But give me a call, please, when you get there, Kate – for old times' sake… I worry… Can't help it."

She slammed the door in his face, got into her car, slammed that door, and took off for home. She had to pull over every so often to cry, during the first stretch. But her 'no- nonsense-self' took charge midway, and she focused on a plan of action. She decided to tell her loved ones very little – only that she and Will were through, that she was too distraught to talk about it, and needed some time to clear her head first. Once Will was gone, she'd tell them the whole sorry story. In the meantime, the last thing she needed was a barrage of advice on 'forgiveness.' She had no desire to forgive Will; she wanted to forget him; and get over him.

From the beginning, Kate had envisioned her sexual relations with Will as both a sacred pleasure and a sacred commitment; and Will had agreed, or so he said, that their coming together was "as spiritually, as it was physically, rewarding." Being Will, he had even joked about it: "You know, though, I'd call any other man who said that a liar!" And Kate had laughed.

It was clear to her, after the confession, however, that he, too, had been lying, or, at best, humoring her, about his feelings. He'd proven himself quite capable of taking the 'sacrament' with a virtual stranger; and, beyond his faithlessness, having the audacity to keep it a secret whilst winning back his betrothed; and then springing it on her, and begging her forgiveness! This was not the sort of behavior Kate expected from a man of character. Will had been faking it; she had fallen for it, and he had let her – that, for her, was unforgivable!

Once again, Will left for Europe without her; and immersed himself in his work. He wired her, though, nearly every day, often with a brief quote – a line or two, on the subject of love. A number of the quotes were Nettie's "jewels" – hand-me-downs, from Kate's letters to him, others were plucked from a book of famous quotes his sister-in-law had given him, and occasionally he offered his own take on one of the quotes.

Seven months later, and running out of material, his persistence finally paid off:

My Darling Will, I've come to forgiveness, at last. It appears from your daily wires that I'm not too late. I thank God for it, and you! Come home, Darling, please! I love you, and need you, K."

The couple's second reunion in New York, March of '33, was even more exciting than the first. They stayed an extra night, and actually left 'Kate's place' on several occasions, to attend the theater, a movie-show, and to walk Central Park in the snow. Will stayed in the States through the sowing at Katelyn, after which they spent the entire summer together in Europe – Kate's first experience abroad, and, in her words, "the thrill of a lifetime." She returned home, alone, for harvest, a month ahead of Will.

Upon sight of her homeland from the deck of the ship, she made an entry into her special diary, entitled, "In My Glory:"

Aunt Nettie made the statement, long ago, after Mama died, that 'only love is real.' And I thought, 'No, Aunt Net, this pain, this loss I feel is also real!' But now I understand. I've come full-circle on a spiritual, as well as an earthly journey. Having forgiven every grievance of the past, my eyes are open! I see that all of the angst my break-up with Will created has come to naught, a faded memory. He and I have been 'to hell and back,' twice, yet our bond is stronger than ever; as is our trust in each other. We remain close, 'souls touching,' we say, whether near, or oceans apart. Our relationship is all that I dreamed of, and more. And I'm 'in my glory,' that being, the awareness that only love is real!

Adding to Kate's joy, on the material plane, things were looking up for the entire country. Franklin Delano Roosevelt had been sworn in as President in March of 1933, and within a hundred days, his 'New Deal' had begun putting America back to work. "This great nation will endure," the President assured his listeners, in regular, 'fireside' radio chats, "…it will revive and will prosper."

Kate believed him. She felt the unreserved hope that he and his policies inspired; saw it lifting the national spirit, and the flagging economy. Signs of a rebound – stores and factories reopened, new projects underway, smiling faces of shoppers and workers, as captured in magazine and newspaper photos – were everywhere, including home:

On Kate's return to Alan House, Mrs. Alan, in a rare display of emotion, wept joyfully as she reported that, for the first time in the soup-kitchen's history, 'business' was on the decline! Over the last six months, she said, the average number of lunches served daily had dropped, from one hundred ten, to eighty-five. Furthermore, Mrs. Alan noted proudly, some of the poor were showing up, not to eat, but to help – to give back, in gratitude, for what they had received! This last piece of news brought the rest of the House to tears. And all through that day, one of the volunteers, or the diners, would break out singing, and even Mrs. Alan, who had voted against FDR, would join in the chorus of his popular campaign song, "Happy Days Are Here Again!"

Unlike Mrs. Alan and her anti-booze crew, however, Kate also supported FDR's push to repeal the eighteenth Amendment to the Constitution, and finally put an end to the disastrous prohibition of alcohol. Kate went so far as to travel to Washington, and join the movement. As it happened, her sister-in-law, Liddy, was a founding member of APL, the Anti-Prohibition League (so named as the antithesis to ASL, the Anti-Saloon League, the temperance group widely known as the 'mother' of Prohibition). Kate took the pledge – "to raise my voice against the tyranny of prohibition until it ends!" and Liddy showed her the ropes. For three weeks, from two days after harvest, till two days before Will's homecoming, Kate, alongside her mentor, marched, rallied, made phone calls, distributed leaflets and gave speeches calling for the Repeal; which, by all accounts, by November of '33, was imminent.

"Isn't it wonderful?" Kate wrote to Liddy, upon returning to the farm, *"our work is not in vain. We'll be celebrating the New Year, and later, my wedding, with perfectly legal champagne! And not a penny of the proceeds to the bootleggers! Ha!"*

Kate had no idea of the negative impact that Repeal would have on her life, though; no idea whatsoever!

Washington, D.C., Dec. 5, 1933

Harry Anslinger, in his pajamas, disheveled and miserable, sat slouched over the breakfast table in the conservatory of his home, staring blankly at the larger-than-life headlines on the morning paper: **PROHIBITION REPEALED.** He breathed a heavy sigh, leaned his elbows on the table, and buried his grief-stricken face in his hands.

His wife, looking on sadly from over his shoulder, slid the paper out of his sight, and stuck a plate of ham and eggs under his nose.

"You must eat something, Dear," she coaxed him, taking the seat beside him, gently patting his hand. "Come, now, I fixed the eggs myself, the way you like them."

Anslinger looked to her briefly. "I can't," he mouthed silently, and hung his head again.

She got up, drearily, covered the food, and put it back on a serving cart. Approaching him once more, she made a last effort to console him: "You knew this was coming, Harry. You did everything you could. Everything humanly possible. Clearly, it was meant to be. We must accept it."

"I can't," he repeated, in a sorrowful whimper.

"Give it to the dog," he said of the food, without looking up. "I'm not hungry."

Across town, an hour later, William Hagar sat, peering at the same heading, in the newspaper on Andrew Mellon's desk. Mellon, also at the desk, had been on the phone, and trying to get off, for several minutes.

Hagar began to fidget, cross his legs, uncross them, tap his manicured fingers on the desk, on the arm of his chair, and hum, nervously. He got Mellon's attention.

"Okay! Okay! Enough!" Mellon shouted into the phone. "I'll do my best," he softened his tone, "but tell her I'm not making any promises. Yeah. Yeah. Good-bye."

"Jesus!" he cursed, as he slammed down the receiver. "Why me?" he murmured dramatically, lifting his tired eyes and timeworn hands towards the heavens.

And then he looked to Hagar: "Anslinger's depressed. He's resigning. His wife's been crying to my sister, my secretary, and anyone else who'll listen. They expect me to fix it – as if I could fix anything in this town anymore!"

"Depressed?" Hagar responded, picking up the paper, waving it in the air. "This has been coming for a year. Where's he been?"

"You don't understand, Bill. Harry lived for Prohibition. When he made chief, it was the happiest day of his whole wretched life!"

Hagar smirked, half-laughed.

"We gotta go see him," Mellon asserted, "right away!"

"Not me!" Hagar declined, loudly. "Make matters worse. Crazy bastard blames *me* for your fall from grace."

They glanced at each other knowingly, for a second, before Hagar broke contact.

"Crazy bastard's right!" Mellon kidded him. "It's all your fault!"

On a stormy afternoon, a few days later, Mellon, having given up on Hagar, convinced Du Pont, who was in Washington on business, to accompany him to the Anslingers. A housekeeper greeted them at the door and collected their wraps, followed by Mrs. Anslinger, who burst into tears.

"Thank you so much for coming, Uncle, Mr. Du Pont," she collected herself, gave Mellon a hug, shook hands with Du Pont, and led them to a cozy, hearth-warmed parlor.

"I'm so sorry to trouble you, on this wintry day, in these terrible times. With all you've been through, I should be comforting you..."

"Not at all, Dear. No need," Mellon assured her, as the three were seated round a coffee table, set with tea and assorted biscuits.

"We're fine, just fine… Monsieur Du Pont, here, and I are realists. We knew the Repeal was coming – saw the writing on the wall long ago." He sighed and paused, but perked up quickly. "And so we did what we had to do, found ourselves a greater cause to champion!"

Mrs. Anslinger nodded, but appeared somewhat confused. She remained silent, brow wrinkled, as she poured the tea and passed around the accompaniments.

It dawned on Mellon then that her comments were not in reference to the Repeal, but to his ousting as Secretary of the Treasury.

"As for me, and my new appointment," he cleverly addressed and skirted the issue at once, "nothing 'terrible' about that either, my Dear!

"On the contrary," he fibbed, "haven't you heard? I actually prefer the new post to the old!"

"I hadn't heard! And I'm so glad, Uncle, truly," Mrs. Anslinger spoke elatedly.

Returning to the problem at hand, however, she came to tears again: "I'm really worried about Harry, Uncle… He hasn't eaten or come out of his quarters in days… He's written his resignation letter; and wants me to send it. He *insists* that I send it! I was hoping and praying you could talk some sense into him. He looks up to you, Uncle, more than anyone – you know that."

Mellon patted her on the shoulder. "I'll do my best, Honey," he said kindly, "I promise you. Come, now," he offered his handkerchief, "dry your eyes, drink your tea, and stop your fretting. Harry'll get over it. We all will. There's nothing else to do!"

"Thank you, Uncle," she repeated, as she wiped her eyes yet again. "And sorry about all the tears. It's just that I feel so bad for Harry. And so helpless…

"Come! Please!" She took a deep breath, got back on her feet, and motioned for the men to rise. "I'll take you to him;

you'll see for yourselves how poorly he's doing, and why I'm so distraught."

They followed her up the stairway in the entry hall to Anslinger's study. She knocked on the door, repeatedly, to no response. Opening the door a crack, she peeped into the pitch-black room, and called out, "Harry, wake up, Dear. It's two o'clock; and you've got visitors. Uncle Andrew and Mr. Du Pont are waiting to see you."

Opening the door completely to light the way, she waved the visitors in; and then she left.

They found Anslinger, unwashed and unshaven, wrapped in a rumpled bathrobe, un-slippered, one sock off and one on, lying on the sofa in the dark – the picture of gloom. As they opened the drapes, Anslinger groaned, "No! Please! No!" and covered his eyes with his arm to block out the light.

"Wake up, Dear, it's two o'clock, and you've got visitors," Mellon mimicked Mrs. Anslinger's sweetness, while rummaging through the papers on Anslinger's desk. He found the letter of resignation, and skimmed it. Holding onto it, he pulled up a seat near Anslinger's head, and pointed Du Pont to the opposite end.

"You can't do this, Harry," Mellon asserted, tapping the letter on Anslinger's chest. "You can't resign! You're not a quitter! Think about it, Harry. Who would they get? There's no one in this country could run that Bureau like you do – they might as well shut it down!"

"It's not like when you were there, Uncle," Anslinger moaned. "I can't do it anymore. They've tied my hands. Cut back my staff, cut off my funding..."

"Hearst is going to help out," Mellon assured him. "He's got ideas for marijuana. Inexpensive ones. You need to meet with him, Harry, right away."

Anslinger shook his head, repeating under his breath, "It's no use, it's no use."

Du Pont grabbed Anslinger's socked-toe, and wiggled it.

"Forget about the Repeal, Harry – that's history. You need to finish the job on marijuana. You're off to a good start with the local bans. You keep that up! Then you take it to the federal level. Little by little, you get that poison off the streets! Just keep thinking of the good you'll be doing the country!"

Anslinger lifted his arm from his eyes, and started to lift his head, but fell back. Looking up at Du Pont squinty-eyed, he spoke, uncharacteristically, in a faint, whiny voice:

"It can't be done. I'm telling you, Mr. Du Pont. Hemp's got a thousand legitimate uses, and more to come. It's not just the farmers, it's the manufacturers, and even the doctors we have to contend with! It's thousands of jobs, and millions of users. There's no *prohibiting* this plant – it can't be done!" He sighed, and closed his eyes again.

Du Pont got a hold of Anslinger's foot now, and shook him to attention: "Listen to me, Harry! All that's going to change! …And I'll tell you why:

"Hemp is expendable – absolute fact! There isn't a single hemp product that can't be replaced with something better. We've already seen it with cloth and paper, and the rest is on the way. We've got synthetics today, Harry, for *everything*! We've even got a synthetic cord in the works – amazing product; it'll make the old rope obsolete within a year, and hemp with it – you mark my words!

"Synthetics are the future, Harry!" He pretended to take a drag off a reefer, and go tipsy. "Hemp is dope!"

Anslinger sat up, smoothed out the sleeves and lapel of his robe, brushed off his shoulders, and yawned. "Marijuana **is** dangerous," he muttered.

"Deadly," Du Pont egged him on, "especially in the hands of children!"

"No one said this would be easy, Harry," Mellon put in. "This is a complicated, gut-retching assignment you've taken on. But it needs to be done. And we're convinced that you, *and only you*, can do it!" He hesitated… "Unless you know someone else?"

Anslinger shook his head 'no.'

"Unfortunately," Mellon went on, "we don't have the pull or connections we had before either. But we've got plenty, enough to see us through. You *will* have what you need, Harry! Don't be afraid to ask!"

"But you'll be abroad, Uncle," Anslinger whimpered, "for months at a time."

"I will, undoubtedly," Mellon conceded.

"But," he gestured toward Du Pont, "we're all in this together, Harry. And Hearst, and Hagar, and Sanford, and their allies are our allies. And let us not forget, the lawyers, obscenely expensive as they are, are on my payroll!"

Anslinger cracked a smile.

Mellon smiled too.

"So, Harry," he wrapped it up, waving the letter of resignation, "can we dispose of this, finally? …Stop all the crying around here?"

'Yes!' said Anslinger, definitively, nodding his head, clearly relieved.

Mellon crumpled the letter, and shot it neatly into a wastebasket. "Good!" he said. "Perfect! How 'bout we celebrate with another round of tea? The biscuits are delectable."

Anslinger was back on the job the following day. Within a week, he had met with Hearst, Sanford, the lawyers, and even Hagar; and within a month, he had finalized a plan to reinstate American Prohibition, albeit with a new drug!

Utilizing the resources of the Federal Bureau of Narcotics, and the fervor of Anti-saloon Leaguers desperately seeking a cause, he would spread the word about marijuana – defined as the "newest and deadliest of the hard drugs" – to grassroots America, and promote its ban. In districts where the bans were already in force, he'd send in federal agents to encourage and assist the local police with raids and arrests. Where feasible, 'investigative reporters,' on loan from Hearst, would cover and sensationalize the stories.

As a final step, he'd push for federal control of marijuana, via nation-wide licensing, taxing, and, ultimately, criminalizing of the drug's producers, peddlers and consumers. Given the merits of hemp, he reckoned it would take at least five years to get a bill before Congress. It wasn't easy, but he did it in three!

Outskirts of Houston, Texas, April 21, 1934.

A police car, labeled 'Precinct 10,' trailed by an unmarked Federal Bureau of Narcotics car, moved slowly down the dirt roads of an impoverished Mexican shanty-town. It was dark – 9:30 P.M., the streets were deserted, and the lights were out in all but one of the shabby, make-shift shacks. It was the one.

Inside the single-roomed, tidily-kept hut, Paco Blanco, a twenty-two-year-old, slightly built, dark-skinned, Mexican field-worker, and three of his workmates of similar descriptions, were seated around a picnic table, playing cards, and smoking cannabis. A solitary lantern, dangling above their heads, provided barely enough light for the men to see. It was their third and final game, they had smoked as many reefers, and gone from silly to half-asleep.

Paco's dog, Chico – a frisky, little, speckled mutt, was lying on the floor next to them, also drowsy. But the sound of approaching vehicles aroused Chico. He began to pace and whine, and scratch at the front door.

"What's the matter, Chico?" Paco queried him, in Spanish. "You were just out."

The dog kept it up, his whine growing louder.

Paco's wife, Maria, a teen-aged, sweet-faced, Mexican-American, peeked out – her big, brown eyes sleepy, from behind a curtained off area of the cabin: "Can't you let him out, Paco?" she asked softly, in English, "before he wakes the baby?"

Paco got up, and went to the door, complaining that the dog had just come in.

"I know," Maria whispered, "but he hears that cat next door – drives him crazy."

The dog flew out the door, yelping, as Paco opened it. The baby started crying from behind the curtain; and the card-players looked at each other and laughed.

Maria returned to her infant; the men to their game. Quiet was no sooner restored, however, when all hell broke loose – a thunderous banging on the front door, a man shouting, in English: "Police! Open up! Now!"

"Policia!" Paco interpreted for his friends, needlessly, as he jumped to his feet.

"Hold on! I'm coming!" he yelled, in English, and ran toward the door, signaling frantically to Maria, who had peeped out again, in her nightgown, and frightened to tears, to get back behind the curtain, and get dressed! She complied.

Paco's mates headed instinctively for the other door, but stopped in their tracks when police started banging there. In an instant, an armed policeman broke through the back door, as Paco let a second armed cop in the front. Chico, still barking, darted in one door, and out the other. On orders, the terrified Mexicans backed against the wall, arms raised.

The baby started to fuss again; and the younger, more jittery, of the cops pointed his gun toward the curtain: "Come out, hands up!" he demanded in English.

Paco leapt between the cop and the curtain, screaming, in English, "Don't shoot, don't shoot! It's my wife and baby!"

The older officer pointed his gun at Paco. "Shut up, spic," he shouted, "Get down! On the floor! Pronto!"

But Paco remained defiantly upright, shielding his family, and pleading with the officers, in English, and in Spanish, to lower their guns.

A nod from the older cop, and armed federal agents, Morse and Ryan, watching nervously from the doorway, stepped in to cover.

The cops holstered their weapons.

With Paco's pals looking on helplessly, the agents cringing, but not interfering, the cops forced Paco to the floor, face down, cuffed his hands behind his back, and kicked him bloody, in the head, and in the ribs.

The younger cop, raging out of control, screamed over Paco's groans: "We say 'get down,' …and you get down, … you piece of shit! …And you shut up!"

Maria, desperate to stop the beating, cried out, with all her might, above the madness, "Stop! Stop! Please! …I'm coming out! …Don't kill us! Please!"

The cops let up on Paco, turned toward the curtain, and drew their guns: "Come out **now**!" "Hands above your head!" they commanded Maria.

But Maria could not obey them; she would not put her baby down. Cradling him with one arm, his whimper muffled against her breast, she held her free hand above her head, nudged the curtain aside with her shoulder, and inched out from behind it, fully frocked now, chin to her chest, her long, black hair shrouding her face and her baby. She stood still, then, eyes to the floor, trembling and weeping silently.

"Put the baby down!" the older cop demanded angrily. "Now, on the ground! Hands above your head, bitch – both of 'em!"

"Do as they say, Maria, por favor," Paco, barely able to speak, agony in his voice, pled with her from where he lay, just a few feet away, on the floor. "They'll hurt you, Maria. *Please*, do as they say!"

Maria caught sight of Paco, the pool of blood around his head, and fell to her knees in shock. "Paco," she cried, "Dios mio! What have they done to you?!"

She managed to crawl to his side, while clutching the whiny baby to her breast. "He needs help! Please!" she begged her captors, as she tried to stop the bleeding from his head, with her hand, the baby's blanket. "Help him! Please!"

The younger cop, infuriated by her noncompliance, holstered his gun, and grabbed her by the hair. Before he could yank her up, however, Ryan grabbed him by the wrist, and squeezed, tighter and tighter, till he let her go.

The cop turned bright red. "Stay out of it, Ryan!" he snarled, "You're not in charge here!" He shook and stretched his hand a few times to get the circulation back, and went for Maria again.

Ryan, wiry, and exceptionally strong for his size, without a word, or even a grunt, wrestled the cop to the floor and pinned him down, and held him down – face down.

The older cop looked hopefully to Morse, but the agent shook his head, and said,

"Uh, uh! We're done here! You got your man… You leave her alone… and let the others go!"

Morse had his way.

Only Paco was arrested, after admitting to providing the "weed" that he and his friends had been smoking.

With the agents keeping an eye, the policemen bandaged Paco's head, and locked him in the wagon. The agents then escorted the sobbing Maria and her agitated baby to a neighbor's home.

The agents and officers conferred, finally, in front of the shack, to get their stories straight.

By this time, half the neighborhood was out, lanterns flickering in the dark, to see what all the commotion was about.

All eyes turned as a third car came slowly down the street, and pulled up behind the agents' car. The driver started to get out, but jumped back in, as the tireless Chico, barking fiercely, hurtled toward him.

"Who the hell is that?" Morse asked the elder cop.

"Looks like that kid reporter," the cop replied. "Must've followed us from the precinct."

"We didn't see any reporters," said Ryan, argumentatively. "And no one, sure as hell, followed us!"

The cop shrugged his shoulders. "Don't worry. He's all right. Keeps his distance."

Chief of the Federal Bureau of Narcotics' office, Washington, D.C., April 25, 1934:

Anslinger, standing behind his desk, was visibly agitated. His eyes darted back and forth between the newspaper he was holding, and agents Morse and Ryan, seated in front of him, looking guilty.

"FEDS BEAT, ARREST MEXICAN FOR SMOKING MEDICINE," he quoted the headlines on the paper, loudly, and tossed it at Morse, who ducked, smoothly, and let it fall to the floor.

"How the hell did this happen, Morse?"

"It didn't, Chief! We didn't arrest him. Never touched him. Cops did. We were just there, after the raid. What we did do, earlier, was shut down a moonshine operation that had killed two people... Not a word in the paper about that!"

"Yeah," Ryan raised his voice, and his messy head. "Hearst's man never showed up. Punk reporter got it all wrong. And the doctor lied for the spic!"

"I don't care what anybody else did!" Anslinger shouted, and went on shouting: "You shouldn't have been there! How many times do I have to tell you? Marijuana is different. Legitimate crop. Legitimate uses. You've got to use your heads; keep your distance. These are local bans. Let the locals handle them...

"I'm not going to have this. I won't be embarrassed again. You will not waste another dollar of the tax-payers' money. Not while I'm in charge here!" He stamped his foot for emphasis.

"Next time, you're out – both of you! No excuses! **Do I make myself clear?**"

"Yes, Sir," "Won't happen again, Sir," came the simultaneous replies.

"Good! Let's get back to the plan. It's starting to work."

"Couple things you should know, though, first," said Morse.

Anslinger gave him a reluctant nod.

"The Mexican and the doctor – neither one of them ever heard of 'marijuana.'"

Anslinger looked at the agent agape. "The Mexican?"

Morse shook his head 'no.' "None of the Mexicans we spoke to. They said the Spanish name for cannabis is 'caniamo' – something like that."

"Get me the **exact** spelling and pronunciation!" Anslinger snapped, "and learn it!"

"Yes, Sir!" said Morse.

"Cops said most of 'em call it 'weed,' or 'grass,' though – they use the English, and the Spanish words," Ryan put in. "Grows like a weed in Texas. Cops laughed when we told them we were after the 'peddlers.' Nobody sells it there, cause nobody buys it. Spics who like to smoke it, go get it in a field, grow a few plants themselves, all they want, free!"

Anslinger shook his head mournfully. He looked as though he wanted to cry.

"Sorry, Chief," "Sorry, Sir," the agents offered, one after the other.

Anslinger nodded thankfully. "Like I said, men," he gathered himself, took the seat at his desk, and spoke in a friendlier tone, "marijuana's different.

"Now we know it's the dope with a thousand names. Doesn't make it any less treacherous. Whatever they call it, it's our job to get it off the streets… That's what we're doing."

He handed each of them a copy of the latest Federal Bureau of Narcotics Bulletin – four pages, composed almost exclusively of marijuana tales, most of which he had written, or co-written, based on Hearst reports. "This just went out a couple of weeks ago, and already our numbers have doubled." He held up a list, with about fifty entries. "Marijuana and hashish banned in these cities and counties. "This is good, but we need more. We need a ban in *every* district where hemp is grown. And we need to get 'em from the ban to the local tax, quickly. "Explain it to 'em, emphasize it – *'unless you raise the price of marijuana, you're not going to curb its use!'*

"As we expected, the Temperance people are doing a great job. Writing petitions, getting signatures, putting pressure on local lawmakers; some of 'em holding rallies, at city halls n' such. Outstanding job! Free of charge!

"I want you to spend more time with them. Wherever you're going – you've got Chicago next, right?"

The men nodded yes.

"You contact the Temperance groups, before you leave. And go see them when you get there. Make sure they know how important their work is, how much we appreciate it. Tell them what other groups have done – try to get a little competition going.

"They might want you to give a little talk about dope, though, for their members, help them understand the seriousness of this drug, and therefore, the urgency of the measures…"

He gave the men a once-over, wincing at Ryan's scruffiness.

"Either of you done any public speaking?"

Morse responded with a pained expression; Ryan horrified.

Anslinger exhaled audibly.

"Okay, okay," he moaned, "I'll write the speeches – short ones. You just read 'em. "And get one of your trainees to take a course, will ya, Morse?" He looked to Morse. "And the two of you take it, too, soon as you can. Before we run out of funds, huh?"

Morse said, "Done, Sir," and made a note.

"I'll be in California, working with Hearst's people, while you're in Chicago. You're all set up for the bust on the Negro musicians, right?"

The agents indicated yes.

"I'll bet they know what 'marijuana' is," Anslinger grumbled. "And the name of their peddler! Hearst has been onto the dope trade there for years."

He paused, and stared pensively into space.

"Thank God he's on our team!" he thought aloud, as he got up, and gestured for the agents to follow.

"Okay, men. That's it till next month. Go get 'em! The lot of 'em! Just remember not to be there when they cuff 'em!

"And don't forget, any violence you hear of, committed under the influence, gets reported back here – on the spot!"

The men uttered, "Yes, Sir," and headed for the door.

"And Ryan…"

The agent turned around. "Chief?"

"Go see Morse's barber before you leave … That's an order!"

Morse burst out laughing.

Ryan grinned, and so did Anslinger – for the first time that day.

Negro nightclub district, Chicago, May 7, 1934, 2:00 P.M.:

It was overcast, and unusually still in the Windy City. Federal agents Morse and Ryan sat waiting, in an unmarked vehicle, on a side street, near the back entrance of 'Shakers,' a former Negro speakeasy-turned-jazz club. Morse checked his watch for the third time since they arrived; it read: 2:06.

"So much for the 'well-oiled machine' they promised us," he complained to his partner, to no response.

He studied Ryan, also for the third time, thinking what a difference a hair cut made. "You almost look presentable,

Wreck," he teased. "We're gonna have to find you a new nickname."

"Enough about the hair!" Ryan returned. "Like I told you, I liked it better before, and so did my girl!"

Morse laughed. He checked his watch again and again: 2:07, 2:08, 2:09… "Damn cops!" he kept repeating.

"Relax, partner," Ryan advised him. "Maybe the reporter was late. Cops seem to know what they're doing here. I got a good feeling 'bout this one."

"Yeah? How'd you feel about Texas?"

Ryan grinned. "See?" he said, a second later, as a squad car, followed by the reporter's car, pulled up a few car-lengths behind them.

Morse and Ryan got out of their vehicle; as two policemen emerged from theirs.

The agents were expecting three cops, but would have been happy with two of the three they favored, out of several they had met at a previous briefing. Instead they got the only two they definitely did not want!

One was a mean-looking, mountain of a man, whom Ryan had openly nicknamed, 'Hulk.' The other, Hulk's partner, although less daunting and younger in appearance, was clearly the meaner and the leader of the two. Both cops had made their distaste for Negroes – whom they faithfully referred to as "niggers" – apparent to the agents from the onset.

"Shit!" Ryan cussed under his breath upon sight of the cops. His palm, on impulse, went up to signal halt. "Give us a minute," he called out to Hulk; and ran around the car to Morse, and led him down the street a pace.

"We're in trouble here, Partner," he whispered. "We need to call the chief – right away, tell him this is a no-go!"

"No-go? I thought you had a good feeling about this one?"

"I did, till I saw who they sent us!"

"Hulk? …He's all right – just looks scary!"

"Not him. The other one – the lead cop. Vicious as a snake! And he's got it in for those musicians, Morse, I'm telling you. I talked to him for *ten minutes* outside after the briefing. He went on and on about those 'uppity niggers, uppity niggers, don't know their place' – must've said it a hundred times! And furious about 'white folks going to the niggers' club, mixing with the niggers, dancing with them, or *worse'* – 'shouldn't be allowed' he said! …He *really* hates the owner – the one they're calling a 'jazz genius;' says there's 'no such thing as a nigger genius'!"

Morse half-grinned. "Sounds like the copper caught his woman out dancing – or *worse* – with one of those Negro fellas!"

Ryan was not amused. "I'm serious, Morse! You think that cop in Texas was angry? No comparison! This one looked like he was about to explode, just talking about 'busting these niggers' – his face all flushed, practically foaming at the mouth! Imagine when we're busting 'em? If they give us any lip? We're gonna lose our jobs if we go in there, Partner. I can't afford to lose my job – I'm getting married this summer."

"You haven't even asked her yet!"

"No, but I'm gonna! And I can't, if I'm unemployed!"

Morse had to laugh. "All right, Ryan, take it easy. We'll figure it out, in a minute. I'll be right back. I'm going to tell those cops to move their car out of sight – down one of those alleys. Last thing we need, if we do go in, is to get spotted – have to *plant* the marijuana!"

"Yeah. Not that either of those two would mind!"

Morse talked to the cops, and they took off for a designated alley. Then Morse had a word with Hearst's reporter, whom he found to be surprisingly mature – twice the age, and far more professional than any of the amateurs he'd dealt with. And likeable. Morse apologized for the delay, but the reporter made light of it.

"I'm used to waiting – or rushing," he said. "Not many crime-stories happen on schedule!" He also agreed, for his own safety, and everyone else's, to stay put in his vehicle, no matter what, until one of the policemen or the agents called him out.

Ryan was sitting in the car, moping, when Morse returned.

"Let's go, Wreck," Morse opened the door for him. "We're gonna do this bust, and do it right! Come on," he insisted, "before it starts raining. We'll hoof it over to that alley," he pointed the way, "and go over it with the cops, step by step, again – make it perfectly clear: *no mistakes, and no unnecessary violence!*"

Ryan cheered up. "You're the boss!" he said good-naturedly, as they started walking. "And, to tell you the truth, Morse, when I saw you talking to that reporter, and remembered the chief saying he's 'the best of the lot,' I figured, Chicago ain't Texas! I mean, I'd hate to see those Negroes get the shit beat out of them, just because white folks like their music; but all that matters, for us, is what gets reported!"

"My thoughts exactly, Partner, which is why we're going in that club!"

Inside the nightclub, a trio of Chicago's top black musicians – a piano player, forty-three years of age, a drummer and a saxophone-player, both twenty-four – had gathered for their routine jam/practice session. Missing – late, as usual, was their bass-player, who was also in his mid-twenties; and missing, indefinitely, was their long-time, lady singer, thirty-two, who'd been living with the pianist, till a few weeks prior, when she left him for another musician.

A Negro cleaning crew, father, mother, and their cute and curvy teen-aged daughter, were in and out, finishing up.

The club – bar, seating, dance and stage areas, which had been renovated recently, and expanded to include the vacant lot next door, was twice as big, some five thousand square feet, as any in the district. Decorated in distinguished black and white, with ruby-red accents; and on the walls, a local artist's rendition of the musicians and their instruments in silhouette, the night-spot was also the classiest in town.

Behind the club, on the ground floor of the building, were a small back room/office, an adjacent galley kitchen, and 'his' and 'her' rest-rooms. An apartment on the second floor, which looked like a miniature extension of the club, was home to the pianist, 'The-Man' Shaker, namesake and co-owner of the establishment, and, his racist critics notwithstanding, a bonafide blues-jazz genius.

The musicians, who had been playing together since the drummer and the sax-player were fifteen, were sitting at the table in the back room, talking business and smoking cannabis, while waiting for the cleaners to leave. Shaker, who'd been hitting the bottle heavily since his woman ran off, was downing a whiskey as well.

The drummer, nicknamed 'Dapper,' for his good looks, sleek physique, and flashy outfits, was rolling a second reefer, when the teen-aged cleaner peeped in.

"We're 'bout done," she announced, her huge, black-brown eyes peering straight into Dapper's. "Floor's dry, but mama said ta leave the windows open – clear out this smoke." She moved her hand back and forth, like a windshield wiper, through the cloud of smoke in her face, and faked a cough.

The musicians chuckled, as they got up and followed her into the club.

"Say, Sassafras, you wanna be a singer?" Dapper caught up with her, flirted with her playfully. "Pays a lot better than cleanin'!

"We hear you singing 'round here all the time – got you a pretty voice, Pretty Girl! Need us a new canary. You heard? Ours is gone – New Orleans. Got her a new manager. ...But I'll manage you, Sass. What do you say?"

"You losing your mind, Dapper? ...You asked me the same questions, day before yesterday!"

"What'd you say?"

"What I said was, 'I heard you got plenty a singers fillin' in; *and*, I got better things ta do'!"

She marched out the front door, banged it shut, but popped back in to shout:

"And quit calling me Sassafras!"

"She be sassy!" The-Man laughed, as he inched his chubby form, precariously, across the lengthy room to the stage area. He flopped down at the piano, which was situated in front of his larger-than-life, black on white silhouette, and tapped his empty shot-glass on the bench for a refill. Although clearly inebriated, he began to play his usual effortless magic.

The sax-player, a tall, blue-black skinned, heavy-set man called, 'Slim,' shrugged his shoulders, and poured The-Man another.

Dapper joined his fellows at the piano. He shook his head worriedly as he watched The-Man gulp down another whisky. Dapper could not understand why one so gifted would do himself in, over a woman; especially since there were plenty of women – good-looking women – eager to take her place. Not that The-Man was good-looking himself; he was short and stout, with a spotty complexion, and a huge nose. But he also had a huge heart, a tremendous talent, and considerable charm, a combination which made him magnetically attractive to women. Everyone else in the neighborhood knew it – why didn't he?

"Play me some of that blues from last night," Dapper requested, holding the reefer to the pianist's mouth. "That last piece… That was some heartache, Man… Nobody wanted to go home!"

The-Man took a drag, smiled appreciatively, let out the smoke, and flowed right into it. "Got me some heartache," he half-sang, half-moaned – in his velvety baritone.

Slim accompanied him on the horn for a while – improvising brilliantly.

"What you callin' that?" Slim asked The-Man, as they came to a pause.

The pianist returned to the opening chords, and mumbled something completely unintelligible.

His colleagues cracked up.

"Sounded like you said, 'Psst da plebb zitszz, fadadaada," said Slim.

"You wanna run that by us again?"

The-Man, chuckling to himself, uttered something totally different, but equally unintelligible.

"And there you have it, folks," Slim laughingly addressed an imaginary audience, "straight from the mouth of Chicago's, Da-Man!"

"That's it! Cuttin' you off," said Dapper sternly, stealing the shot-glass off the piano. "Can't be drinking all day, *and* all night! Bad for your health, and bad for business!"

"Three weeks now!" Dapper went on scolding, "How you gonna get us a steady singer? Get you a new woman? ...Can't even talk!"

The-Man, unperturbed, plucked the remains of the reefer from Slim's grasp, and took a huge drag. He burned his thumb in the act, however, and let out a howl.

All three musicians were laughing again, when the cleaning girl rushed back in, all flustered.

"Sassafras!" Dapper exclaimed. "You changed your mind already?!"

She ignored him, and, noting The-Man's drunken state, spoke directly to Slim.

"My daddy smells trouble – lotta traffic out back." She pointed a finger toward the office. "Cop cars, comin' an' goin'. Two other cars, three, four whiteys, waitin' watchin', checkin' with the cops. Daddy thinks two of 'em are Feds."

"Feds?!" Dapper repeated skeptically. "Tell your daddy Prohibition's over!"

"I'm tellin' *you!*" she snapped back, "and you better listen! When my daddy smells trouble, there's trouble!" Out she strutted, without a good-bye.

Dapper hurried to the back door, Slim went out the front, to have a look. It was all clear out front, but Dapper saw the reporter, and the agents, in their respective vehicles, parked in back. His heart started pounding. "I'll be damned," he muttered to himself, "if they don't look like Feds!"

He ran around the office, frantically, locking up doors and windows, collecting his illegal weed, butts, and paraphernalia, and throwing them into a satchel. The phone rang, startling him, just as he was finishing. He stopped, stared at the noisy contraption, and finally answered it, begrudgingly.

It was the bass-player, Albert Mood, known as 'Moody Two.' Albert's father, Luis Mood, who had made his fortune as a bootlegger, was co-owner of Shakers Club, as well as several other 'goldmines' in the neighborhood.

"Where the hell you been, 'Two'?" Dapper screamed at the musician. "Always late! No respect for nobody!"

"Never mind that! …You been smokin' that 'marijuana' in the club?"

"Yeah! And so have you! But I'm clearin' it out – now."

"That's good …Might be cops headin' your way, Dapper. They're lookin' to shut us down – you know that! *I told you not to bring that shit in the club*!"

"What cops?"

"The ones sittin' out here, in front of my girl's, *for an hour* – just took off. Met up with some Feds, too. They gone now – all of 'em, your way!"

"**Feds!**?" Dapper yelled, as he hung up the receiver, and flew into the club.

"Let's go, boys! Looks like a bust!" he alerted his mates. "Right now – out the door," he pointed his satchel toward the front. "That was 'Two,' on the phone. Cops on the way!"

With The-Man in the middle, supported by his fellows, all three musicians were out the door in a flash. But not in time to make a getaway. A police car was just pulling up. Hulk and the lead cop leapt from the vehicle, guns drawn.

"Halt! Police! You're under arrest!" they shouted, to no one there!

The musicians were already back in the club, securing the door.

The police were cussing, foot-stomping mad! And baffled – they could not imagine who had tipped off the Negroes. Nobody, apart from a few trusted colleagues, and the Feds, who had arranged the bust, knew about it. The plan was to catch the musicians off guard, while they were jamming, and smoking their illicit weed; and while the club doors were open, for early staffers and suppliers, coming and going.

Now, the police would have to break into the building, which was built like a fortress; and they knew it. The solid wooden doors of the club were reinforced with metal plates, and all sorts of oddly placed locks, bolts and crossbars. Decorative iron security bars, which could only be unlocked from the inside, inhibited access through the ground-floor windows; and the second floor apartment was likewise secured.

Using a crowbar, every which way, the police attempted to remove the security gate from one of the windows, unsuccessfully. Hulk then threw his enormous weight against the front door again and again, to no avail. Finally, the lead cop tried to shoot the locks open, top to bottom, for nothing. There were a few small holes in the doorframe, but the door itself remained intact. Hulk went at it again – not even a wobble.

Morse and Ryan rushed to the scene at the sound of gunfire. They agreed with the police that without additional men and equipment, which were not immediately available, it would be easier to force the musicians out, than to enter the building. They put up signs on the club doors and the grassy patches at the front entrance, declaring the establishment CLOSED, till further notice, by authority of the Chicago Police Department and the Federal Bureau of Narcotics.

With Hulk and the agents covering the back and sides of the building, the lead-cop took a tommy-gun between the security bars at the front windows, and smashed and blew holes in them, one after another. Megaphone to his mouth, he then ordered the musicians to come out – "now, hands in the air!" His voice, punctuated by a round of gunfire, echoed forebodingly through the halls: "You've got a minute, Boys. *One minute*! ...Or we're comin' in after you, shootin' mad!"

It was an empty threat, though, and the musicians knew it. Dapper had already flown the coop, furthermore, and was hiding behind a garbage bin out back. While the cops were busy trying to break in the front, he had unlocked the window bars on the sides and back of the club, so that he and his mates could make an escape from any space where the coast was clear.

Dapper chose a narrow window for himself, through which only he, of the three, could fit. It was located in the stairwell to the rear of the building, just out of sight from where the agents and the reporter were parked, and close – less than fifty feet, to an alleyway entrance. With his mates assisting, he swung the bars open, and squirmed his way out. They handed him his satchel, and wished him luck. His moment came shortly. At the crackling of gunfire out front, he assumed, correctly, that the agents would head to the front; and he took off, flying, in the opposite direction. He had mistaken the reporter for another agent, however, and as his wide eyes met the newsman's, he realized, despairingly, that his nightmare had just begun.

The reporter, despite his promise not to, got out of his car, and chased the musician. Dapper ran like lightning, though, and quickly disappeared into a maze of alleyways. To throw the hounds off, moreover, he tossed his satchel into an alley on the left, and then turned right, full speed, into the next alleyway. The satchel caught the reporter's eye, and he hurried to fetch it. Finding it empty, he put it back, returned to his vehicle, exasperated, and started blowing his horn – "ah-hooga, ah-hooga, hooga," unrelentingly. Morse and Ryan came hastening to his call.

The police stayed behind to watch for escapees. Before long, they heard rustling sounds on the left face of the building. The lead cop gestured to Hulk to stay put, and peeped around the corner. He saw that Slim had just jumped out of a window, and was about to help Shaker do the same. The cop drew his gun, stepped into view, startled the musicians, and mocked them with wisecracks, "Where're you goin', Boys? Lookin' for trouble?"

"No, Sir," said Slim, "We don't want no trouble!"

The cop, shaking his head in feigned regret, could not contain his smirk. "If you didn't want no trouble, nigger, you should've come out in front, hands up, when I called ya…

"You on the wrong side, too late!" He glowered at Slim, and then at Shaker. "You niggers got yourself in a shit-load-a-trouble!"

Shaker, the rush of adrenaline snapping him out of his stupor, ducked out of sight, crawled along the wall about fifteen feet, and took cover behind the bar.

The cop tried to lift himself up to where he could see the run-away, while still holding on to his gun – impossible! He went berserk, shooting wildly into the ceiling over the bar, screaming for Shaker to return: "Now, Boy, or you will be one sorry nigger!"

Slim made a dash for it while the cop was distracted, but u-turned, and surrendered, at a warning shot, and a command to "Halt or die!"

Hulk came around in a panic, expecting to see blood.

"Cuff this nigger!" the lead cop demanded, shoving the musician, who went stumbling into Hulk. "Put him in the wagon! …Shoot him if he runs again!" Shaky and frantic, the cop reloaded his weapon, climbed halfway into the club; but quickly changed his mind, dropped back to the ground, and raced around to the other side.

To mislead the cop, Shaker had left a window and its gate wide open on the right side of the building. The cop smelled the set-up, however, and carried on to the rear, gun drawn. Sure enough, he found Shaker sitting on a window sill, about to make the leap. The musician, spotting the cop at once, flung himself around, slid to the floor, and scrambled out of the room. Up in a flash, he slammed the door shut, just as the cop came in through the window. The key was in the lock – a stroke of luck; he turned it, tossed it, squeezed out the nearest opening, and ran with all his might toward the alleyways, straight ahead.

A moment later, there was chaos, in slow-motion – people darting about and screaming, a barrage of gunfire, and then another. Shaker slowed down, and veered to the right, looking over his shoulder, as the racket grew louder. The Feds were coming at him from some distance, yelling, but apparently not at him, "No! …No! …Don't! …No!" And then they stopped dead; and Shaker saw the horrified expression on their faces. He felt an excruciating pain in his right hand; there was blood and flesh and bones flying, in slow motion! He remained upright, somehow, and pressed on. Slim and the gigantic cop came into view then as well, shouting 'no,' in long, drawn-out syllables: … "Naaoooo!"

Shaker heard another shot, felt another searing pain – his shoulder was on fire! He stopped, spun around, shrieked, at the top of his lungs – but emitted no sound, and collapsed to the ground.

Morse and Ryan rushed to the fallen man's side. They took off their shirts, rolled one into a makeshift tourniquet, and tied it above his wrist. They made the other into a pack, pressed it against the hole in his shoulder, and prayed that the bullet hadn't hit an artery.

Ryan "un-arrested" Slim, and removed his handcuffs. The two climbed into the club, called for an ambulance, and returned to Shaker and Morse through the front door, with supplies: a cot, clean shirts, clean bandages, and a bottle of whisky. With extreme difficulty, (Hulk had gone off looking for his partner, to "calm him down"), the agents and Slim moved Shaker onto the cot, and carried him to the portico in front of the club. There they would wait for the ambulance, undercover, and close to the street; the air being heavy with rain.

Shaker came to while they were moving him. He looked up at Slim, who was smiling at him, kindly, and tried to smile back, but could not. "Slim," he moaned, "can't feel my hand." He began to whine then, deliriously, almost inaudibly: "My hand, Slim… It's gone… Slim?! …Slim?!" His bearers put the cot down, lifted his head up, gently, and gave him a few sips of whisky. He did half-smile finally, and then blacked-out again.

Once the men had Shaker situated, Ryan took off for the scene of the crime. "Don't cuff him!" Morse called after his partner. "Yeah, yeah," Ryan shouted back, thinking, "How 'bout I kill the bastard instead?" As the agent turned the corner to the rear of the building, he came face to face with the cops. They seemed to have talked things over satisfactorily, and were heading out front, toward their vehicle. Ryan went with them, uninvited. "Where're you goin'?" he asked Hulk, as they approached the car.

"No place," answered the lead cop, "till we get our stories straight."

"Get *this* straight, Copper," Ryan spoke in a loud and certain voice, "the only 'story' we're gonna tell is the truth! …The truth! truth, truth," he fired the word at the cop, as if to force it into his skull.

The cop was unaffected. "Fine!" he replied, rather smugly, and began to pace and ramble alongside the car. "Truth is, that nigger got what he deserved! It's his own fault – that's the truth! I gave him plenty of warning… Four warning shots," he stepped closer to Ryan, caught his eye briefly, "you heard me! At least four… Kept on running – got what he…"

Ryan hit the cop so fast, he never saw it coming! Right hand to center chin, knocked him out cold! He fell back against the hood of the car, and then slumped sideways onto the street, smacking his face on the curb, splitting his already swollen lip. Hulk bent down, checked his partner's pulse, and his wound, pressed a handkerchief against the latter, and indicated that he'd live.

"Too bad," the agent muttered under his breath. Nevertheless, he gave Hulk a hand. They lifted the cop off the street and laid him down on the back seat of the squad-car. Ryan then disarmed the cop, and removed the entire cache of weapons and ammo from the vehicle.

"I'll return these to your station later," he said to Hulk, as they carried the stash to the portico. "You can keep your gun, Bud, but I need the bullets. He might want to 'borrow' the gun when he comes to... I think he's done enough shooting for today... Don't you? ...Hulk?"

The giant complied without a word. He then returned to his partner, who was coming around, to the blare of an ambulance siren. The cop, still wobbly as he stepped out of the police-car, leaned against it, and watched, dispassionately, as the emergency crew arrived, picked up the blood-soaked Shaker, and sped away noisily.

The moment the Feds and Slim took off, however, the cop perked right up.

"Let's go find that runner," he suggested to Hulk, excitement in his voice, and started walking briskly toward the street behind the club.

Hulk followed, but hesitantly, advising his partner that he wasn't going "anywhere," unless they stuck to "the plan."

"Yeah," uttered the lead cop, clearly unenthused.

Hulk stopped in his tracks. "I ain't going!" he repeated resolutely.

"I said 'yes'!" the lead cop shouted at him, and then eased his tone, tried to make light of it. "What're you deaf, Hulk? I said, yeah, '*yes*,' the plan, we stick to the plan.' ...Hulk!? That's what they're callin' you, right? The Feds?"

"Yeah!" Hulk responded, almost proudly, pacing again, "that crazy Ryan's idea."

"Crazy he is," the lead cop agreed, adding, "nigger-loving son-of-a-bitch! ...But the name – it suits ya!"

Spotting the police, the reporter started blowing his horn again, and waved them over. He showed them the satchel the Feds had found; told them one of the musicians, wearing a silvery stage suit, had come running out of the club with it, at the first sound of gunfire. He pointed towards the alleyway where the bag was recovered.

"First cross-alley to the left," he noted. "Feds never found the Negro, though... Guns kept going off – yours, I guess?" The cops indicated 'yes.' "Then it got quiet," the newsman continued, "and the Feds got back on his trail. Back and forth they went, two, three times. Bag was empty, though – no dope... Negro must still have it on him."

"Nah," said the lead cop. "Probably flushed it, or dumped it.

"Doesn't matter, though," he lied, straight-faced. "We found another whole bag in that fancy flat upstairs. And, we got witnesses, seen every one of those niggers buyin' it."

The reporter asked the lead cop what all the shooting was about.

"Warning shots," he answered.

"Warning shots? All of 'em?"

"Yep!"

"And how'd you bust your lip, officer? Looks bad?"

"One of the musicians tried to run... One thing led to another..."

"One of the musicians?" the reporter took a note.

"Yep! Bunch of nasty niggers! Smoke that dope all day long; makes 'em violent!"

After running, haphazardly, nearly non-stop for over an hour, Dapper, exhausted, panting, and worried sick that one of his mates had been shot, crouched down to take a breather, behind a stack of crates near the back door of a restaurant. This had not been his lucky day! Not one of the dozen of his friends and fans – mostly women, who lived in these back alleys were at home. And their doors were locked. Nor would any of the restaurant owners offer him shelter. Too risky, they told him, regretfully; couldn't afford to have the cops shut them down.

Most of the locals who frequented the club had day jobs, though, and would be home by five or six o'clock. Dapper checked his watch – it read four-ten; and decided to wait it out. He brightened up as one pretty woman, in particular, came to mind. He'd been meaning to call her, anyway; she'd take him in, of that he was certain.

The sound of distant thunder distracted him, and his brow knit as he looked to the clouds; they'd gone from streaky gray to billowy black. He looked down, then, anxiously, at his pricey lame' suit. "Not rain, Lord," he prayed aloud, "don't let it rain. Not yet!"

It was already drizzling across town, where Morse and Ryan sat in their car, in the parking lot of a hospital, waiting for Slim, to report on Shaker.

Ryan studied his partner and shook his head. He could hardly believe it: Morse looked 'uncollected,' and almost slovenly – clothes all wrinkled, blood-stained, hair every which way.

"Say, Bud, don't beat yourself up," Ryan offered. "It was my fault. …I should've stuck to my guns. I knew that son-of-a-bitch was trouble. There was no doubt in my mind. I should've called the chief – Texas fresh on all our minds, he would've said 'forget it!' And that poor bastard would still have a hand! … I feel sick to my stomach every time I think about it."

"Listen, Partner, number one, he's not that 'poor' – got more money than both of us put together! And, two, he's not that innocent – made his money bootlegging!"

"That wasn't him, Morse! That was his partner, Luis Mood! All that Shaker ever did was play the piano – make dance music, ...and that bluesy stuff, tears your heart out. And now he's got no hand!"

Ryan hung his head, and sighed. "I'm starting to hate cops, Morse. Don't want to work with them, don't even want to look at 'em anymore."

"C'mon, Ryan! We've run into a few bad apples lately. They're not all bad. You, of all people, should know that. How many cops in the family – ten?"

"Five. Great cops, every one of them! But from a different generation, Morse. You don't find 'em like that today – decent, proud, respectful of the law, and of people."

"There were crooked cops in your father's day. I remember you telling me."

"Crooked, yeah. A few. Took bribes, shit like that. But not deranged, Morse! They weren't full of hate! Didn't go around blowing people's hands off, for no reason. Cop like that wouldn't have lasted five minutes in my dad's unit. They weren't even allowed to use the word 'nigger'!"

"I guess," Morse acknowledged, "times have changed."

"Here it comes," he said, morosely, of the storm clouds moving in. "Just what we needed... Oh, God! And here comes Slim... Shit! ...He's crying, Ryan... He's all broke up! Oh, my God! ...I was afraid of this... Shaker's dead, Ryan! ...He's dead! I knew it!"

It was beginning to sprinkle where Dapper was sitting. He jumped up, and shook himself off. He needed to find shelter – a porch, an overhang, any little space, where he could hide, and stay dry for an hour or two. He thought about returning to the club – the one place they wouldn't be expecting him. He'd find shelter there – hide in the garbage bin if he had to, suit n' all.

He took off smiling. But, suddenly, he was back in the nightmare!

"There he is!" he heard the lead cop shout. "Get him! ... I'll go around!"

Dapper ducked, and tried to think, and not to panic. There was only one way out of his tight spot – an open basement window next to the restaurant's back door. He crawled to it hastily, and stuck his head in. As his eyes adjusted to the darkness, he breathed a sigh of relief. An old icebox was sitting against the wall, under the window. He could carry on, head first, brace his arms on the appliance, throw his legs over, and escape!

He was half-way home when a huge hand pulled him out by the seat of his pants.

"You crazy or somethin', boy? That's breakin' and entering?"

Dapper felt the blood rising again. "No Sir, nothin's broken," he answered meekly, motioning toward the unmarred window.

"Nothin' to break it with." He showed the towering giant his empty hands.

Hulk cracked the window with the butt of his gun.

"You callin' me a liar?" He taunted his trembling captive, pointing the gun to his head, and gesturing for him to get up.

Dapper stammered, "N, n, no, Sir," as he got to his feet, and raised his arms slowly.

The lead cop had caught up with them now, and was looking on – a misshapen smirk on his broken lip. "Taking a swing at an officer, I see," he put in. "That'll getcha extra time!"

"No, Sir," Dapper answered. "Ain't swung at no one."

"Take another swing at me," said Hulk to the musician, "go ahead."

The bewildered Dapper stared at him, agape.

"You better do what he says, nigger," the lead cop advised, poking the musician with his stick, and letting out a snigger.

Dapper refused, "Can't do that, Sir! Can't do that!"

"Do it, or I'll shoot ya dead!" Hulk threatened.

"He ain't kiddin,'" the lead cop warned, "and I'll say you went for his gun!"

Not knowing what else to do, Dapper lowered his arms, raised his right, and punched the cop in the mouth, full force, drawing blood.

Hulk ran his fingers over his bloody lip, and winced. And then he smiled. "You're under arrest, Boy," he said, almost apologetically, "for assaulting an officer of the law."

Chief of Federal Bureau of Narcotics Office, Washington, D.C., 8:00 P.M., that night:

Anslinger had stayed after hours, waiting for word from his agents, in Chicago. He was about to leave, when a telegram arrived from Hearst's reporter. It said, simply:

Headlines of Chicago papers to read:
"MARIJUANA-CRAZED MUSICIANS ASSAULT POLICE."

"Nice," said Anslinger, out loud to himself. "Very nice. Finally!"

Katelyn Farm, earlier that day:

The afternoon was dreary and drizzly; the living room of the Burnett's home dimly lit, the fresh flowers fading. Kate was at her desk, at the bay window, writing to Will, and missing him, terribly. She smiled at the thought that he was with her, in spirit; she knew this to be true, and found some comfort in it. Nevertheless, her body ached for him, longed for his physical presence, the lying next to him, the warmth and scent of his skin, the sound of his laughter.

She laid down her pen, breathed a sigh, crumpled the page, and threw it into the waste basket. The hounds at her feet looked up at her, sad-eyed. She gave them each a pet, and started anew, determined not to send a single complaint, not a negative word, to her love:

My Darling Will,
Thank you for your letter. I relished it, curled up in bed with it, read it again and again, held it to my heart. I felt so close to you, almost as if you were here – almost! Of course, I love your wires too, Darling. And marvel at them, the immediacy of them, the speed with which you can impart to me a bit of news, a loving thought, from across the world. 'Tis a wondrous age we live in!

She raised her eyes to the sound of the front door opening. Noble entered, and walked toward her, without a word, his head hung low. He was holding a file of papers. The dogs rushed to greet him. He bent down and petted them dutifully, silently.

"Hi, Daddy," Kate welcomed him. "How was the meetin'?"

Noble grunted unintelligibly.

"What's all that?" She gestured toward the papers.

Noble mumbled low again, took a seat on the sofa, and motioned for her to join him.

"Look like you lost your best friend," she said, and sat down beside him, and kissed him on the cheek.

He handed her the file. "The League is petitionin' three counties, includin' ours, to license hemp growers," he said gloomily, "on advice from the federal government."

"License? Why?"

Noble swallowed hard. "You remember me tellin' you, years ago, what happened when my daddy told me and Uncle Ben, when we were kids – I was maybe twelve, Ben thirteen, that some men, Negroes – Caribbean folk, as I recall, liked to smoke dried hemp leaves? Got 'em drunk?"

"I remember it well. You said that you and Uncle Ben tried it, but nothing happened."

"Well, we didn't get drunk. We just choked and turned green. So we figured it must've been a different kind of hemp."

"So?"

"So, the Bureau of Narcotics is sayin' that it's all hemp, any hemp – our hemp! That hemp contains a narcotic. Their letter to the president of our League says…" He pulled the letter out of the papers Kate was holding, and found the passage to which he was referring, "… right here, that Mexicans who smoke 'marijuana' – Mexican nickname for hemp – are committin' violent crimes under the influence of hemp."

"But there aren't any Mexicans in this county!" Kate pointed out.

"That's what I said! But the president, Dennis Baxter – I think you've met him…"

Kate nodded yes.

"… said plenty of Negroes smoke hemp too."

"Not our men!" Kate jumped to her feet, and started pacing. "We would have heard about it!"

"That's what I said! I told them the story 'bout me and Uncle Ben.

"'The Bureau of Narcotics is wrong,' I said. 'Not all hemp contains a narcotic. And even if it did, the dumbest thing we could do is tell people about it, especially youngsters. They're bound to want to try it, just like me and Ben!'"

"What did Mr. Baxter say?"

"He got all snippy. 'So, Noble, you're sayin' you know better than the Federal Bureau of Narcotics?'

'You're damn right I do!' I told him. 'I know those people, had lunch with 'em. They're a bunch of self-serving, self-righteous political pawns. They don't know a thing about hemp. And if you don't drop this licensin' rubbish, now, Baxter, consider me resigned from the League!'"

Kate's eyes widened. "You said that?!"

"I did. And then I got up to leave, and turned to June, and said, 'I expect my fiancée 'll do the same!'"

Kate gasped. "What did June say?"

Noble shook his head, remembering the look on June's face, and Lucy's. "Nothin', June or Lucy – stunned, speechless, both of 'em!"

"No wonder! Doesn't sound at all like you, Daddy!"

"There's more, Kate," he spoke despairingly. "Baxter kept baitin' me. 'Don't be silly, Noble. It's just a license! We need to keep track of growers and traders, make sure no one's peddlin' this dope to our kids.'

"I was too mad to answer, or even look at him. So, he gets snippier: 'We don't need your signature anyway, Noble. Got more than enough, *thank you*.' He waved the petition at me, smirkin'.

"I yanked it out of his hand, crumpled it, started rippin' off pieces, throwin' 'em at him. He jumped up, tried to grab it, I dodged him, kept it up. 'Now you don't!' I said at the last, and stormed out... Be damned if he didn't come after me! Follow me to the car, pullin' on my shirt, while I'm tryin' to climb in. 'Let me give you some advice, Noble,' he said.

"I said, 'No, lemme give you some, Baxter,' and I turned around, and popped him one, right in the kisser! He fell on his face, Kate! Bloodied his nose. Got up right away, though. June and Lucy rushed to help him, in tears. I gave 'em my handkerchief, and took off."

Kate could hardly believe her ears! She didn't know whether to laugh or cry. In all of her years, she had never seen or heard of her father 'popping' anyone.

"Truth is, Kate," Noble went on, "I was more annoyed with myself than him. Didn't mention it to you, figured you wouldn't approve, but at the last meetin' I signed a petition to ban 'marijuana' in our county. June had asked me to sign it; said it was the worst drug she'd ever heard of; showed me what the Bureau of Narcotics had to say about it..." He gestured again to the papers Kate was holding, "in their Bulletin...

"I was suspicious, of course, cause Anslinger heads that Bureau. But then I read about it – sounds awful, Kate, just awful! I figured it can't be all lies. So I signed the petition. Wish I hadn't... Needless to say, there was no mention of hemp in the Bulletin. He's too smart for that."

Visions of an anti-hemp conspiracy began to spin, like a kaleidoscope of horrors, in Kate's head. It made her feel physically ill. She returned to her seat, closed her eyes, and prayed for strength.

"The ban passed overnight!" Noble continued his tale of woe. "Tobacco got behind it, oddly enough... Maybe because marijuana's smoked? And now this... If it's true that marijuana and hemp, any kind of hemp, are the same, we've got problems, Kate. Big problems. We've got to call Anderson, right away. Get to the bottom of this."

Kate was of the same mind. Mike Anderson would know. She glanced at the clock on the mantle. It was almost five-thirty; Mike would be leaving the office. "We'll call him at home tonight," she said. "And I'll speak to Will's parents 'bout the petition tomorrow. It won't pass here with Fairfield against it, Daddy, don't worry! But, if I may say so, Darlin' Father, you've got some apologizin' to do!"

Noble gave her an appreciative smile, and went to the phone. "I already told the girls I was sorry, so very sorry... Went straight to their house, n' waited, all nervous..." he sighed. "They said they understood, though; my livelihood, n' all. Said they believed me, too; it's not our hemp, has nothin' to do with us. Amazin' women, we're so lucky to have them, Kate..."

Kate agreed, and thanked the Lord.

"I suppose I owe it to Baxter, though," he murmured, "and to myself, get it off my chest."

"But," he raised his voice, and spoke with conviction, "I'm through with the League, Kate. June can do as she pleases, but I'm done. Turns out you were right about those people, most of 'em. Nothin' makes them happier than forcin' their ways on others, by law! Amendments to the Constitution?! Incredible, what they've gotten away with! Prohibition's dead, so now they're onto the new forbidden fruit; and hemp – God help us! More crime, more corruption, disrespect for the law... It's just not right, Kate, not in the land of the free!"

4

The Hemp-Mobile

Mike Anderson wasn't at home when the Burnetts phoned. They learned from his secretary, Aggie, the following day that Mike had gone to Nebraska, in response to an urgent call from a former client, named Watts. Aggie said the trip had something to do with the 'hemp-mobile, and that Mike would be returning in a week or two. It was nearly a month before the Burnetts heard from Mike, however. He wired them from a train station, on his return to Richmond; said he'd be home the next Tuesday, and would pay them a visit on Thursday, if convenient.

Noble called Aggie to confirm. The latest news was good, the secretary told him – "very good," for hemp-folk, and for the nation at large.

Kate was out in the fields at first glimmer on that Thursday. She and Joe Mays had been trying to fix their favorite tractor – a theretofore trusty, old Allis-Chalmers – for days. They had had the machine humming, finally, the night before, and were feeling quite pleased with themselves. But on that morning, the temperamental engine failed to start. Nothing. Dead.

Kate was beside herself. Will was returning from Europe on Monday, and he and Kate were scheduled to leave for England a few weeks later. She had promised to give him her undivided attention in between. Meanwhile, there were two hundred fifty acres of Katelyn to be plowed and sown. The Burnett's new tractor was in good order, but the labor was intensive, and required a second, at the least.

She agreed with Joe and her father that "enough was enough." The machine was worn out. It needed a complete renovation. Upon hearing that the local mechanic was backed up, however, and that he might not even look at the vehicle for days, she talked Joe into giving her one more go at it. They hitched the tractor to Kate's car, towed it to the top of the hill above the barn, double-tested the rope, and climbed in; Kate into the tractor, Joe, reluctantly, into the car.

She made a few adjustments, and gave him a nod. He started up, but looked back at her with a worried expression. She shot him another 'go ahead.'

He turned off the engine. "You sure this's a good idea, Miss Kate?" he had to ask.

Kate smiled at him, and nodded 'yes.' "I told ya, Joe," she spoke loudly, "ol' man Williams fixed his just like this: one, two, three!"

"Yes'm," Joe responded warily. "One, two, three. But how 'bout lettin' *me* drive the tractor?"

"Now Joe, don't tell me you're from the 'men do it better' school too?" Kate laughed.

Joe gestured 'no,' and muttered, "nothin' like that, Ma'am."

"You of all people," Kate carried on playfully, "married to a woman, does any man's work, and then some!"

Joe smiled, looked to the Heavens for help, and re-started the car.

"Let 'er roll!" yelled Kate.

Joe hit the pedal, and 'let 'er roll,' down the hill, tractor in tow, in the direction of a plowed field adjacent to the barn. The tractor engine turned, and then started, within a few seconds.

Kate jumped to her feet victoriously, free arm raised to the sky.

"What'd I tell you, Joe?" she shouted. "Let's park 'em, and unhitch 'em!"

There would be no 'two' or 'three,' however. The tractor engine began to sputter and jerk, and stalled out, fast as it had started. Kate lost control, hit a bump, was thrown forward, whacked her head on the dashboard, and tumbled out of the vehicle.

Joe, horrified, pulled the car over, and rushed to her aid, screaming and praying aloud: "Miss Kate! Miss Kate! Sweet Jesus! Have mercy!"

Kate looked up at him, half-dazed, totally embarrassed.

"I'm fine, Joe. Don't worry," she murmured undecidedly. "But the tractor!" she cried, pointing to the disaster in progress behind him.

Joe turned around, held his hands to his head, and continued to pray out loud. He had had the presence of mind to park the car sideways, to keep it from rolling down the hill. The tractor, however, had already passed the car, severing the towing rope with its huge steel blade, and veering off course in the process. It was on the move, picking up speed, and heading directly for the barn!

Joe took off after it, flying, to no avail. Luckily, he stopped and screamed again, "Nettie! Get out!" just seconds before the runaway vehicle rammed through the back of the barn. Nettie and Noble, alone in the building, heard his cry, and got out in time.

Apart from Kate's pride, and the goose-egg on her forehead, no humans or animals were injured in the accident. Kate, however, retreated to her room, sat in front of her vanity mirror, and bawled for a half hour afterwards. Nettie, hovering over her, applied cold compresses to her head, and tried in vain to console her.

"Could've been worse, Missy, that's for sure," Nettie rationalized, when sympathy failed. "The Lord was with ya'll."

Kate shook her head 'no,' then, 'yes,' half-heartedly.

"If the back wall of that barn wasn't padded with all that hemp, tractor could've plowed right through, n' caved in the roof! ... If I hadn't gone to the barn with the mail, curious as I was, n' left the door open, we might not've heard Joe yell, n' got ourselves killed!"

"I suppose," Kate sighed. She looked up. "What was so curious 'bout the mail, by the way? ...Not another offer from tobacco?"

Nettie nodded, and held up two fingers. "They ain't givin' up! Guess they don't know you're fixin' to marry a Fairfield," she laughed. "They don't know your daddy either! He didn't even open the letters. Said for you or me to do it. But to let him know if they offered a million!"

Kate's faint smile became a wince. "Ouch! Ouch!" she cried, "I can't smile, or even frown, without it hurtin'!"

Nettie examined the swelling again. "But it's gettin' better, Honey," she advised. She pulled a clean cloth from her apron pocket, arranged another compress from the basin of ice and water on the vanity, and pressed it firmly over Kate's wound.

"I've been thinkin' about the blessin' of this ice here, too, Missy. Did you know we were plumb outta ice, just yesterday? And then the ice man came – early! Well, we thought it was early, but turned out right on time! This bump on your head would've been twice as big," she lifted the pack slightly, took another quick peek. "Yep, twice as big," she repeated with a nod, "without these packs. Praise the Lord!"

"Praise the Lord," Kate echoed loyally. "And thank you, Aunt Net, as always, for lendin' me your healin' hands, and ignorin' my childish weepin' and whinin'. It's just that I'm so sad. And cross with myself. There's so much work to be done. Now I've added to the load. Not to mention the expense."

"Was just an accident, Honey. They happen now and then, usually a lesson to be learned from 'em."

"You think I'm bein' too hard on myself?" Kate asked her, laughingly, as if she didn't know.

"Always," Nettie answered with a smile, "n' I don't much like it!"

Their giggly, come-lately respite was promptly interrupted by the sound of angry footsteps down the hall.

Kate's quarters, another of her 'favorite places in the world,' had been converted from two bedrooms into a spacious bed-bath-sitting-room suite, and occupied an entire side – some eight-hundred square feet – of the second story of the Burnetts' home. The sitting area featured two picture windows, set at a right angle, overlooking the hemp fields to the north and west of the farm. The sunsets over the Appalachian foot hills in the distance were extraordinary, especially from the 'rocking-chair' balcony off the bedroom. A flat-stone plaque with the word 'sanctuary' scrolled on it – a gift to Kate from her brother – was mounted alongside the doorway to the suite, which was situated at the far end of a long, parquet-floored hallway.

Noble knocked once on the door, loudly.

"Enter, Daddy, please," Kate bade him, and gave him a warm smile; as did Nettie.

Noble furrowed his brow. "Thanks to the hemp stored in the back," he said soberly, "damage to the barn and the tractor are minimal. But..."

"Nevertheless, I'd like to pay for them, Daddy, from my savings," Kate spoke up.

"Don't interrupt me, Kate – I'm not in the mood! And I'm not here to lecture you 'bout the accident. I know they 'happen' now and then. Heard Miss Nettie, and your mama before her, say it often enough!

"What I came to say, first off, is that 'headstrong' and farmin' don't mix! You cannot 'force' a farm to do your will, Kate, or adjust to your schedule. Farmin' takes allowin'; allowin' things to unfold as they will, and allowin' nature to take the lead. You understood that as a little girl!

"Here you are, a grown woman, tryin' to rush what won't be rushed; thinkin' you can get it all done in one season, so you can get married, and look after your husband, in the next. Ignorin' what everyone else thinks! It won't work, Kate, for the farm, or the marriage!

"Second, seems to me you have a choice: Continue to be a partner in the farm, and make *that* your priority, or begin to make a new life with your soon-to-be husband. I suggest you choose the new life. Joe and I can run this farm, just fine, by ourselves, especially with the mill down.

"The boys," he nodded toward Nettie, as he referred to her teen-aged sons, "are strong young men now, smart as they come. Be done with their schoolin' shortly, and happy to get that mill up and runnin', or do whatever else needs doin'.

"Meanwhile, we've got plenty of help – regulars, and a hundred extra hands if we need 'em… And that about sums it up."

Kate had pouted silently through the lecture, her eyes darting back and forth between her father's stern visage, and the reflection of her own misery in the mirror.

"Headstrong?" was all she could utter, feebly, when the scolding was over.

Noble smiled, and softened his tone and demeanor:

"Don't get me wrong, Kate. You've been an outstandin' partner, and the best of friends, in these hardest of times. Don't know what I would've done without you when Uncle Ben passed. Might've sold the damn farm, n' withered away myself. But that's passed too. Lord willin', I'll be workin' this land well into my eighties, like my grand-daddies did, happily.

"For now, I'm worried about you, Kate. And your future. It's been a rocky road for you n' Will…"

He paused and looked up at the sound of the dogs' territorial bark.

"Must be Anderson," he muttered, checking his watch, "early, as usual." He caught Kate's eye, "You up for some good news, partner?"

Kate smiled and nodded 'yes,' a palpable wave of relief lighting up her face.

Noble turned to Nettie. "Leftovers or eggs – whatever's easy 'll be fine for lunch, Miz Nettie, bein' we had an accident n' all."

"Won't be makin' do, Mr. B.," Nettie replied. "Made ya'll chicken' n' dumplin's early this mornin', n' tomata-soup. Puddin' for dessert!"

"You are indeed a blessin', Mrs. Mays," Noble remarked as he took leave. "Meet ya'll downstairs. And hurry, suspense is killin' me!"

"Daddy?" Kate called after him.

Noble did an about face.

"I'll thank you not to mention the accident."

"Oh?" he teased, "you think he won't spot that nose on your forehead?"

Nettie had to laugh. And so did Kate, although it hurt.

Mike Anderson was already out of his car, and petting the dogs when Noble came out to greet him.

It was a most pleasant spring afternoon, sunny, blue skies, light breeze, seventy degrees. Noble was feeling fine for the first time that day; and the sight of his wholesaler, who had arrived in a shiny, new automobile; wearing a spiffy new outfit and carrying a fancy new briefcase, nearly made him jump for joy.

"Welcome Anderson! Good to see you, Son!" he spoke in a vigorous voice. "Looks like business is even better than you reported!" He made a sweeping gesture from the car to the briefcase.

"Things are definitely pickin' up, Mr. Burnett," Mike answered. "Good to see you, too, Sir."

They shook hands warmly, back-patted each other, and strolled leisurely around the house to the hemp fields behind it, the dogs leading the way. Noble wanted to show off his new crop, which was exceptionally vibrant that year.

Mike was impressed. He climbed up on the lower rail of the fence bordering the field, and gazed upon the endless sea of green, smiling and breathing deeply.

"Now this," he declared, "is what the oil fields of tomorrow are goin' to look like. And smell like. Clean, green, and fragrant!"

"Amen!" Noble affirmed.

They carried on to the back porch of the house, where they sat and chewed the fat about the weather, the dogs, and finally, the price of hemp, which had risen slightly, for the first time in five years. Noble attributed the rise to the 'New Deal' policies of the Roosevelt administration; but Mike was certain it had more to do with an increased industrial demand. He would explain, he said, once Kate arrived.

"I'm here!" she announced blithely, opening the French-doors from the living-room to the porch, and waving the men in.

"The table's set, soup's hot, and Miz Nettie's in the kitchen warmin' the casserole. Lunch will be served momentarily, gentlemen, if you please." She led them into the dining-room, taking hold of Mike's arm, and gushing, "So nice to see you, my friend, I declare! And absolutely cannot wait to hear the news!"

He could hardly respond, for staring at her. She looked so different, pretty still, but almost like another person. She was sporting her customary long, dark, A-line skirt, a white, collared blouse, buttoned-up, and a pastel-colored cardigan. But she was also wearing bangs, wispy, wavy golden locks that covered her previously barren forehead, from her hairline to her brow-line!

Noble held back a chuckle long as he could, and then was out with it. Kate blushed, excused herself, and ran off to the kitchen to help Nettie.

"Her mama used to appear with a strange new hair-do every so often as well," Noble whispered laughingly to Mike, as they took their usual seats round the dining-room table; Noble at the head, Mike to his left, the place set for Kate to Noble's right.

The dining-room of the Burnetts' farmhouse, like all of the main rooms, was airy, bright and picturesque. Kate had replaced the original, smaller windows with giant, picture windows, wherever there were views. She had also added screens and screen-doors to the remaining windows and entrances, to let in the nearly constant breeze, and keep out the bugs. The fresh, cheery ambiance, together with Nettie's cooking, and, best of all, at least for Mike Anderson, the nearness of Kate, made business lunches at the Burnett's a sheer delight.

A few bites and 'oohs' and 'aahs' into the meal, at the request of his hosts, Mike began telling his tale:

"Well, as you know, 'bout five weeks ago, I get this call, from an old customer of mine, Watts, who's been farmin' out in Nebraska for a couple of years. He asks me to come out there, by the ninth of the month. Says it's an opportunity I won't want to miss, and he'll pay my train-fare and put me up.

"Now I know this Watts to be a serious type; not the kind who'd lead me on a wild-goose chase; my daddy knew his daddy, and such.

"So, I take the train. When I get there, on the ninth, he tells me he's growin' hemp for Henry Ford – *the* Henry Ford. He says Ford's been experimentin' with engines, and various plant fuels, and has decided on hemp; all of which I already knew, and had passed on to you."

The Burnetts acknowledged, remembering it well.

"The real news was that the engine had been perfected, finally, n' every kink worked out on the chassis. On Ford's orders, ten of the new vehicles were bein' assembled, with minor variations. The first had been completed on the day I arrived, and was scheduled for a test run the next mornin'. And I was invited!"

"But not to drive it? You didn't actually drive it? Did you?" Kate asked excitedly.

Mike smiled from ear to ear. "Yes, Ma'am... I did! ... It was thrillin', felt like I was makin' history!"

Kate and Noble expressed their amazement, and begged him carry on.

"So, early that mornin' Watts takes me from his farmhouse to Ford's secret plant. We pass miles and miles of hemp fields on the way – green everlastin'! Watts said he and his crew alone had sown *ten thousand* acres of hemp! No one knows how many farmers are growin' for Ford, or how many acres they're growin', but, educated guess is, Ford's the biggest grower in the U.S.A. today.

"The auto factory looked huge to me, although I'd never seen one before. Watts said it was 'tiny.' Garage doors in the front of the buildin' were all closed when we arrived. No sign of life, except maybe twenty, twenty-five cars, all Fords, parked toward the back. We went to a side door, and knocked, and waited. The man who finally answered recognized Watts, but shook his head 'no,' while givin' me the once over. Watts showed him a pass, from the 'head-office,' for two, n' we got in.

"It was early, 'bout ten to nine, but the set-up was already underway. A crowd of about thirty men, mostly mechanics, in overhauls, were gathered around the hemp-mobile, watchin' the chief mechanic, and Henry Ford himself do a final inspection.

"I had to keep movin' in and out, findin' spaces between the taller blokes, to see. Ford looked pretty fit for an older guy, distinguished, I'd say, a touch of gray at the temples, and finely attired.

"The crowd was buzzin' from the time we entered, but the second Ford gave the signal, there was silence... He took the moment! Dazzled 'em, as he climbed into the vehicle, dramatically, checked the dashboard, n' pulled the starter! 'Vroom,' 'vroom,' 'vroom' – turned and started immediately!

"The old man threw up his arms; and the crowd went crazy, applaudin', cheerin', some of 'em jumpin', kickin' their heels! It was as if they knew somehow, just by the hum of that engine, that this would be the first, fully successful run!

"The garage doors flung open, and Ford was off, down the driveway, on to the main road, five miles to a turning point, and back, triumphantly!

"'Perfect!' he declared, upon gettin' out of the car. 'We did it, finally, gentlemen. Congratulations!' He shook hands and back-slapped his mechanics; and then he opened the driver's door.

"'Who's next?' he shouted.

"Of course, we all said 'me,' raised our hands, n' lined up.

"The shocker was every one of us got a turn! We went out in pairs, each man taking a turn at the wheel, either outbound or inbound.

"Like I said," he looked to Kate, "it was a great day for me."

"And a great American story you've got there, Anderson," Noble offered. "Hard to imagine, though, that it didn't make the papers, not a hint. I know Ford's been workin' in secret, but now that the car's perfected, why bother?"

"There's still a lot of work to be done, Sir. It's one thing to create a 'model' of a totally new vehicle, another to mass-produce and distribute it, and the paraphernalia that go with it. Watts thinks it'll take a year, or two or three in this economy, before all that can be set up."

"Even with Ford's resources?"

"Yes, Sir, at least a year. In the meantime, Ford doesn't want his 'enemies' at 'Big Oil' gettin' wind of his scheme. He calls them a 'greedy, ruthless lot.' Despite the fall of some of their allies, he says, they still have plenty of friends in powerful places.

"For now, the rules remain: No cameras, no reporters, no outsiders. With few exceptions, Ford's employed only long-time, well-trusted insiders on the project, and paid them well. Pretty much worked. There've been a few leaks, as we know, some rumors; but as nothin' came of any of 'em, they eventually faded."

"Weren't they suspicious of you, Mike?" Kate asked.

"They would've been, had I come lookin' for them. But they called me in. They needed someone to run a hemp-oil refinery. Watts told 'em I'd have leads, which I did; and I could be trusted, which I could.

"I met with Ford, day after the test, n' I've been on the job ever since. Course, that means I'm sworn to secrecy," he looked straight into Kate's eyes, "n' so are you!" And then to Noble, "n' you, Sir!"

Kate solemnly raised her right hand.

Noble swore, "Not a word, Anderson!"

"And Aggie?' Kate asked. "I imagine you had to tell her."

Mike shook his head. "No specifics. All she knows was that the news was good, but remains a secret; and that Ford hired me to do a few related jobs. I also took a lesson from Ford: When I got back, I asked Aggie not to discuss the hemp-mobile, or even mention it, to anyone, for any reason. She gave me her word; and I gave her a bonus!"

He grinned, his eyes fixed on Kate, till she smiled back.

"Now that ya'll 're in the secret society," he went on gladly, "There's more: I came home by way of Chicago, to see a man about the refinery. Heard him give a speech for the Hemp-Oil Institute, while ago; liked what I'd heard. Turns out this guy, Taylor, is experimentin', secretly, too."

"Guess I have an honest face?!" He looked to Kate, smiling.

"Yeah, yeah, honest as they come! ...Carry on, Anderson!" Noble kidded and distracted him at once.

"Yes, Sir," Mike went on good-naturedly. "So, Taylor takes me to his factory, and shows me a type of plastic he's manufacturin' from hemp pulp – hurds. Tells me there's *a thousand different uses* for this plastic, dependin' on thickness, pliability, heat resistance – what they call 'grades.' And there's already a huge demand for this plastic – even in this economy!

"I asked him why the secret. He said he's waitin' for a patent on a process he's devised to make one of the grades even better, faster, n' cheaper. Till then, he says, he's workin' under wraps – Chicago bein' a hotbed of industry spies and crooked politicians, all lookin' to muscle in on somebody else's boon!"

Mike shrugged his shoulders, and carried on: "Still, I consider what he said good news. He, and a growin' number of industrialists agree, and so do I, that these plastics, together with the new auto fuel, are the road to recovery."

Noble wondered if 'hemp, as the road to recovery' amounted to good news or bad; given all the secrecy surrounding these new products, and the untold difficulties of getting them to market. He shook his head approvingly, but withheld comment.

Kate broke the silence: "I declare, that's excitin', Mike. Thank you for confidin' in us."

"There's more!" Mike suggested, staring at her yet again.

"Go ahead," she encouraged him; as did Noble.

"Follow me," the wholesaler spoke mysteriously. He led them out the front door to the automobile he'd arrived in, where he stopped, and turned to face them. Flinging his arm out flamboyantly toward the vehicle, he announced:

"Ladies and Gentlemen, introducin' the brand new, one of only ten in the world, hand assembled, 'Model H,' from Henry Ford!"

"No?!" they exclaimed simultaneously.

"Yes!" Mike assured them. "It's a hemp-mobile! Go ahead, touch it, knock on it. You'll see. The body's made of hemp-based plastic."

He stood back and watched and smiled, as they handled and examined the vehicle excitedly, inside and out, and with his permission, under the hood. Nothing pleasured him more than seeing Kate happy, especially when he, personally, had been cause to the effect. He couldn't stop smiling, or take his eyes off her.

Noble caught it again, and interrupted, clearing his throat, and speaking loudly:

"Well done, Anderson! Congratulations! And thank you, Son, for sharing your secrets, and your 'under-cover' car with us!"

"My pleasure, Sir." Mike replied truly. "The auto's not mine, though, unfortunately. It's goin' to whoever gets the refinery position. I'm just breakin' it in. ...How 'bout lendin' me a hand, Sir?" He returned to Kate: "Miss Kate?"

"THE MODEL H! BY HENRY FORD! DREAMS DO COME TRUE!" Kate headlined her journal that night, and entered:

Dear Diary,

Daddy and I drove a 'hemp-mobile' today, one of only ten in existence! It was a thrill, to say the least, and inspired us with hope for the future. Ironically so, as we could hardly tell that we weren't in an ordinary car.

And the good news kept coming! Mike is working for THE Henry Ford, and has signed us up to grow 'fuel' for Ford, once the new model goes into production. Can you imagine?

All this after the most dreadful morning – the dead engine, the accident, the bump on my head, the scolding, the silly bangs!

But even that sad story had a happy ending. Mike had no sooner left, when here comes old man Williams, down the drive, on his new tractor, fitted with fancy rubber tires. He'd seen daddy and Joe take ours in to the mechanic, and since he was done with his for the week, he wanted us to use it – wouldn't take no for an answer!

I thanked him, hugged him, and kissed him on his shiny head. That was all the reward he needed, he said, but he'd take another kiss when I return the tractor.

Daddy drove him home, and as Aunt Nettie and I waved him good bye, shouting, 'Thank you, Kind Sir,' again, she turned to me and remarked:

'I told you, Honey, that accident's OVER!'

Amen!

K.

Caught up in the exultation over the hemp-mobile, and unwilling to spoil it, the Burnetts had failed to ask Mike Anderson what he knew of the hemp-marijuana connection. Kate phoned Mike that evening, though, and told him the tale of Noble and the licensing petition. Due to the Fairfields' pull, she said, licensing had ceased to be an issue in Fairfield County. Nevertheless, she believed there was cause for concern. The drug marijuana remained illegal in every farm county in Virginia; and Temperance League officials were being told wrongly that fiber-grade hemp and marijuana were one and the same.

Mike agreed, calling the situation "extremely disturbing." He said he had heard about the so-called connection, and the new constraints, several months prior, but had assumed that the problem would go away, once the facts were established; those being, that marijuana and industrial hemp are *different*, and that the latter is devoid of medicinal or narcotic properties. What worried him now, though, he admitted to Kate, was that the Federal Bureau of Narcotics seemed to be 'pushing' the licensing laws, and that the man who headed that Bureau was "the world's most frustrated prohibitionist."

He promised Kate he'd look into it, thoroughly, and keep her posted.

Working from dawn till dusk over the next two days, with top-notch machinery, the help of the entire Mays family, their regular field-hands, and every other hand available, Kate and Noble were able to sow their final two hundred and fifty. They were exhausted, but contentedly so, and up at dawn again on Sunday morning. They took their coffee on the back terrace, and watched the sunrise in silence, smiling and breathing in the beauty.

"Isn't life sublime?" Kate whispered finally.

"Hmm," Noble agreed. "And funny!"

"Speaking of which, I noticed this mornin' you've pinned back your bangs, and your bump's 'bout disappeared."

Kate grinned, then rolled out her lower lip in a fake pout.

Noble chuckled, and glanced at his watch. "How 'bout joinin' us, then, for church and lunch in Richmond? Got an hour to get ready, Kate… June and Luce would love to see you; they ask for ya every time."

"Sorry, Daddy. I'm headin' to the city myself, tomorrow. Will's comin' home, remember? …Maybe I'll join ya'll next week."

"That's what I told the girls last week."

"Well, I'll be in Richmond next week; make it easier."

"We've got a date then."

"Tentative."

Although devout as a child, Kate wasn't much of a church person as an adult. Indeed, when Kate's mother died, suddenly, Kate, barely fourteen at the time, became angry with God, and stopped attending church altogether. She found peace through forgiveness, however, with Nettie's counsel over several months. Continuing with daily prayer and meditation, she then developed a personal relationship with her Lord, coming to know Him as Infinite Love, and taking great comfort in the knowing.

Contrarily, while she acknowledged the universal truths in the teachings of her childhood religion, much of what Kate heard on the rare occasion she attended church was at odds with what she 'knew' about God. Talk of 'hell-fire and damnation,' above all, made her uncomfortable. She feared not for herself, for her God was infinitely loving, but for those, including her father, who believed in a God with suspiciously human traits.

"I'm packed!" Kate announced proudly, as she and the dogs greeted Noble in the driveway, upon his return that evening. She gave him a big hug. "And – surprise! – supper's almost ready... Hope you're hungry!"

They ambled toward the house, and stepped inside. He sniffed the air and smiled. "Mmm,... Smells like Miz Nettie's," he said, crossing his fingers and holding them up.

Kate smiled back. "Don't worry. Recipe came straight from her file, followed it to the T."

Noble checked his watch. "Can you give me an hour, Kate? I've got some papers to review, and thinkin' to do."

"Take your time, Daddy. Supper'll stay warm in the oven. Think I'll catch the sunset from my rockin' chair tonight. Too tired to saddle Georgie."

She returned to the front door and opened it. The labs were sitting just outside, waiting. She usually rode her horse into the sunset each evening, and the dogs tagged merrily along.

They jumped up, all excited.

"C'mon, boys," she waved them in. "Up we go! Show's on the balcony tonight!"

Noble, in spectacles, was settled into his winged easy-chair, a brass reading lamp adjusted to the papers in his lap, when Kate returned. She took a seat on the sofa across from him. He looked up at her pensively, tapped the papers on the arm of the chair, and spoke softly:

"These are Aunt Beth's property deeds. And a slew of offers from tobacco. I've been thinkin', Kate. Maybe now's the time to buy her out. Now that we've seen this 'hemp-mobile' is not just talk. Even if it takes a few years to make it available, n' even if we don't really get to grow for Ford, the demand'll be there. We'll grow for ourselves, as always.

"I feel sorry for Aunt Beth, Kate. She really wants to move to the city. Be with the kids. And the little ones now. She feels she's missin' out.

"You know. You've heard her. And we both know she'll never sell to tobacco – too stubborn…"

"You think she might?' he asked, when Kate failed to respond.

"She'll never sell to tobacco, Daddy. But not because she's stubborn. She thinks tobacco killed Uncle Ben."

Noble peered at her over his glasses. "What about the booze!"

Kate looked back at him, as if over glasses. "Never saw him drunk, Daddy – ever! Or even tipsy… But I remember that cough; and Aunt Beth frettin' about it!"

Kate saw the hurt on her father's face. She rushed to him, sat on the arm of his chair, wrapped her arms around him, kissed the top of his head.

"I'm so sorry, Daddy. I know how much you miss him. I miss him, too. He was a darlin' man…

"And…" She slid off the chair, stooped down in front of him, to see his face, "if you think the time is right, let's do it!"

He smiled approvingly, and patted her on the cheek.

"Do me a favor, though?" she asked him, on second thought.

He nodded.

"Don't mention this to Will just yet. He would not be happy to hear that we're expandin', in the middle of the Great Depression; especially since the land we're buyin''s over-priced, what with tobacco, includin' Fairfield, competin' for it.

"He thinks the Depression will outlast demand here. Farm-land's cheaper in Kentucky and the Carolinas, n' that's where tobacco's headin'. He's been after me to sell my share of the

145

farm, since I'll be livin' in Richmond soon. Says he'll beat the highest bid I get, render me a 'woman of means'!"

"I told him 'bout our plan to hire a manager once I'm gone. And that I hoped to remain your long-distance partner, talk with you daily, by phone or wire, if not in person.

"What'd he say?"

"What he said was, 'Fine. It's your call, Kate,' but his face showed disapproval and disappointment."

Noble shook his head. "I don't know, Sugar. Lie of omission is still a lie. Might be askin' for trouble."

"But, Daddy, we can't tell him *why* we want to buy – we gave our word."

"Tell him just that, we've got good reason, but we're sworn to secrecy."

"I suppose… But the timin' has to be right. Don't want to hurt his feelin's."

"Fine, it's your call, Kate."

Kate followed her father's advice, however, and told Will about the acquisition directly upon his return. Will's unexpected response left her totally in awe of him, and even more in love with him.

Will said that he respected Kate and Noble's "decision of the heart," and their concern for what Noble's brother would have wanted for his wife. Quoting Nettie, "God works in mysterious ways," he added that such decisions often reap a profit, as well as goodwill, in the end.

"You never know!" he suggested to Kate: "Your 'secret sources' turn out to be right, hemp saves the world, Anslinger turns on tobacco instead, and our heirs will be thanking you and your daddy, not me and mine, for their inheritance!"

"Highly unlikely!" said Kate, with an exaggerated drawl, and a giggle.

But the ironies and caprices of fortune were not lost on either of them. Indeed, their discourse on the subject, time and again, had served to unite them. In this instance, they promised each other to act on their instincts whenever they matched, and to seriously consider the other's position whenever they differed.

Accordingly, they agreed to cancel the formal arrangements for their wedding, and ask their parents to give the money to the poor instead. In lieu of the traditional fanfare and expense, they would take their vows, quietly and informally, on their upcoming voyage to England, on the deck of the ship, at sunrise, on their first day at sea.

The set up was uncommon, and romantic; and Kate was overjoyed! She'd been dreading her own wedding, thinking of it as a farce! The idea of spending hundreds of dollars on a gown and veil that would be worn only once was ludicrous to her, especially since the mandatory 'whiteness' of the outfit was a symbol of 'purity' that she no longer accepted, nor portrayed. Nor could she see herself repeating the standard church vows – to love, honor and *obey* her husband? What of partnership? Oneness? What of the God-given right to free will? No! She and Will would write their own marital vows, tailored to their own prerequisites, and commit, not just till 'death did they part,' but till the end of time!

Noble was a bit disappointed. He'd been looking forward to the big affair, to walking the beautiful bride down the aisle, and welcoming Will, whom he already loved like a son, into the family. The peacemaker in Noble had also hoped that a publicized marriage between a prominent Virginian tobacco-man and a glamorous Virginian hemp-woman would help reduce the tension between the two industries, at least in the home-state.

Hemp and tobacco had been competing for the same farmland across the rural South for over a century, with tobacco winning steadily, eventually becoming 'king,' and wielding tremendous power, both political and economic. Resentment among the hemp-farmers grew concurrently, and at the turn of the century, many took sides with the Temperance Movement, which denounced tobacco as well as alcohol, and suggested that both should be illegal. Now the bitterness between the sides was mutual, and, with the outlawing of alcohol in 1920, erupted into an all-out feud.

The legendary generosity and modest behavior of the Fairfield family had long confused the issue in their county. The last hemp-man to publicly criticize the Fairfields, back in the late 1890's, was shunned by his own clan, until he apologized. By 1930, however, it was a different story: Times were hard in rural Virginia. Only five hemp-families, out of more than twenty, remained in Fairfield County, the rest having escaped, after selling out to tobacco, for top dollar. Fairfield Tobacco and two of its chief competitors held seventy percent of the county's prime farmland, and the tobacco business, defying the hard-times, was booming! With few exceptions, the remaining hemp-folk were beginning to hate the Fairfields!

Despite the letdown, Noble took the news of Kate and Will's elopement in stride; and gave the 'love-birds' his wholehearted blessing. He told them, laughingly, that he never thought he'd see the day when he'd be thrilled to have his daughter marry a tobacco-man. But that day had come. He was thrilled, honored, and delighted, for the couple, and for himself.

Will's parents, Joan and Jack Fairfield, were not the least surprised to hear of the elopement. Will had been muttering complaints about "all the to-do" since his wedding date was announced. The senior Fairfields had kept silent on the matter, assuming that for Kate, like most women, finally becoming the bride, the center of attention on the 'biggest day of her life,' would be a girlhood dream come true.

Once Will had won Noble's approval, however, he spoke to his parents directly, albeit playfully, about the switch. The three were seated around the L-shaped mahogany desk in the seniors' office, reviewing a contract, when Will said, out of the blue: "Who do I see about changin' the rules?"

Joan and Jack looked up from their work, glanced at each other, shrugged their shoulders, and turned to Will with questioning eyes.

Will peered back at them, smiling fondly, thinking what a handsome twosome they made, how fit they were for their age – well into their sixties; and how lucky he and his brother were to be of their bloodline.

Joan's face was lovely, fine-boned, and color-rich. She had honey-toned skin, ocean green eyes, and her silky, auburn and silver hair fell naturally into a pageboy, just above her shoulders. Jack's face was a show of contrast, rather than color, but equally striking and distinguished. His eyes were brownish black, as was his hair, apart from the splash of white at the temples. His skin was fair, and highlighted by dark brows, lashes, and mustache. He had high cheek bones, a wide-set jaw, full lips, straight teeth, and a 'Tyrone Power' nose.

Both Will and his brother, James, who were close in age and looked to be twins, took after their father, each with a notable exception: James had inherited his mother's green eyes, and Will her tawny complexion. All three of the men were tall – six-one-six-two, wide-shouldered, and lean, as well.

"Rules?" "What rules?" asked Joan and Jack, respectively, when Will failed to respond.

"The weddin' rules," he replied, "the ones that make 'traditional' compulsory, even if the bride and groom don't want it."

"The *bride?* Doesn't want it?" Jack could hardly believe it.

"Nope! I inquired about her feelin's on the affair the other day, and she gave me her 'gargoyle' face."

"What's that?" they asked at once.

Will squinted, wrinkled his nose, flared the nostrils, opened his mouth, curled the top lip over his teeth, tongue out toward the chin, and growled, "Ahhhh!"

His parents cracked up, but thought he was kidding, as usual.

"I'm serious," Will assured them. "I know it's hard to imagine, one so beautiful, makin' a joke of her face, but it's true. She does several of these 'faces,' for laughs; mostly from me!" He smiled delightedly at the thought of it. "Her latest, 'confusion,' is *really* funny. Crosses her eyes, like a bat, twists the rest of her face and *tongue* in different directions – hilarious!"

"Not so funny, Will," Joan objected. "She could hurt her eyes doin' that!"

"Yeah...You tell her, Mom... I have to laugh."

"Anyhow," Will continued, "her 'gargoyle' implies '*extreme* aversion.' She's been goin' along with the weddin' because she thought that's what *we* wanted. ...Sweet girl! She knew ya'll were forced to have a 'rich-peoples' weddin'.' But since ya'll went through with it, she figured we were expected to do the same.

"I set her straight; told her you've been snubbin' richness ever since. She knew all about the early Fairfields – down-to-earth, not at all 'showy. They were 'folk-heroes,' out in the country, she said, for that alone... But since ya'll lived in Richmond mostly, and rarely made the newspapers, she thought ya'll were just 'private' people.

"No, I said, they're 'anti-rich'!"

Both parents grinned, but Joan corrected him: "We're not anti-*rich*, Will, for goodness sake! All our friends are rich! We're anti-polo, -debutant ball, that sort of flauntin' it thing."

"I know, Mother, and I feel the same, always have... Well, maybe not about the debutant balls – I resented missin' those..." The three shared a chuckle, and Will continued:

"But Kate knows where you're comin' from now; says she loves ya even more."

"And we love her, Will, like a daughter, already, you know that," Jack offered.

"I do; and so does she," Will confirmed

"Makes me want to cry," Joan murmured, "bless her heart! Let her have the weddin' she wants, Will!"

Will nodded in agreement. "I get emotional over her too, Mama," he added, "And, I'm glad ya'll are fine with it, figured you would be; 'cause we're breakin' the rules, my Katie and me – the big weddin''s off!"

The 'weddin',' however, turned out to be bigger than the bride and groom thought. It took place, as planned, at sunrise, on the ocean, as their ship, destined for England, took leave of New York Harbor. The two were dressed, inconspicuously, they hoped, in the outfits they wore on their very first date; Will in a white dress-shirt and a tan sport-coat, no tie; Kate in a lengthy, bias-cut skirt, and a lacey, pink, long-sleeved blouse, no hat.

Despite their casual garb, and dark though it was when they boarded, the movie-star-ish couple drew attention straightaway. A few minutes later, at first glimmer, the ship's chaplain led them from their cabin up to the deck, and over to the railing, facing east. As they stood before the cleric, breathlessly, hand in hand, a few curious passengers began to inch their way towards them. And then a few more hurried over, and a few more. Before they knew it, some forty persons had gathered in a semi-circle around them, all eyes fixed expectantly on Kate, who was poised to speak, the rising sun encircling her in an ethereal golden aura.

She hesitated, for a moment, not knowing whether to proceed. Will gave her a reassuring smile, squeezed her hand. She mouthed a silent 'I love you;' he mouthed back, 'Me, too;' and gazing into his eyes, she commenced with their 'Wedding Prayer:'

"In beauty, wonder, and awe," her voice rang out, melodiously, *"under Heaven's glorious light, from sea to sky... With boundless passion, and a heart full of love and gratitude,*

I, Kate Lynette Burnett, take you, William Blain Fairfield... to be my husband..." She paused to wipe a tear...

Will, ready with his handkerchief, gently dried her eyes, and then his own, kissed her cheeks, and urged her on:

"*The Lord as my witness,*" she continued emotionally, "*I promise you, Will, my life-long fidelity, my eternal friendship, and my undyin' love and devotion.*"

Will, tears streaming again, half the crowd sniveling with him, lifted her hand to his lips, kissed it tenderly, lowered it, slipped the wedding ring on her finger, and repeated the vows to her.

The chaplain spoke his piece then, briefly, followed by the pertinent questions to Kate and Will, (re-worded slightly, as per their request). Both answered "I do," most solemnly, and the chaplain pronounced them husband and wife.

The crowd went wild, clapping, hooting, cheering the couple on.

"You may kiss the bride!" the chaplain shouted over the noise to Will, who had already swept Kate into his arms.

The hubbub grew louder as the couple kissed; but the chaplain soon placed a finger across his lips. "Shh... Shh... Please... " he begged, motioning for quiet, "There's more!" And all complied.

Kate and Will bowed graciously toward their audience, and to the cleric. Turning to each other, they fixed their gaze, clasped both hands, and completed their 'Prayer' together:

Here we are – husband, wife; a few words spoken, forever changed,
Where we were two, now we are one, heart and soul; and so shall it be,

In this precious moment, ever and always, by the grace of our Lord,

the strength of our will, and the gift of our sweet, holy love. Amen.

The two embraced yet again, kissed unabashedly at length, and sighed and wept for a moment on each other's shoulder.

There was a soft, intermittent applause from the crowd through the final embrace, but mostly the onlookers watched, and wept with the newlyweds.

"Why are all these people cryin'?" Will whispered to Kate, in jest, when they came up for air, "they don't even know us!"

"They're happy for us, Will," she responded, ecstatically. "They're cryin' tears of joy – so sweet!"

"Indeed!" he agreed; "Let's go meet them, invite them to lunch!"

She took his hand, and they made their way through the crowd, introducing themselves, shaking hands, hugging those with open arms, thanking all for their good wishes. The last man they greeted asked Will, quite loudly, if he was one of 'the' Fairfields, of tobacco fame.

"Distant cousins, unfortunately!" Will fibbed. "Nevertheless, Sir, I must say, I feel like the richest, luckiest Fairfield in the world on this day!

"And," Will raised his voice, and addressed the entire crowd, "Kate n' I are invitin' ya'll to our weddin' bash this evenin'. Champagne and hors d'oeuvres at seven, dinner at eight, followed by dancin'. I've already arranged for the band to play till 2:00 a.m.... One must dance, after all," he threw up his arms exultantly, "on the happiest day of one's life!"

The crowd cheered, and shouted, "See you at seven!" as the bride and groom took last bows, turned, and scurried off the deck. One of the onlookers had somehow gotten hold of a bag of rice, passed it out by the handful, and led his fellows in a chase after the newlyweds.

Kate and Will picked up speed, laughing and screaming like children, finally out-running their tail. They were out of breath and speckled with rice when they reached the cabin. "Now that," said Kate, "was a weddin' adventure! Thank you, Darlin', I loved it!"

"My pleasure, *Wife!*" he replied, with a satisfied smile. "But I can't take credit for the crowd, or the rice... Must've been the chaplain. We'll double his tip... later!"

"I thought we were invitin' our new friends to 'lunch,' by the way?" Kate questioned him, as he unlocked the door.

"We were," said Will, turning to her with that certain look, "but then I remembered – we need to get this marriage consummated!"

She laughed luxuriously, and then wildly, as he lifted her into his arms, carried her over the threshold, and plopped her on the bed, just like in the movies!

5
The Association

Katelyn Farm, spring, 1935:

Kate, Noble, and Mike Anderson were at the dining-room table, usual places, surrounded by paperwork, coffee cups, and the scant remains of dessert. Mike stood up for a moment, handed a list to Noble, and one to Kate.

"Okay, then," he said, looking from one to the other, "it's settled. You're roundin' up the growers, I'm gettin' the manufacturers. Already have a few of each signed up. But the pitch is the same:

"This is the *American* Hemp Association we're endorsin', headquartered in Kentucky. (One of my clients is lettin' us use his office address in a small town near Lexington. We'll switch to my office later, once we're rollin'.)

"Purpose of the group, same as the state groups, but nation-wide: identify and protect the common interests of hemp growers, manufacturers, and consumers. It does so by keeping its members informed about all things, hemp-related, that might affect their interests – laws, market trends, inventions, scientific findin's, whatever...

"The information gets to members in quarterly bulletins – brief, couple of pages, typed up and mailed out. It's also passed at meetin's, twice a year. And here, again, a few of my clients are willin' to fib a bit, call the state meetin's they held at their

155

factories, last few years, 'American.' Won't hurt anyone, no reason for anyone to question it!'"

He looked to Kate, whose brow was beginning to pucker.

"We're all goin' to have to fib a little, Kate, as a precaution. We can't have it known that *we* are the founders of this association. We have to pretend we're just ordinary members, rank and file, relatively new. Harmless fib. No one gets hurt. But we're protected."

"From what?" she begged to know.

Mike exhaled loudly, and focused on her.

"You remember those 'enemies' of Ford I told you about?"

She nodded. "Big Oil."

"Right, among others. They're still around, and so are their connections in Washington, and elsewhere. Last thing we need is to be singled out by these people as 'trouble-makers.' Ford says they have no qualms about destroyin' a person's reputation or livelihood. And, he added, he wouldn't put it past them to do *violence* against a major trouble-maker. Now, it's possible that Ford's exaggeratin'. He's been known to do so. But why take chances? Like I said, 'harmless fib.'"

Noble concurred: "Makes sense to me."

Kate, however, looked unconvinced.

"I could tell you stories, Kate," Mike persisted, "but I'd hate to scare you."

"Go ahead, Anderson," said Noble. "You'll scare me, not her!"

Mike laughed, but then took a serious tone:

"One of the biggest growers I know, Matthew Harris – he's a distant cousin, actually, out in Kentucky, filed a suit against his county over the licensin' law; on the grounds that the hemp he grew, accordin' to two local doctors, (who specialized in medicinal research), had no narcotic in it whatsoever. The county contacted the Federal Bureau of Narcotics, and they sent a couple of agents to investigate.

"Now, these Feds understood that Matt Harris is well-liked and respected by the Sheriff, and everyone else in that county. So, they go to the doctors, and try to intimidate them. They tell the doctors their studies are 'invalid,' because the hemp they sampled was fully matured, and could well have contained the narcotic at an earlier stage.

"The doctors said, fine, they'd take samples of Harris' hemp at various stages, and do another round of tests. Easily accomplished, at the time. Harris had three thousand acres planted, one sown in April, another in May, the last in June.

"However, the doctors argued, they had tested samples of medicinal hemp at full maturation, and, unlike the fiber-grade hemp, the medicinal did contain mind-alterin' properties. Not 'narcotic,' to be sure, but 'mind-alterin',' which can be mistaken for narcotic. What that study showed, the doctors said, was that medicinal hemp and fiber-grade hemp, while in the same family, are *not* the same plant.

"Therefore, the doctors told the Feds, the original studies were valid; and they refused to withdraw them as evidence in Harris' case. They would carry on with the other round of tests, but only to gather 'additional' proof.

"The agents returned to Washington, mission unaccomplished. But they didn't 'go away.' A few days later, the doctors, and Matt Harris received notice from the U.S. Treasury that they were being investigated for income-tax evasion! And both the doctors, and several of their family members, reported being followed."

"That's outrageous!" Kate interjected.

"Appallin'!" Noble agreed.

"It gets worse, folks," Mike responded. "But I can stop here?"

With a nod from Noble, Kate replied, "No, no, Mike, carry on, please... I have a question, though, if I may?"

He indicated yes.

"Did you get the names of the agents?"

"I didn't, Kate. But I assumed they were Anslinger's sidekicks – Matt mentioned somethin' about the 'scruffy one.'"

"Why am I not surprised," Kate murmured, with a sigh.

Mike gave her a nod, and continued: "Where was I? ...The doctors... one of them finally succumbed to the pressure, and withdrew his evidence. So, the agents return, and go straight to Matt Harris, try to reason with him, convince him that marijuana is the worst drug in the world, and must be controlled; that the licensin' law has nothin' to do with him, personally; it's about stoppin' the spread of a dangerous substance.

"The agents were stunned, however, to hear about the doctors and their families bein' followed, and the shady tax-evasion probes! The agents swore they knew nothin' of these intrusions; and seemed to be annoyed, and embarrassed by them.

"'Then who the hell is houndin' us?' Matt wanted to know. 'And why?'

"The agents shrugged it off, hintin' that someone at the Treasury must be usin' 'scare tactics,' to try to get Matt to call off the suit, and nothin' would come of it.

"Matt believed them. But he wasn't goin' to let the Treasury get away with harassment. He was suin' the county, he told the agents. And that was final!

"Turns out, though, the doctors gave the Feds too much information. The agents snuck back out on Harris' property at day's end, and took samples of hemp from his 'medicinal' bushes. The 'evidence' was tested, found positive for 'medicinal' properties; and the agents took it to the Sheriff's office – he happened to be workin' the late shift that night.

"Round about midnight, the Sheriff was bangin' on Matt Harris' front door. Matt's housekeeper answered, scared out of her wits. Harris came runnin' down the stairs in his bathrobe, yellin' 'what the hell's goin' on, Joe?' – Matt and the Sheriff were pals, fishin' buddies.

"Sheriff showed Matt the bag of narcotics found on his property, and said he had come to take Matt in.

"'In the middle of the night? You gone crazy?' Matt screamed.

"Then Matt noticed the hemp was from a medicinal bush, and really got riled up: 'This isn't what I grow! This is medicine, Joe! And you know it!'

"So, the Sheriff gives him the facts, regretfully: 'Matt, you've got these bushes on your property, there's a narcotic in 'em. Law says you need a permit to grow 'em. Now, unless you show me that permit – which I know you refused to buy, I gotta take you in, Buddy, just for the record. Your foreman, too… My job's on the line here.'

"Matt said okay, he'd go. But he put his foot down about the foreman. He said he wasn't goin' to let that Negro go to jail. The man was the best worker he ever had – smart, honest, and law-abidin'. And he wasn't goin' to have him 'marked for life' over some stupid law that had nothin' to do with him.

"Sheriff didn't like it, but he went along; said he'd tell the Feds that Matt didn't have a foreman, that he was his own foreman.

"Matt was gettin' dressed, when the fire bell started ringin', and the dogs howlin'. Now the foreman's wife pulls up in a truck, blowin' the horn, screamin, 'Field's on fire, field's on fire. Hurry!' Bunch of little colored kids crowded in the truck were cryin', shakin', all scared. Housekeeper took 'em in the big house; put 'em to bed.

"The agents were outside, waitin' in the Sheriff's car, while all this commotion was goin' on. They all pitched in the bucket brigade with the rest of the hands… managed to hose down the barn, save it, and the animals. But not the Negroes' cabins, burnt to the ground, all three of 'em, n' their belongin's.

"Harris lost a third of his crop, and the rest of his heart. He'd lost his wife to cancer the year before; and now this.

"Last I heard, he's sellin' the farm to tobacco."

159

Kate broke into tears. "You'll get no resistance from me, Mike."

"Me either," said Noble sadly. "We will fib!"

Mike nodded gratefully, and carried on, "Sheriff vowed to catch whoever set the fire and bring 'em to justice. The agents swore, at the risk of losin' their jobs, that they'd look into it, and report back. So far, the main lead, the man who was followin' the doctors around, has disappeared. He was a smoker. Might've been him snoopin' around on Matt's property that night. Neighbor's watchdog was barkin', like crazy, just before the fire started, and the neighbor saw a strange car pullin' away ...Maybe the dog spooked the driver, he tossed a butt, and the fire was an accident."

"Maybe not," said Noble. "And that's a scary thought!"

That evening, Kate and Noble, on horseback, dogs trailing, took to the dirt road around their freshly plowed fields. They rode in silence for a long while, losing themselves in the wonder and beauty of their surroundings. The winter had been severe; the first crocus had yet to bloom. But in the rosy remains of daylight, the dark, rich earth took on a metallic sheen, and its stones shone like rubies and opals.

As father and daughter completed the circle, thoughts of the day, the trials and tribulations of a fellow hemp-farmer, returned.

Kate moved in closer to Noble, and broke the silence:

"Something Mike said over lunch gave me an idea, Daddy."

Noble looked to the heavens for help, jokingly.

She smiled.

"It occurred to me that if we could talk just one big oil company into investin' in hemp-oil – just one. And if that investment paid off, it would turn this whole mess around in our favor."

Noble took his time mulling it over, and then shouted, "I like it!" and took off speedily toward the barn, yelping, "Yee-hoo!"

The dogs and Kate followed suit.

The hemp-farmers spent the next two weeks close to each other, and to the earth. They worked hard in the fields, sowing two-thirds of their land, their last sowing together as house-mates. The rains came, the parched earth drank in the moisture, and the rains abated, in perfect time.

Will arrived on schedule, and came to fetch Kate. But much to her and Noble's delight, Will chose to spend a week in the country, to "watch, listen, and unwind."

He and Kate picnicked daily in her 'favorite place,' and made love under the tree where her father had proposed to her mother. And they laughed, it seemed they never stopped laughing, both of them finding each other, as well as themselves, highly amusing.

Almost overnight, the tiny green hemp plants began to sprout from the moistened soil. And soon, from Kate's balcony, the glistening, verdant fields stretched far as the eye could see.

It was a blissful, 'soul-touching' week, for the couple; and the lingering fears Kate had about moving to Richmond were laid to rest. *"The inevitable change is upon us,"* she wrote on the eve of the move, *"and, more than ready, I welcome it, my arms wide open, my heart overflowing with love!"*

She was already with child, and sensed it, could almost see it in the mirror. She was afraid to mention it, though, and get Will's hopes up, in the event that it turned out to be wishful thinking.

Her first week as a city-girl was a whirlwind of surprises. Will bought her a piano – a Steinway, no less, and arranged for her former, much-loved teacher, Mrs. Olsen, to work with her again. Kate had learned to play at age seven, and was said to be 'gifted.' She gave it up, though, when her mother died; due to the difficulties she incurred as a teenaged farm-girl, in getting to the city on a regular basis, without a chaperone.

Will also set about buying for her a ten-acre stretch of her 'favorite place in the world.' The site included the hill on which he would build her 'dream-home,' the lake and the meadow above which the home would be perched, and the acreage necessary to connect the homestead with the main road to Richmond.

In the end, Noble chose to gift the land to Will and Kate, and to their offspring, as part of their inheritance.

The foundation of a U-shaped home, a downsized version of Bobby and Liddy's, was already up when Kate was presented with her gift. At the ceremony, Will promised her, Noble as his witness, that they would divide their time "as equally as possible" between the countryside, the city, and Europe.

"Are you ready to be a gypsy?" he asked her, playfully.

"I am!" she replied, all smiles, "the happiest gypsy in the world. And I thank you both," she looked adoringly from one to the other, "from the bottom of my heart."

Toward the end of her first month in Richmond, Kate awakened one morning with the dawn, feeling queasy. She was lying on her side in bed, her back to Will, who was nestled against her, arm over her waist. Seeking comfort, she snuggled even closer to him, and sighed as he responded with a sleepy kiss to the nape of her neck. But a huge wave of nausea followed. She lifted his arm off her body, sat up, and took a sip of water from the glass at her bedside. One sip, and she barely made it to the bathroom!

Will awoke to the muffled sound of her retching.

Dr. Frederick Linden, the Fairfields' family physician of twenty years, who had delivered James and Tess' babies, confirmed that afternoon what Will and Kate so happily anticipated: They were going to have a baby, early in the new year. They phoned their parents with the joyful news, and spent the remainder of the day at home alone, in Richmond, snuggling, giggling, and playfully debating which of their impromptu romps under the 'engagement tree' had been the 'one.' Overwhelmed with excitement, they fell asleep, intertwined and fully clothed, before dark.

In the morning, as soon as Kate's tummy was settled, they plotted their course for the coming months. Will called off his travels, and Kate agreed, dutifully, not to drive for the duration of her pregnancy. She'd have Will's houseman, Toby, on call as her driver, though, till the end. Through Kate's second trimester, the couple would divide their time between Katelyn, where they were overseeing the construction of their new home, and Richmond, where Will would tend to work, and Kate to volunteering. To be safe, they'd spend the last three months, including the holidays, close to the doctor, in Richmond.

During their very first stay at the farm, however, Will began to question her judgment, and wish he had kept her city-bound. They were chatting with Noble one morning at the fence behind the farmhouse, he and Kate on the trail side, Noble on the field side. Joe Mays, who was deeper into the field, checking for cutworms, spotted something suspicious, hollered out to Kate, and waved her over. On impulse, skirted though she was, she nimbly jumped the fence, and rushed to have a look.

Noble never gave it a thought; Kate had been jumping fences, in britches and skirts, since she was a toddler. But Will was aghast. Without a word, he flew over the fence, ran to where she was crouched down among the roots, planted his boots firmly in her view, along with his extended hand.

She looked up, her big smile fading, as she realized from the expression on his face, what she had done. She gasped, took hold of his hand, and got up. "Oh, I'm so sorry, Darlin'," she spoke sincerely. "I frightened you! I wasn't thinkin'. I promise to be careful, Will... No more jumpin' fences, never again, truly."

She hugged him to no response, then backed away, cocked her head, and smiled at him, her eyes softly pleading.

He nodded his acceptance with restraint.

A week later, he still hadn't let it go, and there was another incident, at their house in Richmond. He was dressing for work in their bedroom, choosing a shirt and trousers from the vast array in his closet, when he overheard Kate on the telephone in the next room:

"...Yes, our farm's to the northwest of yours... No, won't cost you a penny, Mr. Adams... Delighted to have you join... Well, so happens my daddy and I and Mike Anderson, our wholesaler – I believe he's done some work for you as well? ... Hmm. We'll be tendin' to business, not far from Emporia, on Friday mornin'... Be happy to pop in, get you signed up, answer any questions you might have.

"Fine, then, Mr. Adams, see you around noon on Friday... Same to you, Sir... Good bye."

Will barged into the living-room, wearing only his boxers and a scowl:

"I think that's too much drivin' in your condition, Kate! Emporia's clear down to the Carolinas."

"Oh, no, Darlin', I'll be fine," Kate dismissed him politely. "Doctor Linden says I can do anything at all, except ride a horse or climb a ladder. And I've added 'jump a fence,'" she noted with a laugh...

"Nice chest!" she flirted with him, flickering her brow. "How 'bout bein' late for work?"

Will ignored her pass, for the first time – ever.

"Still," he insisted, "I'd feel better if you'd call him, Kate. Check with the Doc. That's a long ride, back and forth. What if you get there, and don't feel up to drivin' back? What then?"

Kate frowned. She resented being treated like a child, and Will knew it. But she didn't want to fight with him either, so she tried her best to stay calm, and apply reason:

"Will, Darlin', Dr. Linden knows that we drive out to the country every weekend, sometimes twice a week. He has no objection whatsoever, hasn't cautioned me even once about the trip, with all of its twists and turns. Emporia's no farther from Richmond than Katelyn. And the road to Emporia's the best in Virginia."

"Who says?"

"Mike Anderson... And he knows; he practically lives on the road!"

"Hmm," was all Will could muster. Everything about Mike Anderson, the slightest mention of his name, rubbed Will the wrong way.

As it happened, Noble had to bow out of the Emporia trip. June's brother, from California, was in Baltimore on business, and wound up with a free day. He wished to pay June an unanticipated visit on Friday; said he was looking forward to finally meeting her fiancé.

Mike Anderson said he'd be happy to carry on without Noble, but he wasn't going to Emporia without Kate. Mike had had Mr. Adams on the verge of joining the Association a few weeks prior, but then had lost him. He didn't want to take the chance again.

"You Burnetts are the charm," he told Noble, referring to Kate's perfect 'reel 'em in' record: Five out of five of the farmers she'd met with had joined the Association. Moreover, their wives had joined; and not just to keep an eye on their husbands! The women found Kate to be "trustworthy," with a "keen business sense." If Kate said that joining was good for the farmer, the industry, and the community, it was good enough for them!

Noble was torn. He was sure that Kate would want to make the trip, with or without him, but he wasn't sure it was a good idea. He believed that Mike Anderson was still in love with Kate. The signs were there, not as glaring as before, but noticeable. Noble suspected that Will noticed too; and the last thing Noble wanted was to stir up trouble for the newlyweds, especially now, while they were 'expecting.' He considered making the call himself, cancelling and re-scheduling with

Adams. But then he'd have to admit to Kate that he had decided for her, or lie to her. He couldn't do either. He told Mike that she'd be coming to the farm on Thursday for a meeting, after which she'd call him, with her decision.

Kate was, in fact, eager to get Mr. Adams signed. Adams was a major grower, fifth generation, like Noble, well-respected and connected. He and his family also ran the South's largest hemp-paper-operation. Throughout the '20's and '30's, they'd kept their mill profitable by producing miniature Bibles on home-milled paper. These reasonably priced, tiny treasures, which tucked easily into a pocket or a handbag, were extremely popular across the Bible-belt of the South. Beautiful as the books were, with rich hemp bindings and gold-leaf adornments, they made excellent gifts as well.

Kate arrived late for the meeting at the farm on Thursday. Will had instructed Toby to drive under the speed limit; and Kate, reluctant to overrule her husband, and put poor Toby on the spot, had remained silent for twenty harrowing minutes. After five cars had overtaken them, however, the last one recklessly, Kate did what she had to do:

Tapping her driver gently on the shoulder, she spoke to him in a 'confidential' tone, just above a whisper, "So sorry, Toby, but I must insist that you pick up speed! I know Mister Fairfield was thinkin' that 'slower is safer,' but clearly he was mistaken!"

"Thank you, Ma'am," said Toby, in a loud, grateful voice, and hit the pedal.

"I thank you," she replied sincerely, "And I'll thank you not to mention this?"

"Yes, Ma'am."

"Nor will I mention it... You have my word, Toby, on my honor. Do I have yours?"

"Yes, Ma'am!"

Kate sensed the tension in the dining-room of the farmhouse from the moment she stepped inside. Her very presence, however, softened the atmosphere. Both Noble and Mr. Headly, the real-estate broker who was there to buy land that was not for sale, jumped to their feet, with sighs of relief. Kate sniffed, and smiled at the scent of another tension-reducer in the air – "peach cobbler?" she asked out loud.

Noble nodded, and grinned. Nettie was making his favorite dessert – smart lady!

Kate greeted the men, Noble first, apologetically, carrying on about the "terrible driver" on the road, who was "backin' up traffic, all the way to Richmond!" She got a kick out of playing with a story, telling her experience, whilst leaving out an 'irrelevant' detail that didn't quite support the point she was trying to make; which, in this case, was that she was late, but it wasn't her fault.

She returned to Headly. "You must be a gardener, Mr. Headly!" she commented, shaking his hand again.

"I am, indeed, Miss Burnett," Headly responded, his smile growing wider, "but how did you know?"

"Why, your gardener's tan," Kate replied, "that healthy, bronzy glow is hard to miss!"

Noble rolled his eyes, and stifled a laugh. His daughter never ceased to amaze and amuse him. She was incredibly charismatic. Since childhood, she had made it her habit to focus on the finest traits, physical, and/or behavioral, of every person she met, and then to mention those traits to the person. She had learned the habit, by word and example, from her mother.

"There's good and beauty in all of God's children," Kate's mama often told her. "If you look for it, Kate, you'll find it. And if you remind them of it – oh, that's the wonderful thing; it'll lift your spirits as well as theirs!"

By the time she came of age, the practice was second nature to Kate. She even found herself using it on Anslinger. Upon their introduction, she referred to the "majesty" of his voice and his captivation of an audience as "Shakespearean." She told Noble later, however, jokingly, that she regretted the compliment; calling it her "most difficult" and "least sincere" ever!

Flattery worked for Kate on various levels. Her enormous physical presence, which she modestly attributed to size, rather than beauty, was intimidating to many people. But only until she paid them a heartfelt compliment or two. The initial reaction of the receiver was usually shock. Here was this golden-haired, goddess-like creature noticing, and drawing attention to the star-like qualities in them! It made her likeable, if not lovable, to virtually everyone; and that made Kate's life easier. All was forgiven her: beauty, brains, education, a fabulous catch for a husband (or a dreadful choice, depending on one's view of tobacco), and even non-conformity. Quirky as she was, Kate Burnett had the world at her back!

She didn't know quite what to do about Mr. Headly, though. He'd been pressuring Noble before she arrived, and now was fixed on her; referring repeatedly to the "deal of a lifetime" he'd offer her and her daddy, if only they'd hear him out.

Noble was beginning to lose his patience. "Like I said earlier, Mister Headly," he cut in, "you come highly recommended. Ol' Man Williams said you were efficient, straight-talkin', and fair. And that's good – wonderful. But I don't need a broker. My land's not for sale; and my mind's made up! I agreed to this meetin' for 'future reference.' The Williams were supposed to tell you that, Sir. I didn't want to waste your time, or have you waste mine!" He chuckled, softened his tone a notch, "Guess they forgot… Gettin' up there in age!"

Headly, whose Ben Franklin glasses and bushy gray eyebrows gave him a professorial look, was fifty years old, of medium height and stature, with a pleasant face, and distinctive blue-gray eyes. He had moved to Virginia from Kentucky two years prior, and planned to stay, he told the Burnetts, eventually to retire on a farm he'd inherited in the next county. He denied ever working for tobacco; indeed, he had dubbed himself the "no-tobacco broker," which kept him in good favor throughout the abstemious South. Nevertheless, he freely admitted that much of the farmland he'd brokered, over his twenty-five years in the business, was now "tobacco-land."

The Burnett's dearest, life-long neighbors, the Williams, were recent beneficiaries of one of Headly's deals. Managing their farm had become increasingly difficult for the elderly couple, and none of their offspring had the slightest interest in growing soybeans or raising turkeys. Because of its location – directly across the road from Fairfield Plantation, the Williams' farm was considered prime real-estate. Had it been on the market, all of big tobacco would have been bidding for it. But the Williams were staunch Temperance-folk. It broke their heart, they told their broker, to sell their land – it had been in the family for two hundred years; but to see the "devil's seed" sprout on that land would've killed them!

Headly's typical "deal of a lifetime" was to let the sellers name their own price. (He'd discovered early on that farmers, in general, were fair; and almost always asked for less than he would have paid). The Williams followed suit; and the deal was done, no haggling, no hassle. Headly purchased four hundred ninety of the farm's five hundred acres; the farmers kept the ten on which their homestead, a wooded area and a vegetable plot were situated. The contract also ensured that the land would not be sold to tobacco, by Headly or any intermediate buyer, for five years. (The Williams, who were in their mid-eighties, figured they might not be around in five years; and if they were, they'd be ready to move to the city, and help raise their grandchildren's children.)

Kate and Noble succumbed to the pressure, finally; and Headly made his pitch:

"I'm offering you a *fifty percent profit* on land you purchased less than two years ago, Mr. Burnett, Miss Burnett, and a written guarantee – same as the Williams', that the land will not be sold to tobacco for at least five years."

Noble replied: "That's a very generous offer, Mr. Headly; like you say, 'deal of a lifetime' – for the right seller! Not me!" he looked to Kate, "– us! I didn't want to get into it," he sighed, "but here we are, might as well tell you why:

"First off," he forced a laugh, "I intend to live more than five years. That's a problem, because the property you want belonged to my sister-in-law, Beth Burnett – good woman, salt of the earth. I promised Beth when I bought it, that while I'm alive, her land would not be sold to tobacco. She hates tobacco; thinks it killed her husband. She's the first to admit that the Fairfield family has done nothin' but good in Fairfield County, and she's very fond of my son-in-law, Will Fairfield," he gestured toward Kate, and smiled at the shock and confusion on Headly's face, "but she hates tobacco anyway. So you see, Mr. Headly, my hands are tied. My sister-in-law's land is not for sale. You could offer me a million for it, and lest I sell my soul, I'd have to turn you down!"

Headly's blue-gray eyes were bulging behind his glasses. He hadn't heard a word Noble said, after unveiling Kate as a Fairfield! How could the Williams have forgotten that? Or failed to mention it? It changed everything!

Kate read his face, and politely explained: "Will and I were married only recently, Mr. Headly, en route to England, where Will's been doin' business for months at a time. We hadn't gotten around to tellin' our neighbors yet. But we plan to, soon."

There was a bit more to the story than Kate had offered. The entire population of Fairfield County knew that Will was courting Kate, back in the early '30's. Upon their engagement, the couple became the subject of endless small-talk; and when they split, there was talk of nothing else! People weren't being mean, as such – most everyone liked Kate and Will. But there was a touch of smugness and jealousy in the gossip. One lady approached Kate at the grocery, and said to her, out loud, turning every head, "Sorry, Honey, but we knew it wouldn't last! Hemp and tobacco don't mix! You, of all people, should've known that!"

Kate had left the shop in tears. But she decided then and there that should she and Will be reunited, they'd keep it strictly to themselves; until such time as they were married, and she was 'visibly' with child. Then, without a word, but a flicker of her ring finger, she'd have the last word: Ha!

Headly thanked Kate for the explanation, and promised to keep the news to himself, so that she and Will could inform whomever whenever they saw fit. In deference to the Fairfields, Headly then clarified his position as a 'no-tobacco broker.' He said that he understood the farmers' love for their land, and their desire to prevent the spread of something (thought to be) 'evil' upon that land. But Headly was not at all anti-tobacco in the political sense; indeed, he was anti-prohibition. He believed that it was wrong, an intrusion on the God-given, Constitutionally-protected freedoms of Americans, for the government to dictate what its citizens may or may not drink or smoke. For Headly, proof of Prohibition's 'wrongness' was that in the thirteen years it was law, great harm, and no good ever came of it – no good, not so much as a dip in alcohol consumption!

Noble was impressed, and Kate even more so. She'd taken a few notes on the discourse. "My feelin's precisely, Sir," she concurred, "and cleverly put!"

It was the perfect moment for Headly to try a new pitch; but Nettie arrived just then with dessert on a cart.

"Excuse me, folks, here's your cobbler," she said, holding the aromatic sweetness under their noses, "still warm, like Mr. B likes it." She put the serving dish back on the cart, filled three bowls, served Headly first, then Noble and Kate.

"Help yourself to the cream," she added, placing the bowl of frothy, white peaks on the table, "fresh-whipped!"

Headly was not at all interested; he barely said thank you. All he could think of was the land that was not for sale. His bushy brows twitched as he pondered his predicament. He wanted that land! He'd be sitting pretty with a large piece of property to the north, and another to the east of Fairfield Plantation. Tobacco would plunge into an all-out bidding war for it. He'd sell, and retire comfortably, at age sixty, to his own farm. But first, to entice the Burnetts! They were a strange, crafty pair, far more business-wise than the ordinary farmer. The deal would have to be absolutely irresistible!

"I'm offering you whatever price you ask, Mr. Burnett, Mrs. Fairfield," he blurted out. "No bickering! And a *ten* year guarantee that the land will not be sold to tobacco! You name the price," he repeated, "tobacco waits ten years!"

Without so much as a glance toward Kate, Noble made light of the offer: "I'd hate to go to hell for livin' eleven years, Mr. Headly. Like I said, the land's not for sale."

"How about sellin' me another parcel, one that has nothin' to do with your sister-in-law?"

"I'd get into trouble with my grandson, then; he wants to grow hemp."

"But hemp's on the way out, Mr. Burnett. Permits required… some of 'em bein' refused."

Noble looked up at him, mouth open, his spoon, with a second bite of cobbler poised to enter. "Not here!" he said haughtily.

Headly ignored Noble's tone, and carried on, "They're sayin' there's some kind of narcotic in it… Does your grandson know that?"

Noble was beginning to steam.

Kate intervened: "We believe that's misinformation, Mr. Headly, and that it'll be cleared up shortly, and hemp will be vindicated."

"But," was all that Headly said when Noble jumped up from his seat.

"This meetin's over, Headly," he announced, "You can either stay, and eat your cobbler quietly, or leave!"

"But," the broker repeated…

"Uh, uh," said Noble. "I want you off my property, now, Headly! Don't Make Me Lose My Temper!!!"

Headly looked to Kate; but she lowered her head. The real estate broker sighed, got to his feet, collected his papers, and trudged toward the exit.

Kate followed him outside, and over to his car.

"These are desperate times for hemp farmers, Mr. Headly," she offered, "My apologies."

"You were just a tad hard on him, weren't you, Daddy?" said Kate, sarcastically, when she returned to the dining-room.

Noble eyed Headly's cobbler; it was untouched. He smiled, slid it over, and dug in. "Lord, that Nettie makes a fine peach cobbler!" was all he had to say.

Returning from Emporia, the following day, both Kate and Mike Anderson were feeling pleased with themselves. Kate, in the passenger seat of Mike's car, was admiring the tiny Bible in her hands. Mike kept glancing at her, as she stroked the cover, the gold-leaf edging, the red-ribbon page-mark of the book. She caught his eye, and smiled at him.

"You were right," she acknowledged, "it is a 'work of art.'"

"I knew you'd get him," Mike responded playfully, "never gave me no fancy Bible!"

Kate laughed, from deep in her belly. But then she flinched, suddenly, groaned, and held her stomach, her face turning white with fear.

"You all right?" Mike asked her anxiously.

"My stomach's been hurtin', on and off since last night, Mike," she sighed. "That was the worst, cut like a knife!... Scared me," she whimpered. "But I'm seein' Doctor Linden, in the mornin'. He's wonderful. Comfortin'."

"Good!" Mike responded. "We're almost home, Kate. Don't worry! ...Want me to speed it up a bit?"

"Ah... yes, Ahhh, no... I, I, I don't know... Oh, Mike, they're gettin' worse... Sharper... I'm feelin' nauseous..."

Mike pulled the car over, got out, and went in the back; quickly cleared everything off the seat, rolled his jacket into a makeshift pillow, and opened her door. "C'mon, Kate," he urged her. "Get in the back, lie down… We'll get you to the doc in no time…"

She did as he said. He handed her the Bible, and she held it to her breast. "He's across from the hospital, right, Kate?" She confirmed with a nod. There were tears streaming down her face, and tough though she was, he was terrified for her.

She felt herself bleeding, as they took off again, and feared the worst – she was losing her baby. She removed her cardigan, with difficulty, folded it up, slipped it beneath her petticoat and between her thighs. "Hurry, Mike!" she murmured pitifully, "Hurry, please!"

Will Fairfield was summoned to Dr. Linden's office an hour later. He came with his mother, they'd been working together, luckily for Mike Anderson.

Will's eyes turned steely as they met Mike's in the waiting room.

Mike shook his head sadly, and handed Will the Bible Kate had been holding. "It's Kate's," he said sorrowfully, "a gift from Mr. Adams."

Will took it without a thank you, not even a nod. He might have caused a scene, despite his mother's presence, had Noble not appeared with June an instant later. Kate had asked the nurse to call for her father along with her husband, as the former was in Richmond as well on that day.

Noble hugged Will. "So sorry, Son," he said, "so very sorry!" And they broke down at once.

Mike Anderson disappeared as Dr. Linden entered the waiting room, and led the family into his private office, to a seating arrangement around his desk.

Kate had had a "miscarriage," very early in her pregnancy, the doctor told them; and offered his sincere condolences. He made it clear, however, that Kate was "fine," apart from the emotional trauma she was experiencing. There were no signs of damage to her organs, and every indication that she could become pregnant again, in the near future, and carry full term. Such miscarriages were not at all rare, the doctor noted, especially early on, in first pregnancies, "for reasons known only to God." In his opinion, he emphasized, there was nothing Kate had done to cause the mishap, or could have done to prevent it.

Will was not so sure. He couldn't help but think that if Kate had been in Richmond, instead of Katelyn or Emporia, she might have seen the doctor at the first experience of pain. The doctor would have surely ordered bed-rest, during which the baby might have grown stronger, and more secure in the womb, and survived the critical period, and survived – period! Will's lawyer's sense told him, furthermore, that since the baby was already lost, the good doctor had 'modified' his opinion, left out the "ifs" and "might haves," to help ease the pain for Kate and the family.

Will drove Kate back to the farm that afternoon, to her sanctuary. She was certain that she'd heal faster there, under Nettie's care, than anywhere else, and she told him so. She slept throughout the ride, as the doctor had given her a sedative – cannabis, actually; but the moment they arrived, she pled with Will to stay with her, to share with her the advantage of the healer in their midst:

"We'll cuddle, comfort each other, cry if we need to, Will. … And we'll be fine… It'll take some time, counselin', prayer… But there was a lot of good news, much to be thankful for, Darlin', despite the sad… So sad," she repeated, and broke into tears again.

Will held her, and sighed. He told her apologetically, though, that he felt the need to be alone, in *his* comfort zone, at least for the evening. He'd work in his greenhouse in the morning, it was in full bloom, and sure to lift his spirits. And then he'd return to the farm, bring her a surprise. He asked if there was anything she needed from the Richmond home.

"My Steinway," she said dreamily, with a slight giggle. She was kidding. But the piano arrived at Katelyn, along with two professional movers, in a Fairfield truck the next morning!

She phoned Will at once, "Will, Darlin', I spoke in jest! You couldn't tell?"

"I figured the roof's up at the new house; and your daddy said the windows went in this week, and the floor in our bedroom..."

"Yes, they're movin' it into our room, as we speak, but..."

"Good! ...I think it'll hasten your recovery, Kate, to have it there. I know how much you love it, losin' yourself in the music."

"Thank you, Darlin'! Just in time. The ol' farm piano's been retired. Tuner says there's no hope for it!"

"We'll get you another for Richmond as well – got *me* addicted to the Mozart, you know!"

Kate smiled, but didn't laugh. She sensed he wasn't up for it.

She played, mostly Mozart, with a bit of Beethoven and Bach, for an hour or two, daily, when they were in Richmond. Her goal, she liked to say, was to play well enough to "deserve" the Steinway. But her teacher, Mrs. Olsen, proposed that Kate had achieved that goal at the age of twelve! And that what Kate needed now, should her desire to play professionally be rekindled, was to replace her teacher with a proper coach-mentor, a 'maestro.' Kate said, "absolutely not!" she was just a farm-girl who loved Mozart, and she was sticking with Mrs. Olsen.

Will's eyes went distant when he returned to the farm the next day. Kate was up and about, feeling much better – far too recovered, too quickly, it seemed, for him. He brought her an orchid in a hanging basket. She thanked him effusively, dubbed it "Gorgeous," and scurried about, looking for the perfect spot to display it. He watched her in disbelief. He was still devastated by their loss, unable to shake it. She appeared to be over it – done, in one day! He found it offensive, and had to leave. "Sorry, Darlin'," he said, "I feel queasy suddenly."

Kate took to her bed, the moment he left, and moaned and mourned for three days. She pretended to be asleep when Will phoned, and asked that no one enter her sanctuary, apart from Nettie, and the dogs. Noble spoke with Will, tried to comfort him. He said that Kate had suffered a "relapse." She was depressed, and wished to remain secluded. But not to worry! She was getting plenty of sleep, which Dr. Linden and Nettie agreed was the "best medicine."

After his second call for Kate, on the second day, however, Will said he was coming to Katelyn to check on her, whether she wanted him there or not! Noble talked him out of it: "Give her another day, Will. She's still upset, but she's chattin' a bit with Miz Nettie, finally. That's only good! She'll come out of it, *and phone you.* I'm sure of it, Son. I know my Katie."

Nettie peeked in on Kate, early, on day three of the seclusion. She opened the drapes, and let in the sunlight, with Kate's permission. She found Kate's little Bible on the floor, across the room from the bed, for the second time, in so many days, and picked it up.

"This your Bible, Missy?"

"Yes, Ma'am… Mr. Adams gave it to me… Held it against my heart when I was losin' the baby… for all the good it did me!"

"Oh," said Nettie, "I was wonderin' why it kept landin' on the floor, such a beautiful Bible." She put it back on Kate's nightstand.

Kate just sighed.

"You angry with the Lord again?"

Kate shook her head. "No, never again. He's my comfort," she touched her heart, and smiled, "Pure Love!" She rethought the question, and went on, wryly, and bitterly, "I'm angry at the 'fates,' whoever they are... fickle, dastardly, little devils! ...One minute they have you in your glory... the next, they take your baby, and make you look guilty!"

"You feelin' guilty?" Nettie asked her.

"No, it wasn't my fault; but I'm afraid Will thinks it was!"

Nettie changed the subject, gesturing toward the tray sitting on the dresser: "Brought you some breakfast, Missy. Oatmeal with peaches, honey n' cream... But first our hugs!" She sat on the bed, leaned toward Kate, and they went through their morning ritual.

Kate ate her breakfast, with delight. But an overwhelming sadness soon returned. She moaned as she put the tray aside, and slid over to the edge of the bed. "What do you think happened, Aunt Net?" she asked tearfully, waving Nettie back beside her.

Nettie obliged, put her arm around Kate, gave her a gentle squeeze. "I was hopin' you'd ask real soon, Missy. From the minute your daddy told me about it, I started prayin' that we'd come to peace with losin' the baby... and affirmed it, over and over, as always: 'Peace is within us, peace all around us. We thank You, and praise You, Lord, for the blessin' of peace.' And the word came, as always, but in a 'question'!"

"A question?"

"Yes, answer n' question in one. It was odd; didn't know what to think at first. But the more I thought about it, the more I saw the sense in it, and the beauty of it: 'What if the baby wasn't ready, and decided to come later?'"

After a moment, a smile came over Kate's face. She leapt from the bed in joy, and twirled round and around, in her sleeveless nightgown, arms flailing. Nettie's answers had never failed to comfort Kate, but this one put her "over the moon," as she liked to say – set her free instantly! If the *baby* had decided that he or she would rather come later, than sooner, who could argue? Or feel wounded? It was, after all, his or her own life!

Nettie stood up, and joined in the twirling, and they giggled, and hugged again.

"You're amazin', Aunt Net! I was certain that I'd considered *every possible explanation* for the miscarriage: It was my fault... But I followed doctor's orders! The doctor was at fault... Nonsense! It was God's will, then? ...But why would God will it? To punish us? Not the God I know! And here you come, with the only explanation that makes any sense, blames no one, and everyone can accept: *the baby decided!*

Nettie reminded Kate that the explanation wasn't *hers*, she had prayed for it, but hadn't authored it.

"In any event, we must tell Will," Kate responded, "end his agony."

"Only if he asks," Nettie advised.

Kate looked hopefully into the healer's loving eyes. "But he might not ask, and continue to suffer."

"It's for him to decide, Missy. First rule of advice: 'Give only when asked for!' I know I told you 'bout that; learned it from the preacher when I first came here; 'take my word, Nettie' he said, or 'learn it the hard way!'"

"But no exceptions?"

"Only one – children! Hardly ever ask. ...Advice might keep 'em out of trouble; or at the least you can say, I warned ya'll!"

Kate laughed, but then groaned. "Can't tell him till he asks?!"

"He might not be ready, Honey. Just like the baby! When he's ready, he'll ask, and be freed, like you were, I hope!"

"All right, then, I'll wait."

Kate phoned Will straightaway. She told him she'd come to peace with losing the baby, after a long talk with Nettie, and that they were praying for his peace as well.

Will read her mind. "I'm not ready to talk to Miz Nettie," he said bluntly, "so don't ask!"

Kate was discouraged, but kept to the 'rule,' and let it go:

"Fine. ...Can you say why, Will?"

"Hard to explain, Kate!"

"Fine. When you're ready, Darlin'. How 'bout comin' out today? We'll drive over to the new house, if you like, and I'll play some for you on my fancy piano? Tuner's comin' this mornin', daddy phoned him."

Will perked right up, he missed the music, he said. He had a lunch meeting scheduled at noon, and then he'd head out.

There were the usual thirty or so laborers at work on the house, and as many on the job along the new entry road, when Kate and Will pulled up to the site. With all of the extra hands on board, the completion of both projects were well ahead of schedule. Between the Katelyn construction, and renovations at Fairfield Plantation, more than half of the formerly unemployed locals were now on the Fairfield payroll. With several new projects in line, the jobs were secure, at least for the year, and hopefully into a recovery. The tobacco-magnates had thus regained the favor of their county-folk, and the tobacco-haters among them were mum.

Kate asked the foreman to give the house-workers a break. She was going to play the piano for Mr. Fairfield, she announced, "Mozart concerto, number twenty-two," specifically, and she did not wish to compete with their hammers. The foreman looked confused. Kate had come earlier with the piano-tuner, and stayed for nearly an hour; but she let the work continue at the far end of the house. "We won't be long this time," she gave reason, "ten, fifteen minutes, Sir; I promise. And then ya'll can get back to work." The foreman smiled, muttered, "Yes, Ma'am," and rang the dinner bell to alert his men.

Kate and Will entered the house, hand in hand, stepped inside their lovely-hardwood-floored bedroom for the first time together, and admired it at length. The spacious room was empty, of course, except for the Steinway, an elegantly sculptured piece, ebony finished, and its matching, velvet-cushioned bench. They opened the windows, at Will's suggestion, to give the workers "a treat." Will sat on the floor, to Kate's right, leaned against the wall, chin up, eyes closed, and waited. He loved the piece she had chosen, it was happy and heartening, precisely what he needed. And Kate had always played it well.

But this time, she played as never before, brilliantly, ten and a half minutes of pure joy! It was as if the music were hers, and the piano an extension of her being. Will jumped to his feet when it was over, applauding loudly, and cheering, "Bravo, Kate, Bravo!" The workers, who'd been watching and listening, entranced, from outside the windows, joined in vigorously. Kate, slightly embarrassed at her un-concert like attire – riding pants, jacket, and jockey cap, stood up, nevertheless, let her hair tumble out of the cap, smiled and took bows all around. She started to cry on the way out – happy tears. To her mind, the performance had marked a milestone in her intermittent musical life. It was the first time she'd done her piano and her beloved composer well. She had a feeling, moreover, that her baby, wherever he or she was, had also seen her perform, and like the workers following her and Will to their car, was still applauding.

Will left on the spur of the moment, though, after dropping her off at the main house. When he returned the following morning, he requested a "serious" talk with Kate. They sat on the sofa in the parlor of her quarters, and sipped coffee. He came right to the point: He needed a break, he said. And unless she felt that it would jeopardize her recovery, he was going to Europe, off schedule, for a few months, alone.

Kate had expected as much, and she told him so.

He made an attempt to explain, although describing his feelings as "irrational and erratic." On the one hand, he said, he knew it was time to accept his loss, and get on with life, as Kate had done. On the other, he felt that his sadness and anger were justified. His loss was great, to get over it too quickly would be to "trivialize" it.

"You think that's what I've done?" she blurted out, in dismay.

"I don't know what I think," he said unhappily, avoiding her eyes. "I'm too close to it, Kate. I know that I love you; of that I have no doubt. Whether I can live with a woman who is as 'headstrong' as you are, after this incident, I'm not so sure."

"What does 'headstrong' have to do with it?" she asked disbelievingly; the answer, "nothing," implied in her tone.

"I don't know, Kate!" he raised his voice, "Maybe nothing!" And quieted down. "But I need to get away, far away. Clear my head, and get a new perspective on this whole thing. Some objectivity. My humor back, God willing... Too many reminders here...

"And James is there," he gestured to the east, "a world away from the scene of my grief. He's the one I laugh hardest with, apart from you... Not that I expect to find anything funny about the miscarriage, ever!

"James'll be glad for the help as well. He hates goin' to the Continent. Keeps sayin', 'These foreigners need to learn English if they want to sell our cigarettes!'" He smiled a bit; as did Kate, and they leaned a little closer to each other, but didn't touch.

"I understand," she said kindly, "and I imagine that distance and laughter, as well as time, can heal. You go with my blessin', Darlin'. I wish you a speedy recovery..." After a pause, she added, from nowhere, "and I release you from your vows for the duration of your stay!"

Will's jaw dropped. "I'm not askin' for that!" he said indignantly.

"I'm givin' it nonetheless, Will. No questions will be asked upon your return, and no confessions welcomed!" She emphasized the latter.

He shook his head in disbelief, "See what I mean about 'headstrong'? We're not in enough trouble, Kate? You're settin' terms? For us? Without consultin' me?"

"They're not terms," she argued, "not at all. I made a simple statement of facts: You're released from your vows during the break, so that 'just in case' you're tempted to stray, you won't be tempted, upon your return, to tell me what I don't want to hear – ever!"

"I see. You should've been born a man, Kate, and become a lawyer. You're very good."

"One does not have to be a *man* to become a lawyer nowadays, haven't you heard?"

He made a face at her, to which she smiled and playfully replied, "Well, you started it!"

He leaned forward, and kissed her tenderly, and then holding her face in his hand, he looked deeply into her eyes, and whispered, "I hardly ever see you as 'headstrong,' Kate; truth is, I see you as a 'strong, independent thinker.' And I admire you for it; and it excites me!"

That did it! They locked the doors, put their troubles and differences aside, and tended to what they referred to as "matters of consequence!" Each of them thought it a blessing that the other was willing to do so when the need arose.

Will stayed in Europe for five months, nevertheless. Kate received a wire or two from him weekly, and an occasional note or letter. He kept her up to date on his recovery, calling it "virtually complete" by the end of his leave. Only one of his notes made the cut for her special journal, though, it read:

James and I split our sides laughing today, over some silly thing he said. 'About time,' I teased him, 'I've been here four months! You're not as funny as you used to be!' And we laughed some more. Sense of humor: returning! I love you, Will

Sowing, reaping, volunteering, and her renewed affair with Mozart kept Kate busy in Will's absence. She also took a three-week sojourn with Bobby, Liddy and their son, Davey, in Washington. Noble and June came for a few days over one weekend to celebrate Davey's ninth birthday. It was a joyful, fun-filled get together, although Will was very much missed by all, and they sent him a wire to say so.

Bobby unveiled his first sculpture during the reunion, dramatically, to music, as well the piece deserved! It was a lion's head, depicted on a three-foot circular stone plaque; the head, almost life-size, was presented realistically; the mane, following the natural formation of the stone, was stylistic, and wild. The guests were amazed, though not surprised, at the beauty and quality of Bobby's sculpturing. Kate and Noble received due credit for having encouraged him to give it a try. Bobby also made an exciting announcement at the unveiling: He and Liddy had made plans to retire early, in their fifties, he said; and, with his daddy's permission, they would soon begin construction on a second home/studio at Katelyn. "Permission granted!" Noble shouted, to applause and cheers led by Davey.

After the elders left, Kate took a few days of solitude, in her favorite courtyard. She read, new-thought authors, and meditated by day; slept under the stars, close to the hearth, at night; and emerged renewed, and ready to work. For the duration of her stay, she assisted Liddy in her multiple careers, as mother, business-woman, and social-activist. They held daily meetings in Liddy's home office, and stayed busy in between on three separate phone lines. Kate learned a lot that week about women's equality, and the lack thereof, in American law.

On the last day of her sojourn, Kate attended an outside meeting with a group of Liddy's closest fellow activists; the five men and women who had been her co-founders in the since disbanded Anti-Prohibition League; and served with her now as advocates for women's rights. Liddy wanted Kate to hear, first hand, what these people knew, and where they stood on the so-called "new" prohibition.

All agreed with Kate that Anslinger was still on the warpath; albeit against a new 'evil,' marijuana. They understood that marijuana was actually cannabis, a benign substance, used as a medicine world-wide; and they assumed that Anslinger was vilifying it just to have something to prohibit. There was very little they could do about it, though, they told Kate, at least for the moment. The "numbers" simply weren't there. Not enough people knew about the drug. The ones who did were misinformed, and many actually favored banning it.

Liddy elaborated, "A lot of people are just tired, too, Kate, worn out from the Depression. They're glad Prohibition's over, but they're also fed up with anti-prohibition. It's been decades now, of 'wets' versus 'dries,' and never-ending conflict!"

The activists assured Kate, though, that they were onto Anslinger, and that the moment there was enough interest, they'd reorganize. And the next time, they promised her, they'd finish the job, and retire "the fanatic!"

Rob Denver, a wild-eyed, young, assistant law professor at Georgetown University, spoke up. He suggested that Anslinger was doing himself in; and they wouldn't have to. The war on marijuana was extremely unpopular among the Feds, Rob explained. There was too much misinformation and too many outright lies associated with it. The war was giving the Feds a bad name, and the agents blamed the commander and chief. Anslinger had lost his two top agents the year before because of it.

Kate was stunned, and asked Rob how he knew.

The professor gave her a wide smile. "We've been lucky!" he said, his comrades muttering their agreement. "We've had an 'undercover' member working as a crime-story reporter for the Washington Times, since the inception of the APL, and he's still with us, in our disbandment."

"I think the agents who quit were the ones you talked about years ago, Kate," Liddy put in.

"Morse and Ryan?"

Rob answered, "Yeah. Ryan's the one who gave the statement to our reporter. Story was, Ryan went to Anslinger and said he wanted to get off marijuana duty, and on to the 'real' narcotics.

Anslinger said no, and Ryan quit. Our man, of course, asked Ryan 'why' he wanted off marijuana; and Ryan told him the same thing he'd told Anslinger: From what he'd seen during five years on the job, contrary to the brainwashing he'd been given in training, marijuana was a 'mild' intoxicant. It made people mellow, and then drowsy. The only violence he'd witnessed during scores of marijuana busts was committed by the police, most of it was unnecessary, and some of it was criminal! Ryan's partner agreed, and Anslinger fired him. Our reporter turned in the story, but the Feds managed to keep it off the press.

"It won't be the last story, though. There's a lot of dissension in the ranks, Kate. It's bound to leak out."

"I hope so," said Kate with a sigh in her voice. "And I thank ya'll for fillin' me in. Like I said, they're tryin' to drag hemp down with marijuana," she held her fist up, jokingly, and got a laugh, "and I refuse to let that happen! ...It's good to know ya'll are with me."

After winning permission from his parents and teachers, Kate took Davey home with her for a week. It was fall harvest at Katelyn, and time, at last, for Davey to participate in the big event. The farm had been sown, a third at a time, in three consecutive months that year. Each third was thus in a different state of maturation; from the woody stalks still standing tall, to the fallen stalks drying out in the fields, to the bundled fibers arranged in teepee-like fashion, and set upright in rows, for the final drying.

Davey took part in every phase. He cut stalks with Noble, the old-fashioned, blade-in-hand way, he walked the middle fields with Kate, turning stalks, for even drying, and he, and Kate, and Noble pitched in with the Mays' boys, and the rest of the hands, to bundle and set up the 'teepee' rows. The boy was a natural farmer. He loved it all: the working hard, and close to the earth, the smell of the harvest permeating the air, and the satisfaction at days end, of knowing that his effort was well spent. "Our crop's the best!" he'd remind Kate and Noble, repeatedly, bringing tears to their eyes, "No other crop serves the people in so many ways!"

Will returned home just after Davey left, and a few days prior to the wedding of Lucy Stevens and Jonathan Ledger, in which Will stood as best man, and Kate as matron of honor. It was a beautiful, traditional wedding, with lots of tears, laughter, and all the trimmings money could buy: wonderful food, live music, and despite the Temperance leanings of the bride's mother, the finest champagne. Lucy looked her loveliest ever, a pixie turned fairytale princess, in billowing, white satin and lace; Jon, her ruggedly handsome golden boy, the perfect prince. At the reception, June announced that she had given the couple, as a wedding present, twenty acres of her countryside estate, on which to build their summer home.

The crowd applauded, Kate was overjoyed, and Will joked, "Good Lord, he's a grown man now, and married, still followin' me around!" Everyone in earshot laughed, including the bride and groom, who spurred Will on, "It's not enough, we're soon to have the same father-in-law? He has to live in the same neighborhood?" Again, there was laughter. But this time Jon replied, brow raised, "I'll get you later, *Uncle* Will (referring to their nearly ten year age difference), when you least expect it!"

Will grinned; and Kate thought to herself, 'he's regained his sense of humor with everyone but me!' And then she thought, 'One more to go, Darlin'!'

She'd been practicing a new affirmation Nettie had shared with her: "Kindness is my path, my power and my glory!" With kindness in mind, she approached Will, delicately, as they were getting ready for bed that evening, at their home in Richmond. She told him she sensed that he was not quite himself yet, that something was still troubling him, if only slightly. He ran his fingers along his jaw-line to the point of his chin a few times, and then nodded and said, "Yeah, I keep thinkin' I'll wake up one mornin' and be a hundred percent…"

"You will, Darlin', soon," she assured him. "But I want you to know that if you think another break would make the difference... I'd miss you terribly... But urge you to go..."

He held her close, thanked her, told her he loved her, and he'd think it over.

Five minutes later, she was at her vanity, in her flimsiest nightgown, brushing her hair. Will sat down beside her on the bench, kissed her bare shoulder, and took a deep breath. After avoiding Nettie on the subject for nearly a year, he said, he was too embarrassed to ask Nettie for her counsel on the miscarriage... But he was ready to hear it from Kate.

Kate's face flushed, she swallowed hard, held back her tears, and was out with it, instantly: "What if the *baby* changed his mind, and decided to come later?"

Will leaned over, caught her eye, and grinned. "That's it?"

"That's it! Aunt Nettie prayed for peace, and that's the answer in a question she received."

He started to laugh. "It makes sense, though! Why didn't I think of that?"

"I asked myself the same question, Will, over and over; and I wanted to tell you, so many times, but I had to wait till you asked – the rules!"

"The baby decided," he said pensively, repeating, "the baby decided! Of course! No wonder I couldn't figure it out!" And, finally, he saw something funny about it. "Kid's headstrong, like his mother, already – not even born yet! ...I'm in trouble!"

Kate laughed. The joke had closed a very difficult chapter in their relationship, and opened a most exciting one.

Katelyn Farmhouse, Fall, 1936:

Noble, bespectacled, Kate, and Mike Anderson were seated around a coffee table on the back terrace, talking business. The weather was delightful, the lunch had been delectable, the

Burnett's fall harvest had made a nice profit, but the mood was blue.

Mike had arrived with bad news. He was no longer working for Henry Ford, and neither was the man he'd recommended to run Ford's refinery. He hadn't heard from Watts, or anyone else, regarding the hemp-mobile in three months. During the same period, the American Hemp Association, for the first time since its founding, had lost more members than it had gained. And the price of hemp, once again, was plummeting.

Nettie, looking uncharacteristically down as well, peeped out from the French doors to say, "Excuse me, folks. Ya'll might want to know. That Anslinger fella's 'bout to come on the radio, recommendin' a movie."

The men got up and followed Nettie in. Kate stayed put, rolled her eyes, and sighed despondently. She knew exactly what Anslinger was up to.

She and Lucy had gone to see the film, "Reefer Madness," on a Saturday afternoon, a few weeks prior. It was a horrible, disheartening experience for Kate. She hadn't even mentioned it to her father, seeing no point in upsetting him.

Noble peeked out on the terrace, and gestured for Kate to come in.

"C'mon... Since when does *he scare you?*" he teased.

Kate trudged in, only to learn that she was right. Anslinger was touting "Reefer Madness:"

"I strongly recommend this film to parents," he began, "but I warn you, Friends, it is alarming! I can only hope that 'forewarned is, indeed, forearmed'!"

"The scourge of marijuana is no longer relegated to Mexicans or Negroes. Or even to adults. Indeed, as this film reveals, curious, innocent children are the dope peddlers' newest targets."

Kate recalled the movie, vividly, appallingly: It opened with a 'doctor,' in a white coat, alerting the members of a parent-teachers association about the hazards of a new drug – a "deadly narcotic," an "assassin of youth," an "unspeakable scourge," called marijuana. The 'doctor' went on to suggest that the drug had caused "incurable insanity" in a number of cases, and that it must, therefore, be "stamped out."

In the next scenes, a pair of dope-peddlers, a man and a woman, argue over whether or not to sell the drugs to school children...It was clear to the viewer that the man would win, and the children would be lured into their den of inequity.

Kate could not bear to see it, but was hesitant to leave. Lucy saw her struggling, leaned over, and whispered, "This is no fun, Kate! Melodramatic, nonsensical! Let's go!"

Kate shook her head 'no.' "There might be somethin' I need to see, Luce. Somethin' important, the mention of hemp, maybe."

"You go, then, I'll stay," said Lucy. "No sense in both of us sufferin'!" she grinned. "Meet you in the car, Sweet-pea – go on now!"

Kate kissed her on the cheek, whispered thank you, and ran out, holding her ears.

"I think it's lies, Kate," Lucy declared, upon entering the car; her sweet little fairy face hardened with anger. "Lies, and *extreme* exaggeration, with the sole intention of creating panic, nation-wide. Once you have panic, the rest is easy: outlaw the drug, which outlaws hemp, and the competition with it!

"What really riles me, though, is that we can't put a stop to it! We have no recourse! Every one of our families has taken on city hall in the past, and beat it! But not in D.C.. We just don't have the connections. Not even the Fairfields. These people have taken the capital, Kate. They've got the upper hand!"

She turned pensive for a moment, and then smiled. "We need to get Will or Jon, or both, to run for office, local, then federal... Get *our* men in there... Then we'll see who has the upper hand!"

They giggled a bit; and forgot about "Reefer Madness" for the rest of the day.

"Remember, Folks," Anslinger went on with his radio address, speaking of the film as if it were factual, "these peddlers are not just greedy and vicious. Most are addicts themselves, and desperate for money to feed their habit.

"It has, therefore, become my unhappy duty to bear this terrible tale. And bear it I shall. For I have seen the devastation of body and spirit that this narcotic wreaks; and I could not sleep at night, were I not to call my countrymen to arms!"

Noble, unable to stand another word, jumped up, clicked the radio off, returned to his seat, and stared dejectedly into space. Mike, looking miserable as well, sighed audibly. Nettie left the room; and Kate rushed to comfort her father.

"I saw it, Daddy," she confessed. "Well, not all of it, but all I could take... Lucy stayed and watched till the bitter end. There was no mention of hemp... Anslinger never mentions it. Maybe he's finally accepted the fact that hemp and marijuana are different."

"I'm afraid that's wishful thinkin', Kate," Mike put in. "He's up to somethin'. I know it! I'm goin' to Washington. There's a young congressman I want to meet, sympathetic to our cause. Doesn't have much pull yet, but we need a friend on the inside up there."

6
H.R. 6385

Katelyn Farm, early Summer, 1937:

As Kate made a good-morning call on her father at the farmhouse, she heard him on the telephone in the parlor. He sounded distressed. She peeked in. "Okay, Anderson... see you shortly... Good luck... Bye."

Noble hung up the receiver, turned to Kate with a furrowed brow, and sat there, speechless, for a long moment.

"I'm testifyin' before a Senate Finance Committee, tomorrow, in Washington," he finally muttered, voice trembling. "Anslinger's pushin' for *federal control* of hemp. And a heavy tax. If we don't stop him, Kate, we may never grow hemp again!"

"I'm goin' with you, Daddy," she responded at once, holding back tears. "I'll call Bobby, and tell him we're comin'."

"What about Will? I thought you were off to Richmond tomorrow?"

"He'll understand. I'll meet him there when we return."

Lunch was rendered a somber affair, Noble advising Kate of the details and the seriousness of their plight:

"Mike apologized for the short notice; said it couldn't be helped. He called it a 'miracle' that he had been there and heard about the Bill at all. He said that Anslinger – 'snake in the grass' – had kept the whole thing hushed up. No mention of it

192

in the press, no talk in the lunch rooms. The Bill got through the House Ways and Means, disguised as 'The Marijuana Tax Act,' without a word, Kate, not a single word, from a hemp grower; which is why I have to be there tomorrow. Hagar, of course, is in cahoots with Anslinger, and one of Hagar's Senator 'pals' chairs the Committee... It's gonna be tough, Kate – tough as hell!'"

Senate Committee Hearing Room, Washington, D.C., 11:00 A.M., the next day:

Kate and Noble, attired, on Mike Anderson's advice, in fashionable hemp-cloth suits, entered nervously, as the proceedings were getting underway. Mike, who was waiting toward the back of the room, was visibly relieved to see them. He waved them over, and had them sit on either side of him.

"Thank you for comin'," he whispered, "... right on time. That's Clinton Hester, for the Treasury, swearin' in. He's one of 'them!'"

Kate eyed the witness for signs of 'enemy-ness;' there were none.

Hester looked to be an ordinary, middle-aged man, dressed in a run-of-the-mill business suit, noticeable only for the rather thick spectacles, which slid down the bridge of his nose, as fast as he pushed them up; harmless, by all appearances.

She scanned the spacious room, with its hundred-plus chairs, agape. It was nearly empty – only thirteen persons, including her party of three, looking on, and maybe a dozen seated and moving about a u-shaped table arrangement, facing the audience, at the head of the room. There were a handful more, kingpins Anslinger and Hagar, first witness Hester, and a couple of unidentified persons taking notes, at a pair of tables to the left of the audience.

But where were the other hemp farmers, she wondered? Where were all the people whose lives would be destroyed by this Bill?

"I tried, but couldn't get any other farmers," Mike spoke to her, voice low, as if he had read her mind. "Too short notice."

She nodded acceptingly.

"What about the senators?" she asked him. "Where's the rest of the 'alphabet'?"

Mike smiled briefly.

There were only three Senators, identified by their name plates, as Avery, Brown, and Cedar, at the Committee table. Kate had a feeling that Brown was the one with the 'enemy;' Avery and Cedar looked too young and too green to be chummy with Hagar.

"They need three votes to get the bill to full Senate," Mike explained glumly; adding bitterly, "If they had needed four votes, Senator 'D' would be with us."

Kate covered her face with her hands, and prayed for strength. She'd been at the hearing two minutes, and was already overwhelmed. Her first impression was that three senators, at least one of whom was affiliated with an anti-hemp conspirator, were about to decide her future, the future of a great American industry, and perhaps the future of America itself. "Why? How could this be happening, Lord?" she begged silently.

Chairman Brown struck the gavel twice, nodding to the witness upon each strike.

"Yes, yes... Thank you, Senator," Clinton Hester began, adjusting his glasses, "I am counsel for the Treasury, and I'm here to explain why H.R. 6385 is necessary."

"Proceed, then, Mr. Hester," the Chairman responded impatiently.

Hester complied, with dramatic flair: "We have a growing problem in the United States, Senators. It's a narcotic, called 'marijuana,' known by its Mexican name, because Mexican immigrants were the first to introduce it to Americans, most unfortunately. Marijuana is contained in the leaves, flowers and seeds of the hemp plant, which are smoked, in pipes or reefers, to get the narcotic effect.

"Leading newspapers, recognizing the seriousness of marijuana addiction and the violence it incites, are advocating legislation to control it. If I may quote from a recent Washington Times editorial?" He held up the article to which he referred.

"Go ahead, Mr. Hester," said Senator Brown.

Hester obliged, "Quote: 'Marijuana is one of the most insidious forms of dope, largely because of the failure of the public to understand its fatal qualities.' Unquote. 'The Marijuana Tax Act' is intended to raise public awareness of the problem, while curbing traffic of the drug."

Senator Avery asked the witness how the Bill would accomplish this.

"It requires that growers of marijuana be issued permits by the U.S. Treasury. And it levies a tax on the crop, to create revenue to control the drug, and to raise the price of the drug on the street. At the current street price, about a dollar an ounce, a youngster can buy a reefer for just pennies. Mr. Anslinger has more, much more, on the dangers inherent in that... I believe he follows me."

"Yes, unless there are further questions for Mr. Hester," Brown looked to his colleagues, "we'll move on." He rapped the gavel twice, to no response.

As Anslinger was swearing in, Kate leaned toward her companions and whispered, "If you'll excuse me, I need some air," and walked out. Mike followed her every step, marveling at how gorgeous she looked wrapped in hemp-sac.

Anslinger passed each of the Senators an inch-thick copy of his 'Marijuana Case Files,' describing it as a compilation of "dozens, yet only a mere fraction, of the violent crimes committed under the influence of this drug." He proceeded to review the cases, in detail, one by one, before Senator Cedar interrupted:

"Mr. Anslinger, can you give us an idea of the 'types' of crimes, an example or two of each, perhaps, rather than a reading of the entire File, which could take all day. You can always go back, if something important gets left out."

Senators Brown and Avery approved with a nod.

"Certainly," Anslinger concurred, and referred his listeners to a few more cases, concluding with his favorites:

"...Returning to page twenty-three, I believe, you'll find the notorious case of one Victor Licata, a young Florida man, who, in 1933, axed his entire family, five innocent persons, to death; the evidence showing that he had smoked marijuana prior to committing the heinous crime.

"Finally, and extremely disturbing, on page forty-seven, a more recent case, from Chicago, of a young girl – thirteen years old, Senators! – who plunged to her death from an apartment building window. The officials called it 'suicide,' but we consider it 'murder,' by the same lethal narcotic.

"And so I must reiterate, emphatically, Senators, what I stated before the House Ways and Means: 'While opium has all the good of a Dr. Jeckyll, and all the evil of a Mr. Hyde, marijuana is entirely the monster Hyde.' We cannot begin to measure its harmful effects."

Mike went to fetch Kate between witnesses. He found her sitting alone under the sun, cross-legged, on a ledge alongside the stairway to the building. She was staring, ironically, at a flag, made of hemp, flying freely, in the light summer breeze. He wanted to hold her close, and promise her that all would soon be well. But he tapped her gently on the shoulder instead.

She was startled momentarily, and then smiled sweetly at him. "Is 'Mud-slinger' done?" she asked him.

"Yes," he said, with a grin, and helped her to her feet. "We need to get back, Kate. Loziers is up next; from the Hemp-Oil Institute. He's good. And he's one of us."

Their man was testifying as they returned to their seats:

"Our members produce paints, and machine oils, among countless other industrial products, Senators. But before we go any further, I'd like to comment on something Mr. Hester said, if I may."

"Certainly," said Senator Brown, "proceed."

"I believe he's misinformed about the smoking of hemp *seed* for narcotic effect. I know, for a fact, that the seed is crushed and eaten as porridge in many countries. And that it's nourishing. We use the seed mostly as animal feed in America, but where available, country folk add it to all sorts of recipes, for flavor and nourishment. In fact, my wife makes hemp-seed muffins quite often – delicious! ...Neither has there been a single outbreak of violence or madness among the consumers of her muffins," he added drolly, smiling at the titter from the audience. "We would have noticed!"

Chairman Brown slammed the gavel. "I see," he countered sternly, "but have you ever *smoked* the hemp seed, or seen it being smoked, Mr. Loziers?"

"No, Sir," Loziers replied, "Never heard of such a thing!"

"Then you do not know 'for a fact' that Mr. Anslinger is misinformed?"

"No, Sir, I do not," Loziers granted. "But the point I came here to make is that this Bill is too all-inclusive – too restrictive and invasive. It would bring the thousands of activities of a great industry under the control of a single government bureau, which may come to crush it, at a time when Americans can least afford it!"

Nearly jumping from her seat, Kate raised her arms in a silent hoorah. Mike and Noble just smiled, shaking their heads, glad to be sitting behind the rest of the audience.

Senator Brown looked anxiously to Anslinger for help: "And what have you to say, Mr. Anslinger, regarding the effects of this Bill on legitimate growers and users. I remind you, Sir, you're under oath."

Although he had every intention of limiting the numbers of permits issued, and eventually doing away with permits, Anslinger replied without hesitation:

"Legitimate growers and users are fully protected under this Bill. Once growers have their permits, they can grow, and do business, just as they've always done."

Mr. Loziers begged to comment further.

"Go ahead, Mr. Loziers; you're still under oath," Brown allowed.

"Yes, Sir. Thank you," the witness responded, "I want to point out that the hundred-dollar tax imposed by this Bill is going to wipe out the small growers that many new industries are depending upon; industries that could make or break the economic recovery of the entire na…"

Anslinger cut him off. "I regret to say, under oath, Mr. Loziers, that my hands are tied in this respect. The revenue from that tax is needed, to control marijuana, which is spreading like wildfire, and wreaking havoc on families and children, as we speak."

Noble got Kate's attention, and gestured for paper and pencil, which she hastily provided from her handbag. Her father looked so downhearted, it made her want to cry; but she offered an encouraging smile instead.

Senator Cedar directed a question to Anslinger and Loziers "Can either of you explain why the use of this drug, unheard of until now, is spreading so quickly?"

Loziers said he was not so sure that the use of cannabis was spreading.

"Of course it's spreading," replied Anslinger, "we wouldn't be here if it were not! I'm at a loss to give you a rational reason why, Senator. But personally, I think it's the work of Satan himself!"

During a break in the hearing, a few minutes later, Kate, Noble and Mike were having a bite in the cafeteria of the building. Anslinger rushed in, headed toward the counter where they were seated, but upon spotting the Burnetts, he turned, and tried to rush back out. A woman colleague pulled him over, though, before he could escape. Noble got up calmly, walked over toward Anslinger and the woman, gave them a nod, and stood back to wait his turn.

Kate looked to Mike wide-eyed, and mouthed a silent, "Oh, my!" as Noble confronted their nemesis:

"Mr. Anslinger, remember me, the 'hemp-man?' How're you doin'?"

"Of course, Mr. Burnett," Anslinger answered nervously. "It's been a while."

"I was just thinking 'bout how difficult this must be for you, goin' after hemp," Noble continued, a biting sarcasm in his voice. "I remember you sayin' how much you appreciate hemp – the flags, the bibles, American tradition, n'all."

Anslinger got defensive, "Who could have imagined this, Mr. Burnett? I hope you don't take it personally. It *is* tough on me going after hemp. But I don't have a choice. It's my job, my responsibility. Marijuana is a vile, addictive substance. We cannot continue to let it grow freely. It's nothing personal, I assure you."

Noble glared at him, face flushed, nostrils flaring, just itching to smack him one. He glanced over at Kate, who was watching anxiously, biting her lip.

"It's nothing personal, like I said, Sir," Anslinger repeated, backing away from the heat. "But, it's not too late, Mr. Burnett. You can still get top dollar for your land, from tobacco. My advice to you, Sir, before news of this gets out, is to…"

"Whoa! Whoa!" Noble cut him off, poking him twice in the chest, "you keep your advice to yourself, Anslinger. It's nothing personal, but I don't like you!"

Anslinger tried, unsuccessfully, to shrug off the insult, as Noble turned abruptly, and walked away.

Next up, when the hearing reconvened, was a Dr. Woodward, speaking on behalf of the American Medical Association.

"Say a prayer," Mike whispered to his companions as Woodward was sworn in, "this doc could be our saving grace."

Mike had approached the doctor only one day before the hearing. But Woodward had agreed to testify on the spot, calling the attack on cannabis a "medical emergency," and an "underhanded government intrusion on the practice of medicine!"

Anslinger looked increasingly miserable as Woodward read a brief opening statement, in which he proposed, in effect, that something was 'terribly wrong' with the government's case:

"The crimes and violent acts described in Mr. Anslinger's case files, allegedly committed under the influence of 'marijuana,' could not have been committed under the influence of cannabis, that is, medicinal hemp, which the government now claims is one and the same as marijuana. Cannabis, as every doctor knows, induces a 'sedative effect,' *invariably*. I repeat, *invariably*; unlike other drugs – alcohol, for instance, the effects of which vary greatly from person to person, and in extreme cases, have been known to incite the types of violence in question."

Anslinger had heard the same from every doctor, public-health and private, he had tried to line up for the government. These doctors had also agreed with Woodward that cannabis was not 'addictive' in the medical sense:

"… not in the sense that alcohol or tobacco are with some people; and certainly not like opium is."

Nor, all doctors seemed to concur, was the use of cannabis on the rise:

"We've seen no rash of misuse, as alleged by the government," Woodward testified, "nor excessive prescribing by doctors or pharmacists."

He went on to enumerate "just a few" of the many conditions and ailments that cannabis had been used to treat "for centuries, with considerable efficacy: migraine headache, neuralgia, insomnia, anxiety, rheumatism, dysmenorrhea, convulsions, loss of appetite, constipation, and pain;" and then he concluded:

"For all of these reasons, Senators, the AMA stands firmly against the passage of H.R. 6385. We feel that the Bill is unnecessary and unfair, if not unconstitutional, and that it will place an enormous burden on doctors and patients, not to mention thousands of farm..."

Senator Brown interrupted Woodward with three strikes of the gavel.

"Excuse me, Doctor," he said hastily; and turned to Anslinger, with a raised brow:

"Is there *anyone else* with something to say on medicinal use?"

Anslinger squirmed and thumbed through some papers before finally giving Brown the nod; the Senator reminding Anslinger that he was still under oath.

"Cannabis will be available by prescription under this Bill. So there is no issue here," Anslinger stated with authority. "However," he added falsely, "I am told that its various uses are limited, and could be abandoned, or replaced, without suffering."

Woodward was visibly annoyed. "By whom? Mr. Anslinger," he demanded, to no response. "I can't imagine any *doctor* making such a statement!"

Brown thanked Anslinger; and asked Woodward if he had anything more.

"Yes, Sir, I do," the doctor replied decisively, and paused at length for emphasis. "The AMA also objects to the term 'marijuana' used here. This term has no meaning whatsoever in medicine or science. Nor does it mean anything in the English language. Nor, I am told, is it relevant to the issues here in proper Spanish.

"We believe the sponsors of this Bill used this 'nonsensical' term, instead of the correct terms, 'cannabis,' or 'hemp,' so that they could carry out their plot in secret, as part of some hidden agenda. Had people known that 'marijuana' is hemp, and that a great American industry would be scrapped, in order to curb the use of an obscure drug, The Marijuana Tax Act would never have come this far!"

"The point has been made, Doctor," Brown countered, "that marijuana is no longer 'obscure,' and that it is inciting violence and madness. Is the AMA offering a proposal on how to contain this scourge?"

"No, Sir," Woodward responded. "The AMA has concluded that the data on cannabis use is unclear; but that if its use is on the rise, 'newspaper exploitation' of the habit, more than anything else, is to blame."

"I see, 'newspaper exploitation,'" Brown returned sarcastically. "So, Doctor, you would come here to criticize what the government is trying to do, and offer no alternative solution, other than to curb the 'reporting' of the problem, instead of curbing the problem itself?" And before the doctor replied, "Is there anything else, Dr. Woodward?"

He struck the gavel once, to the doctor's faint, "No, Sir," and then announced a short break, after which the Committee would hear from a final witness, Mr. Burnett, a hemp-farmer, and representative of the 'American Industrial-Hemp Association.'

Upon mention of an *'American'* Association, Anslinger and Hagar looked at each other, stunned.

Kate and Noble, also confused, regarding the word *Industrial*, turned to Mike.

"I threw it in," Mike confessed, in a whispered tone, with an impish grin, "figured it would align us, and our testimony, with Loziers and the industrial sphere. Which is where we belong, rather than with the medicinal; wouldn't you say?" They said yes. "I think we need to make that clear, here, and to our members, in the next bulletin. In fact, unless you have some objection," he looked from one to the other, "I suggest we add the 'Industrial' to our title, permanently."

Again, they concurred.

The three huddled outside the entrance to the building during the break, reviewing the testimony. They were thrilled, of course, with Dr. Woodward's performance. Kate gave Mike a hug, and thanked him effusively for finding "a voice of sanity amid the mayhem." Noble congratulated Mike as well, noting that Loziers had also done them proud.

Lastly, they discussed Noble's upcoming testimony, and agreed to some minor changes; after which Noble returned to the hearing room, alone, to collect his thoughts.

"Good luck, Daddy! Don't let the bullies wear you down!" Kate called after him.

"Good luck, Mr. Burnett," Mike joined in, with a 'thumb's up.'

Noble smiled bravely, waved, and went inside.

"I'll bet that Brown scares the other Senators to death," Kate remarked to Mike. "He was just plain rude to Dr. Woodward."

Mike paid her no attention, for once. He was too busy worrying; his eyes fixed on the door through which Noble had just entered, and disappeared.

"I feel like I've thrown your daddy to the wolves, Kate," he sighed. "It doesn't matter what he says, or what Woodward said. Neither Avery or Cedar has the guts to buck Brown.

"All we need is one vote, Kate," he went on, despondently. "One lousy vote. I should have come sooner. I could have found someone."

"You did your best, everything you could, Mike," she comforted him. "And we're grateful to you." She smiled at him, sincerely.

On impulse, he brushed the back of his hand along her cheek, tenderly. She bowed her head, and looked away from him.

"I'm sorry," he whispered.

"I know," she replied.

At the same time, in a small office near the hearing room, Congressman Hagar backed Anslinger against a wall.

"What the hell happened to your Public Health doctors?" he demanded.

Anslinger answered huffily: "I told you, Bill, we had a doctor problem. They all backed out at the last minute; said their data would hurt our case. What could I do? Haul them in anyway?"

"That's great, Harry, just great! And who do you have to offset this poor, suffering farmer up next?"

"I've got nobody!" Anslinger shouted. "These people showed up at the last minute. I have no idea how they got in, or who contacted them. I've never even heard of an 'American' Industrial Hemp Association!"

Five minutes later, Noble was testifying on behalf of the 'Association,' although declaring himself a "beginner, rank and file" member:

"What we're asking for, Senators, is fairness, to the industry, and to the farmer. My forebears, along with George Washington and Thomas Jefferson, were among the first hemp-farmers in Virginia. Jefferson and my grand-daddy also tinkered with machinery for hemp-processin' – together once, I'm told, quite successfully, for the good of all. Like our foundin' fathers, I hope to pass my land and the great hemp traditions on to my children and grandchildren.

"My grandson, Davey, who is about to turn ten, would take over now, if I let him…"

Noble's smile was returned by all three senators; and he carried on:

"Why should my family be penalized, and our kindly crop defamed, for somethin' that has nothin' to do with us? We do not grow marijuana. We never have; and never will. We never even heard of the drug till just recently.

"If the government needs revenue to control marijuana, let it tax the buyers and sellers of marijuana, like it does with the liquor industry, among others. Let there be license requirements for growers and distributors, to give the government some control, and to ensure the protection of children. Finally, let the fees and taxes be steep, to discourage the use of marijuana.

"But let us not burden the *hemp* farmers, Senators! Let us not confuse marijuana with industrial hemp, the most useful plant on God's earth!

"Accordin' to medical research," (he held up a copy of the evidence submitted in Matt Harris' case, noting that the Senators had been provided with the same), "fiber-grade hemp is 'useless' as a drug, completely devoid of mind-alterin' properties. But it makes the world's finest paper, a sturdy, affordable cordage, an excellent cloth;" he stood up briefly to show off his hemp-cloth sport coat; "dozens of industrial staples, as specified by Mr. Loziers. And hundreds of new products, includin' hemp-based plastics, are in development. Is it fair to burden the thousands of producers and millions of users of these products as a means of controllin' the profits and habits of a few?

"And will it work? Will the government gain the 'control' it seeks? …Have we learned nothin', Senators, from the colossal failures of Prohibition? The culture of crime and corruption it set off? The disregard for law? And what of the smudge of tyranny it left on our history? What would our Founding Fathers think of an 'Amendment to the Constitution' that fosters a government intrusion on the personal freedom of its citizens? Is that not the 'opposite' of what they envisioned for this great land?"

He paused for effect, and a sip of water.

Kate scanned the faces of the opposition: Hagar and Brown looked pained, Anslinger nauseous, Avery and Cedar concerned.

Brown nodded sullenly; and Noble continued:

"Let us not be fooled, Senators, the Marijuana Tax Act is the beginning of a new Prohibition. And the new is set to be more disastrous than the old, an infringement upon our economy and our recovery as well as our freedom. Can you imagine, Senators, within a single generation, a prohibition that wipes out the hemp trade in America, while the trade in marijuana rages on, illegally? A new source of revenue for the underworld and its thugs? How would we explain such a folly to our children?

"What will we tell the children, Senators?" he repeated the thought slowly, looking each senator in the eye; and once again, in an emotional whisper, "What will I tell my grandson?"

"We ask that you be prudent, Senators, as well as fair. The Marijuana Tax Act is neither. Do the right thing! Do your country a great service! Stop the madness and injustice, before it's too late – vote this bill down! ...We thank you."

With an exuberant, teary-eyed Kate in the lead, the entire audience, all twelve remaining persons, jumped to their feet and applauded Noble; drowning out the persistent rap of Brown's gavel.

The Chairman remained speechless for nearly a minute after the applause died, nervously contorting his face, shuffling papers, checking out the reaction of his cohorts. Finally, he cleared his throat, and asked Anslinger if he had any closing remarks.

Anslinger spoke only briefly, but condescendingly, triggering boos and hisses from the fired-up audience, followed by a rapping and a scolding from Brown.

"It is unfortunate that innocent hemp farmers should be 'inconvenienced' by this Bill... But the government has no choice... It cannot ignore the spread of marijuana addiction, much less the crime and violence the drug incites... The government is duty-bound. It must do everything it can to protect the public from the evil of this narcotic, beginning," he tapped the Bill on the table, "with the passage of H.R. 6385."

After the hearing, Mike asked Kate if she would be willing to meet with a new contact that he had made in Washington; a first-term, pro-hemp congressman from Ohio, who might be able to help them. Kate agreed, and upon leaving Noble off at her brother's home, she and Mike returned to the Capital, and met with Representative Calvin Mead, in his office.

Mead, thirty-five, had a pudgy face and pink cheeks, which, despite his dark moustache, gave him a boyish appearance. He was obviously taken by Kate's beauty, nearly jumping out of his seat to meet her, extending his hand nervously over his desk towards hers, and gawking.

Mike was amused.

"You must be ah, ah Miss Burnett," Mead stuttered. "Pleasure to meet you, indeed. Indeed!"

"It's 'Mrs. Fairfield,' actually," Kate replied, shaking his hand, "but please call me Kate. Nice to meet you, Congressman."

All were seated at Mead's invitation. He managed to take his eyes off Kate long enough to rummage through some papers, while filling her in:

"I think you're going to be pleased with what I've come up with, Mrs. Fairfield – eh, Kate, albeit a bit late."

Finding what he wanted, Mead looked up at her again, with big eyes, and a broad smile.

"I don't know if Mike told you, Kate, but there's no one in Washington who wants to stop this hemp bill more than I do."

"He did tell me, Congressman. That's why we're here," she responded, and turned to Mike for confirmation.

Mead adjusted his privates, quickly, while she was looking askance, after which he proceeded to tell her his story anyway:

"The two biggest employers in my hometown, in Ohio, are dependent on hemp oil and fiber. One of them is my father! As you can imagine, he's not too happy that H.R. 6385 got through the House Committee without my notice." He looked to Mike, and continued, sarcastically:

"The Marijuana Tax Act! Who could've known this had anything to do with hemp? Anslinger – viper that he is! To pull this off in the height of a depression. It's treasonous!"

After an uneasy silence, Mike spoke up:

"Say, Congressman, how 'bout we go over the details of our plan with Kate?"

Mead nodded, turned to Kate, and, in an instant, went from an insecure, bungling beginner to a confident, crafty, practiced politician making his pitch:

"As I'm sure you know, Kate, Mr. 'Holier-than-thou' Anslinger, personally, is clean as a whistle. The man's a fanatic, clearly. But it's not about greed with him. Amazing, when you consider that Andrew Mellon is his uncle!"

Kate's brow went up at the last remark; and Mead corrected his statement:

"Well, actually, 'his uncle through marriage.' But the point is, despite being thick as thieves with Mellon for decades, Anslinger never invested with Mellon, and never amassed a fortune – not that he needed one; his wife's loaded!

"What Anslinger has gained through 'Uncle Andrew,' however, is the only thing Anslinger ever wanted: control, power over other people, his will as 'law of the land'! He's addicted to power. He'll do anything to get it, including team up with the likes of Hagar; which he did, a while back. Huge mistake! He wound up having to cover for Hagar, whom, we now know," he waved a report at Kate, "was in on *all* of Mellon's shady deals; and then some!"

He paused, smiled at Kate seductively, and handed her the report. She took it, straight-faced.

"Nobody in Washington knows about Hagar's misdeeds yet; well, they suspect," Mead continued, "except us, our tiny inner circle. There's enough in that report, we think you'll agree," he stopped to get a nod from Mike, "to make Hagar and Anslinger back off the hemp bill – today!

"And here's the beauty of it: If you go in with us, Kate, you don't even have to mention the bill. All you have to do is meet with Hagar and Anslinger, five minutes each. I've already arranged the appointments for tomorrow. You say you're from the 'Association,' a new member, just like your daddy. You received the report, anonymously; you have no idea why. You skimmed it, thought it might be important, and brought it to their attention. They'll get the message!

"That's it! Done! We all go home, get on our knees, and thank the Lord this national nightmare's over!"

Kate was beginning to look upset, tears welling. She turned away from the men, and breathed deeply, and audibly.

Mead and Mike made eye contact, and shrugged their shoulders.

"Tell her what Hagar's been up to," Mike suggested, hoping to turn her around.

"A lot!" Mead said excitedly.

She turned slightly toward the Congressman, not to be rude.

He nodded a thank you, and went on:

"That Hagar did not go down with Mellon will stun anyone who reads this report. He was in on every scam! Plus, he was a bootlegger! His father-in-law owns the biggest distillery in Canada. The Fountains got regular shipments all through Prohibition, while Hagar was *boisterously denouncing the Repeal!* It's hard to imagine the nerve of this man!

"And here's the topper, Kate: The Feds, under Anslinger, raided the Fountains twice in '32. We've got police reports, names of witnesses, and so on. But there're no federal records of it. They've disappeared! There was no press coverage. And Hagar was never charged."

"The cover-up!" Mike proposed.

"I like to call it *collusion*," Mead one-upped him, "in bootlegging and tax evasion."

"Collusion," Mike repeated, with a grin, "has a nice ring to it!"

Kate let out a sigh, and turned again to face the men fully.

"Blackmail..." she uttered, with a distant look in her eyes, and placed the report back on Mead's desk.

Mike scanned the room nervously, trying to hide his frustration. He raised his eyebrows toward Mead, looking for help, but Mead, too, was at a loss.

"I thought you understood, Kate," Mike said finally, "these hearin's are a formality. The powers that be have already made their decision."

"I won't be a party to blackmail," she insisted. "If that's what it takes to 'win,' as you define it, I'd rather lose."

"We don't think of it as 'blackmail,' Kate," Mead responded readily. "And the irony is, neither would Hagar, or Anslinger. It's the way the game is played here in Washington. And, if people like us don't learn how to play it, people like them will continue to win, and run the country! Is that what you want? ...We don't think so!"

"This is only the *beginnin'*, Kate," Mike took over. "You see that, don't you? The beginnin' of the end. First, it was the licensin', local, now they want federal. Then came the taxes, same deal. Then the bans, local, and from here, unless we act, they will get a federal ban! Hemp'll be a memory in this country, before we know it; that's their goal!

"And they think it's justified; they believe their own lies! They've convinced themselves that if they go down, the country goes down. Better to get rid of hemp, in the name of marijuana. ...They're doin' it, as we speak, Kate! The biggest American growers, includin' my 'friend,' out in Nebraska – you know who I mean – did *not* get county permits this year! Who do you think was behind that?"

Kate shook her head dejectedly.

"Mike, Congressman," she looked to one, and then the other, "if you're right about the conspirators, and I think you are, how can you ask me to stoop to their level? My principles be damned? As long as I beat them at their own dirty game? ... Which is not a given, by the way. Witnesses can be bought... Or worse, threatened! Or harmed! ...I don't even want to think about that... I'm sorry; there *must* be a better way."

"It's too late, Kate," Mike argued. "The verdict is in! Unless we take them down – now!"

"Then history will have to rescind the verdict, in its own time... I cannot do what you're askin'."

7
The Reprieve

Katelyn Farmhouse, Autumn, 1937:

Kate, curled up in her 'sanctuary' with a book of affirmations (which read like something Nettie might have written), looked up excitedly at the sound of a certain bark from her dogs. She rushed out of the room, down the hallway and the stairs, to the dining-room window, and then out the front door at the sight of a car pulling up. It was Will! He flew out of the vehicle, and she into his arms, smothering him with kisses.

"I take it you missed me!" he said cheerily.

"Terribly... my Darlin'," she replied between kisses, "I never... want to be away from you... ever... again..."

He backed away to look her in the eyes.

"You mean it, Kate?"

"With all my heart!"

"No more stayin' behind, then... If I go, you go?"

"Like your shadow!"

"I will have to return, Darlin', once or twice – maybe three times, and then I'm finished over there.

"At last!"

He kissed her, at length, on the mouth, lifted her off her feet, and whirled her around, till she shrieked with laughter.

The dogs whined and wagged and nosed Will, trying to get some attention.

He put her down, finally, and tended to the hounds, briskly. "Yes, yes, good ol' boys. I missed you, too! Sweet boys!"

The hum of an engine grew louder, as Noble approached on the tractor.

"Will, you're back early!" he shouted over the racket, "Welcome home, Son!" He shut off the engine, climbed down, and joined in the hugs.

The respect and genuine affection between her father and her husband was a source of great joy for Kate. She stood back, beaming, as she watched them interact.

"Good to see you, Noble," said Will, "and lookin' fit, as always, pleased to say."

"Thank you. And same to you, Will, truly… How's it goin' in Europe?"

"So far, so good, Sir, with the business. Bit tense in Germany, though; gettin' ugly. Luckily not where we are."

"Thank the Lord… Well, you're just in time for the harvest, Son… Big one! May be our last, though," he looked to Will with mournful eyes. "Didn't get our permit."

Will shook his head sadly. "That's a shame, Noble. Terrible! I'll talk to my daddy bout it; see if he still has connections in the right places."

"Bobby's workin' on it, too," Kate noted. "And, of course, we can pray. Aunt Net says prayin' makes you feel a whole lot better, even if you don't get what you wanted!"

"She's usually right," said Noble, as he climbed back on the tractor. "I'm beginnin' to think she's psychic as well! She's cookin' somthin' special for supper tonight; said she had a feelin' someone special was comin' home!" He laughed. "See ya'll at six, 'love-birds'!"

Kate and Will laughed too; and promised to be on time. Then they hopped into Will's car, and drove over to the new house. She had so much to show him. He followed her around dotingly from room to room, admiring each piece of new or refurbished furniture; and out into the courtyard, where the

English garden they had modeled after James and Tess' was coming along beautifully. The hedges had grown nearly a foot in Will's absence; and one of the Mays' clever boys had managed to shape them exactly as described.

"That boy's got English blood in him!" Will kidded, to her grin.

Kate had saved her favorite renovation for the last. Will caught her tender glance, as she took his hand, led him back inside, through the main rooms, and into the nursery adjacent to their bedroom. His eyes went teary as she opened the shutters, and the light came flooding in.

The room was furnished and fitted to perfection: a crib, a matching armoire, cradle and rocking chair, with stuffed cuddly-bears of all sizes scattered about. The walls were papered in a pastel, carousel print, predominantly mint green, suitable for a boy or a girl, complete with matching valences, bed skirts and linens.

"It's gorgeous," Will declared, taking her into his arms. "All that's missing is the baby... Let's go make one!"

"Maybe we should wait, just a bit, till we're finished in Europe," Kate offered smoothly. "Wouldn't want me crossin' the ocean in my 'condition.'"

"Good point!" he agreed. "So, let's go practice!"

They closed the shutters, and off they went, arm in arm, giggly with anticipation.

The couple left for Richmond the next day, and spent the week; Will catching up with company work; and Kate, along with Lucy, doing double time at Alan House.

Kate and Mrs. Alan had come to an edgy 'understanding' regarding Kate's marriage. Mrs. Alan had hinted that if Kate didn't mention 'it,' neither would she; and that no one would be the wiser for it. The ancient one had confirmed, furthermore, that Kate had always been her 'favorite' helper, and that she therefore assumed that if Kate had married a Fairfield, that that particular Fairfield must be endowed with "redeeming qualities" which set him apart from the ordinary tobacco-man.

This condescending attitude on Mrs. Alan's part irked Lucy Ledger no end. Lucy knew through her mother, who was best friends with a former Fairfield banker; that Will had been funding Alan House, anonymously, for years. Lucy suspected that Mrs. Alan knew it too, but wasn't admitting it, even to herself. June had made Lucy promise to respect Will's desire to remain anonymous. But as time went on, and Mrs. Alan grew snobbier, Lucy was finding it harder to bite her tongue.

Although unaware of the funding, Kate had also been tempted, time and again, to tell Mrs. Alan off. Kate, too, had refrained from speaking out, because, truth was, as much as Kate loved and admired her husband, she understood Mrs. Alan's resentment of tobacco and its peddlers.

Kate's Uncle Ben, like Mrs. Alan's husband, was the only man in their family, over several generations, who smoked; and the only one who had died significantly – more than a decade – younger than his counterparts. Both Kate and Mrs. Alan had heard of other families with similar experiences.

Indeed, by the 1930's, it was becoming increasingly clear, to doctors and people in general, that smokers, by and large, were not as healthy, and died younger than non-smokers. This disparity was particularly evident in states like Virginia, where tobacco was prevalent, and even poor folk grew, cured, and smoked their own.

Will and his family were also aware of the hazards of smoking, and often expressed their concern about them. Will once told Kate, laughingly, though, that his mother was "anti-tobacco" when her children were growing up. Smoking was prohibited in the Fairfield home, and even outdoors when youngsters were present. He and James were informed, early on, that tobacco, like alcohol, for some people and *all children* was addictive, and therefore bad for their health. Both of his parents had also insisted, then as now, that Fairfield's advertising, worldwide, be directed exclusively toward adults.

Upon returning to the countryside, Kate learned that Mike Anderson had phoned her twice, from a hotel in Louisiana, and had left a number, but no message. Noble paced nervously in the next room, as Kate returned the wholesaler's call.

"I'm in oil country," Mike reported. "Pretty grim, Kate. Depressin'. I hope we can do somethin' about it... be a good deed."

"Very." she affirmed.

"I'm stayin at an inn on the main route here, lookin' toward the sea. Two giant oil rigs out there in the distance, boomin'! Huge clouds of black smoke surroundin' them, both of them. I don't know how the people who live here breathe, Kate! There's this oily film on everything; it's killin' the trees; gotta be bad for the lungs!"

Kate didn't know what to say. She'd seen magazine photos of oil fields, looking exactly as he'd described them; and photos of oil-workers and their clans, reminiscent of coal-miners, with their distant, sad eyes, and tar-streaked faces.

"I've got some potentially good news, though," Mike broke the silence, "and I wanted you to hear it first."

"Oh, thank God!" she responded; peeping out at Noble, giving him a happy face. He took a seat, and breathed a sigh of relief.

"Looks like your idea might work," Mike proposed, a strange mixture of elation and reservation in his voice. "There's a chance at least... I've been talkin' to two V.P.'s all week... Ah... Listen, Kate, I'm in an open lobby here, can't get too specific..."

"That's okay, Mike. Go ahead. "

"Anyway," he lowered his voice to just above a whisper. "Can you hear me?"

Her free ear covered with her free hand, she replied, "Yes, clearly."

"So, these V.P. s say they're ready to do a hemp-oil refinery, create a 'new division' of Big Oil. They almost sound excited about it, Kate! And they've got *three* big growers with permits."

"That's wonderful, Mike! Great work, my friend, so quickly."

"Yeah... Thanks... Won't be easy from here, though. We need *five* more growers, just to get started. And the Treasury is stingy with these permits, Kate. At a hundred dollars apiece, you'd think they'd be pushin' 'em.

"I do have leads, though, bunch of 'em. Headin' north tomorrow; see what I can do. I'll keep you posted.

"How's the harvest, by the way?"

"Best ever, Mike. No exaggeration." She laughed. "I know I always say that, but it's true this time! Ten feet tall, swayin' in the breeze. Beautiful. Almost makes it sadder... Poor daddy, gets teary every time he thinks about it... Thanks for givin' us hope, Mike."

"My pleasure," he muttered, after a long pause, adding, "Say a few prayers, huh?"

"Of course," she replied. "Be careful, Mike."

"Yes, Ma'am."

"And keep in touch."

"I will."

"You have our number at the new house?"

"Yes," he said. "Good bye."

He was lying about the number – he had refused to take it from Noble; and he didn't keep in touch.

Fairfield Home at Katelyn Farm, New Year's Eve, 1937:

The living and dining rooms of the new home were decked with boughs of holly, silver bells, and red ribbons, and re-arranged for a party; half the furniture carted off to the garages to make room for dancing.

A hired pianist, "Swing Man," and two accompanying musicians, were warming up around the piano. Nettie, Toby, and Belle were scurrying about with final preparations. Kate, dressed daringly, in a black, halter-neck, bias-cut, evening gown, (with a bit of silky fabric veiling her back), was on the telephone, as Will, sporting a dark suit, and tie, and a very-British, white vest, came looking for her approval.

She gave him a big smile, tapped her hand over her heart to indicate excitement, and then hung up the phone and stared pensively into space.

"Something wrong, Sweetheart?" he asked her.

"Hope not. That was Aggie, Mike Anderson's secretary. She said that Mike hadn't returned for the holidays, as planned. But he's scheduled to close the oil deal, middle of January."

"Sounds like good news to me."

"I suppose," Kate muttered weakly. "But she also said he thinks someone's been followin' him."

Will mulled it over for a moment, and then said optimistically: "Industry spies! Let them follow... Maybe they'll *all* get into hemp oil!"

Kate smiled at him, stood up and started swaying to the music, swirling up close to him, flirtingly.

"Want to dance with me, Mister?"

He wrapped his arms around her, and whispered in her ear, "All night long!"

The party was a huge success, swing-dancing and merry-making till 3:00 in the morning; after which all of the out-of-town guests were put up, twenty or so at Fairfield Plantation, just down the road, and ten at the Steven's estate, next door.

Kate and Will awoke to horrible news, however. As they were popping corks and cheering in the new year, Mike Anderson had been killed in an auto accident in the Smokey Mountains of Tennessee. A man driving behind him had witnessed the tragedy, and reported it to the nearest police station. Conditions on the road were terrible, he said, wind, snow, visibility poor. He was following the lights of the automobile ahead of him, when suddenly it spun out of control, and vanished. He pulled over where the car had disappeared, and to his horror, saw that it had skidded through a railing, dropped over a cliff, crashed, and burst into flames.

It was nearly a week before Mike's charred remains were returned to his family.

A light snow was falling, and it was bitter cold in Richmond on the day of the funeral. A minister prayed at the foot of the coffin, surrounded by mourners, in heavy coats under black umbrellas. His words, though few, seemed to hang in the air, like the clouds of mist from the mourners' breath:

"Heavenly Father, as we sadly commit our beloved Michael's body to the earth, we loyally entrust his spirit to your loving care... We beseech you to bless his loved ones, his mother and sister, especially. Their loss is great... And so tragic in its suddenness."

Kate could not stop crying; nor had she had a decent night's sleep since news came that Mike had passed. She felt guilty. She had sent him on the 'wild goose chase' that had resulted in his death. He wouldn't have been in those mountains, on that snowy, slippery night, she told herself, if it weren't for her, and his unrequited love for her.

She took to her bed after the funeral, and lay there moaning.

Nettie let her mourn for a day or two, and then began leaving little notes at her bedside, referring to Kate and the mourner as separate persons: "How much longer do you think 'she' needs to be sad? Remind her that the Lord has forgiven her, forgiveness being His way. Can one forgiven in His eyes be guilty in yours?"

Will read the first note, and repeated the question: "How much longer are you goin' to mourn, Darlin? It's a terrible thing, you've lost your friend, but life must go on."

"'She' needs the rest of the week," Kate sighed.

"Fine! I'll be back on Friday to get you. We'll stay a while in Richmond. You'll visit with Lucy, help out at Alan House. It'll do you good, Kate; lift your spirits, always does. Agreed?" She agreed.

He found her exactly the way he'd left her, however, when he returned; in bed, bedraggled, eyes red and swollen, fixed in a blank stare.

Now, he was losing his patience. "I'm takin' you into Richmond, if I have to carry you, Kate! You can't go on like this!"

"When are we leavin'?"

"For Richmond? Soon as you're ready."

"For Europe."

"Ahhhhh – the twenty-fifth, ten days or so.

Kate sniveled, and struggled for the right words: "I do so want to go with you, Darlin', but I cannot bear the thought of travelin' yet. Can't we please put it off for another month? I'll be fine by then, Will, I'm sure of it.

Will shook his head.

"No, Kate, I'm sorry. The situation in Germany is deterioratin'. We've got to clear out of there, before it's too late. We could lose everything if we don't.

"To tell you the truth, I was plannin' to leave you in England, with Tess and the girls; and goin' to Germany alone, just to be safe... Maybe I should do the whole trip on my own this last time... give you a while to recuperate..." He smiled at her. "Start missin' me again... What do you think?"

She hugged him around the waist, and kissed his abdomen again and again. He lifted her up and onto the bed, and they made love, as if no one had died, and nothing could ever come between them.

A few days later, Will returned to their home at the farm to find Kate at her desk, engrossed in paper work. She looked groomed, slightly made-up, her hair washed and shiny.

"I see you're feelin' a little better, Sweetheart, hmm?"

She turned to face him with a smile: "A lot better, now that you're here."

"What are you workin' on?"

"Re-doin' the new year Association Bulletin. Addin' a few words about Mike, and askin' for volunteers to fill in for him."

Will shook his head and wrinkled his brow.

"No, no, no…" he moaned, pulling up a chair, and coming face to face with her: "You cannot take up where he left off, Kate… absolutely not!"

"I'm lookin' for someone else to do it, Will," she argued. "In the meantime, my name's not goin' on anythin', and I'm not takin' calls. Aggie's keepin' his office open for at least a month. What harm is there?"

"A lot! If 'they' want to find out who you are, Kate, 'they' will. You need to get out of that Association. It's dangerous! And I'm not the only one who thinks so; just ask your daddy."

"Well, I'm not gettin' out! And I resent your tellin' me what I have to do, Will. I may be depressed, but I'm not feeble!"

"I'm tryin' to protect you, Kate. You're too bull-headed to see…"

"I don't need protection!" She stood up boldly. "I've thought it through; I know exactly what I'm doin'… And who are 'they'?"

Will, shaking his head again, took hold of her hand, and pulled her gently back to her seat.

"I didn't want to tell you, Kate, add to your burden," he said solemnly, "but it seems I have no choice:

"Mike Anderson's car was *rammed* off that cliff on New Year's eve. It's possible that the crash was accidental, a 'hit and run.' But the police suspect otherwise. They think he was murdered, Kate! They're lookin' for his *murderer*!"

Kate stared at him agape, her eyes flooding with tears.

"Now, are you goin' to promise me, here and now, to stay out of his affairs. Or let me leave for Europe *very* angry with you?"

She let out a wail, ran to the bedroom, and threw herself face down on the bed, arms flailing, sobbing hysterically:

"It's my fault," she cried. "He's dead, and it's my fault. I should have warned him. God help me! It's all my fault!"

Will trudged into the bedroom after her. He sat beside her, silently, running his fingers along his jaw-line. He had no idea what she was talking about.

Kate, keeping her word, hadn't told a soul about the meeting she'd had with BJ Jackson a few years prior. Bobby and Liddy had arranged the meeting at their home, reluctantly. Kate and Will were estranged at the time, and BJ admitted to knowing it. Nevertheless, BJ assured Bobby and Liddy that he had no ulterior motives. He wished to meet with Kate only to warn her of the "clear and imminent danger" she could find herself in as a hemp activist. He'd been privy to information that had scared him, he told the couple, and that he hoped would scare Kate, feisty and determined though she was, into lying low.

When BJ finally got together with Kate, he made a pass at her, jokingly, to break the ice:

"Bobby and Liddy had me promise not to make any advances toward you, Kate. But I told them plainly that you and I are old friends, and I could never be rude to you. Should *you ask me* to take you out to dinner tonight, I would have to say yes!"

Kate laughed heartily, and promptly invited him to join her and Bobby and Liddy for dinner that evening, in Washington, at The Fountains.

"I'd be delighted," he happily replied, "but please let them know that I'm picking up the check."

"You'll have to discuss that with Bobby," she said, "He likes to pay – makes him feel wealthy!" She chuckled.

"Bobby's not the problem," BJ whispered, looking over one shoulder and then the other, as if someone might be eavesdropping, "he's reasonable, lets me take a turn now and then. It's that sister-in-law of yours, your mentor! She corners the waiter ahead of time, and *insists* that he bring her the tab. It's embarrassing, Kate! I swear, she's the only beautiful woman on earth who competes with men for everything, including the check! Where'd she come from?!"

Kate smiled and shook her head. "I don't know, BJ, she's *your cousin*!"

They shared a good laugh, and then BJ turned serious:

"Listen, Kate: I know that you're aware of the anti-hemp conspiracy afoot. Bobby told me that you have your own secret sources."

"We do, daddy and I, through the grapevine, so to speak. We're members of a hemp association. But we keep a low profile. We don't reveal secrets, even to each other, when called for. And we *never* expose sources."

"Good! Wonderful! I have your word, then, that what we discuss here today is strictly between the two of us?"

Kate raised her right hand, and swore, "Absolutely!"

"On the other hand," BJ qualified the restriction, "should you find it necessary to protect your daddy, or anyone else, Kate, you have my permission to tell them that you have it from an *inside source* that the anti-hemp conspiracy is real, 'life and death real,' you can quote your source on that! And that it's huge, and growing. Hemp has a lot of new uses, and that means new enemies, in the works. Also – *extremely* important, at least one of the conspiracy's founding members has ties with the underworld, and hit-men on his payroll! In other words, since all of this is the unembellished truth, you may advise your people, for their own safety, NOT to get on the conspiracy's list of troublemakers!"

BJ went on to tell Kate, without mentioning names, that one of his clients had masterminded the conspiracy. This client, BJ submitted, was perhaps the richest man in the world, was heavily invested in the petro-chemical industries, which gave him his anti-hemp leanings, and at the same time held a very influential post in the federal government, which gave him power. Upon discovering that a new, hemp-based industry was about to put Big Oil out of business, the client rounded up a few hemp-threatened cronies, and they figured out a way to destroy hemp first.

"They got lucky, Kate!" BJ mourned, as he finished the story. "Everything fell into place, as if the fates had planned it! It made me sick; these were not nice people! But I was in too deep to get out hastily. I didn't want *me* on their 'hit-list' either!"

She nodded sympathetically; and he knew she understood. Then she cocked her head and smiled at him. "So tell me somethin' I don't know, BJ! ...And by the way," she chided him, "why is this the first I've heard from you?"

"You were engaged to Will Fairfield, for openers!" he answered loudly and defensively. "I figured you were *out* of the hemp business. And your daddy's not the 'trouble-making' type. I assumed that both of you were safe. And then I heard that your daddy, too, was about to marry a millionaire, and retire. Still, I told Bobby to warn him about the conspiracy. And he told Bobby to tell me he was already warned! ...Your daddy never liked me, Kate; you know that!"

She chuckled a bit. "Yes, but I never understood it, BJ. What'd he have against you?"

"He never mentioned it?"

"Not a word."

"Well, on the first day I met you, Kate... I don't know what got into me, apart from being young and foolish and brazen. And infatuated! I took your daddy aside, and told him that I intended to marry you! And I asked for his permission to take you out to dinner that night, with Bobby and Liddy as chaperones.

"He said 'no,' point blank. He said he'd already lost his son to the 'Washington crowd,' and he wasn't going to 'facilitate' the loss of his daughter. And that if I was still interested when you turned eighteen, 'and not a day before,' I should ask you, not him, if you'd like to go out to dinner!"

Kate had to laugh. She was beginning to see where her feistiness came from. Her father had always kept that side of him hidden.

BJ chuckled too, and then sighed and returned to the business at hand:

"I do know a few things that you don't know, Kate," he proposed, his mysterious eyes catching hers. "I got lucky too. My client was forced to 'retire' from his post, about a year after I started with him. And to save his face, which coincidentally saved my backside, he was given an ambassadorship abroad. The man was gone! Out of the country! He wanted me to carry on with the hemp crusade here. But one of the other conspirators had it in for me and my fellow lawyer, and everyone knew it. I told my client that unless he was staying

Stateside, or breaking ties with the hateful conspirator, he needed to find a new lawyer. He understood.

"Of course, he warned me before he left that '100%' of the information I'd been privy to was classified; 'top secret,' he called it; 'vital to our nation's security and prosperity,' and all sorts of nonsense! But I agreed, 100%; and I was free. I moved my office from Washington to Alexandria, and I stopped working for politicians.

"Here's what worries me, though, Kate: Not everyone who wanted out has fared so well. At least three people, one of them my lawyer pal, who had balked at what the conspirators were doing, and then tried to quit, wound up missing, disappearing! Two of them for over a year now! And the third turned up dead, Kate! Auto accident. Now, it could very well be coincidence; missing persons and fatal accidents happen. Neither of the missing men had families in the area. Maybe they just moved out of town, thinking they'd get blackballed here; not so farfetched. My friend was fed up with Washington politics *before* all this. Maybe he'd had enough, and returned to Canada, where he was born. I've got someone looking for him, carefully. And maybe the accident was really an accident. The police had no doubt."

He exhaled loudly. "But I have doubts… I've never seen a more sanctimonious, self-serving lot, Kate. They think they have *cause* to do what they're doing, and that God is on their side! …makes them extremely dangerous. So, if you're bent on saving your crop from this unholy war against it, proceed with caution, my friend – please!"

Kate promised BJ that she'd be careful as well as discreet, and thanked him for confiding in her. She was, indeed, grateful to him. Nevertheless, she was not impressed. She interpreted the information he'd given her, not as a startling revelation, but as a confirmation of what she already knew; mainly through Mike Anderson and his 'insiders,' including Henry Ford. Ford, after all, had warned Mike that Big Oil and its allies could very well resort to violence. She told Mike about the confirmation, but, much to her dismay down the road, she omitted the tale of the missing persons.

What did impress Kate, indeed, astounded her, during her journey to Washington that year had nothing to do with the anti-hemp conspiracy. Kate had walked into Liddy Burnett's office, in the second-story wing of Bobby and Liddy's home, and found Liddy smoking a cigarette, in a fancy holder, like a movie-star! Kate could not get the scene out of her mind:

Her jaw dropped; and Liddy burst out laughing.

"Don't worry, Darling," Liddy teased, "I only smoke Fairfields! And I'm not at all addicted, I simply enjoy my cigarettes. As does Bobby, on occasion." She whispered then, "Especially after 'intimacy!' Heightens the afterglow, Kate; you really must try it!

"Of course, we never smoke in front of Davey; it's not for children. But for adults, apart from 'addictive types,' why not? Indeed, I'd *recommend* it for working women." She took a drag... "Helps me concentrate," ...blew out the smoke, in Kate's face. "I find it relaxes, gives me a boost, and increases my effectiveness, at once!"

London, England, March, 1940:

Will, in pajamas, taking long sips from his first cup of coffee, watched for Kate from the dining-room window of their apartment. She was making her usual morning rounds; to the office to fetch the mail, to the bakery to fetch the baguette, and so on.

The Fairfield flat was tiny, compared to their American abodes, but cozy and well-situated; a ten-minute walk to Will's office, and along the way, a French bakery, and all sorts of specialty shops. It also featured a single luxury: a private bath, with a claw-foot tub and shower combination. Kate took a bubble-bath daily during their stay, and sang her heart out. She liked the way the tub amplified her voice. Will liked it too. He peeped in on her often.

"Perfect pitch!" he'd say, "You need a manager?" And she'd giggle.

Despite the mounting threats of war, the couple had been blissfully happy in England throughout the first half of their six-month stay. They loved London, second only to New York, with its theater, dining, museums and galleries; and they shared a fun-filled, loving relationship with James and his family, with whom they'd spent their first Christmas abroad.

At the same time, they were anxious to return to the States, to start a family of their own; and for Will, to initiate a private law practice in Richmond. Will would never say so to his parents, whom he adored, but he agreed with Kate that promoting the use of tobacco around the world was not the noblest way to earn a living, nor the best example to set for their children.

Will poured himself a second cup of coffee, and started to pace. Kate was late. He was about to phone the office, to see if she'd been detained there, when he spotted her, finally. He smiled broadly. She stood out so from the rest of the crowd. She was wearing an English raincoat and floppy hat, but her gait and her expression were thoroughly 'Yankee,' and she smiled as though she were proud of it! Will waved to her, but she never looked up, before disappearing into the lobby of their building.

He took a seat at the dinette table, and waited for her to climb the stairs.

She practically burst into the flat!

"You won't believe this, Will," she spoke elatedly, waving a little pamphlet at him. "It's from the Department of Agriculture, practically *beggin'* farmers to grow hemp! Says they need it for the war effort; rope for ships, transport, all kinds of things."

"And, look," she handed him the newspaper, "it all makes sense when you read the headlines: 'U.S. SUPPORTS WAR EFFORT,'"

Will was astonished as he scanned the pamphlet, and then the headlines, and back to the pamphlet.

"We still need a permit," she carried on, "but look here…" she pointed out a passage, "They're forgivin' the tax! Isn't that amazin'?"

"Incredible!" he agreed. "Your daddy sent this?"

Kate sighed dejectedly. "'Fraid not. It was Joe. Daddy wants no part of it."

"He'll change his mind, Darlin'. He's still bitter. Can't blame him. He'll come 'round. You'll see. Two, three years without a crop. That's a misery for a farmer. He's not goin' to pass up a chance to grow."

Kate sat down beside Will, and took his hand. "I've got to go back, Will," she said emphatically. "Even if daddy does change his mind. There's too much for him to do alone. Besides, I really want to be involved in this revival."

Will pulled his hand abruptly from hers.

"What about what I want, Kate? What we agreed we wanted? You were goin' to help me start a practice when we got home. Remember? Get me out of this business? The stench of tobacco?"

"I never used that language, Will," she rebutted, "I'm not that rude!"

"And we were goin' to have our baby. Finally! Remember?"

"Of course I do, Will! And I will help you, I promise, right after the harvest.

"And I hope we conceive the moment you're home, on the farm, as before, where we shall nurture him or her, full term."

"In the country?" he challenged her. "Where you can jump fences? Take regular road trips? An hour's drive, at least, from the doctor? You'd take those chances again?"

Kate gasped. "What are you sayin', Will?" she demanded, voice raised.

"I'm saying that you're behavin' selfishly again! And that it's gettin' to be a habit with you. And that I'm tired of it!"

"Let me set you straight, Mister!" she stiffened up and snarled. "If I were thinkin' only about myself, I would not be here, in Europe, in the middle of a war, sellin' cigarettes to soldiers!"

Will slammed his hand on the table, harder than he meant to – gave him a start, and sent his coffee cup and spoon clamoring.

Kate backed away from him, trembling. She'd seen him angry by now, a number of times, but never violent! It frightened her. She felt alone, suddenly, and far from home.

As angry with himself as with her, Will jumped up from his seat, jaw clenched, stormed into the bedroom, and slammed the door, again, harder than he meant to.

She collected herself, some documents, and a stack of money, threw them into her purse, grabbed her coat and floppy hat, and left the flat.

As Will sat sulking, and staring at his unpacked suitcase early that evening, the doorbell rang.

It was James.

"How ya doin'?" he asked Will

"Lousy!"

"I came to tell you that Kate's gone home, Will. She was up at the house, cryin' her heart out to Tess. We tried talkin' her into stayin', or at least makin' up with you first. But you know how stubborn she is!"

"Her ship's gone already? That's impossible!"

230

"She caught a flight to Lisbon; and then she's gettin' the Pan Am to New York."

"Sweet Jesus!" Will exclaimed. "She's flyin' across the ocean, alone, for the first time? I haven't even done it yet!"

"Me either!"

"I swear, James, she's the nerviest woman I know!"

"Nah, I heard her brother's wife takes the cake!"

"Yeah, Liddy – she's Kate's idol, of course. But Bobby says she's 'almost normal' now, since she became a mother."

James could not resist: "Well, therein lies your solution, my son. Get your woman with child!"

Will laughed; then sighed despondently.

"She was cryin'?" he asked.

"Yeah. Well, you scared her, you bully!"

"I didn't mean to; damn, flimsy English furniture!"

James changed the subject: "Tess says you should come for supper, 'bout seven."

"Tell her thanks, but I don't think so. Gotta finish packin'."

"You're not leavin' till late tomorrow," James argued. "C'mon Will, it'll do you good. Play with the girls a while. They're goin' to miss you, you know."

Will exhaled audibly as they walked toward the door. "Yeah, I'll come," he said finally, "see my girls. Then off to the war zone!"

"Oh, I almost forgot," said James, "Kate wanted me to make you promise to be careful in France."

"I'm always careful... See you at seven, James, bye." He tried to close James out, but James stuck his foot in the doorway.

"Not so fast! ...Kate made me promise to make you promise, on the assumption that you're a man of your word!" He grinned.

Will sighed, rolled his eyes, and smiled a bit. "Yeah, yeah, I promise. See you at seven, brother. Thanks!"

He closed the door, leaned against it, and ran his fingers along his jaw-line to the point of his chin a few times.

Kate was back in the Americas within forty-eight hours after she'd left Europe. She was in a state of utter amazement throughout the journey, depicting it in her diary as "an otherworldly experience." Still, she understood that this was only the beginning; the world was shrinking before her eyes. "What a glorious time to be alive," she wrote, "Praise the Lord!"

A while later she noted, as an afterthought: "What a glorious time to be a woman! There're two of us on board, unaccompanied, along with twenty men! We can do anything – Ha!"

All Kate thought about on the train ride from New York to Richmond, however, was Will, and their senseless spat: "Lord, I love him so," she moaned to herself. "Why do I quarrel with him? Why can't I just let him have his say? Accept it as another point of view? I've had conflicting viewpoints on certain issues myself, from time to time. Why, then, must I always be right, and make him wrong? Help me, Lord!"

She had wired Will's parents from New York that she was returning; and they sent Toby to the train station in Richmond to pick her up. The Katelyn dogs leapt and howled ecstatically at the sight of Will's car in the countryside, and again as their mistress exited the vehicle, knocking her over as she crouched down to greet them.

"Hello, hello, my friends, I'm so happy to see you, too. Yes, yes, my sweet boys!"

Nettie appeared on the front porch, smiling radiantly. "Missy Kate! What a surprise! Come, child!" she held out her arms, and Kate came running.

"Good to see you, Aunt Net. You're lookin' fine; praise the Lord. How's everyone else? ...Daddy?"

"Everyone else is fine, Missy. Well, your daddy says he's fine. But he's been cooped up in his room 'bout a week now, sorry to say. Don't think he's 'sick,' but he's 'down' – won't see the doctor, and he's not eatin' much. Says he just tired, Missy. All started when a 'Mr. Stokes' came callin' last week."

Kate's eyes welled up with tears at this report. Her mother had complained of feeling "tired, and achy all over," but no chest pains, a week before she died of heart failure. The thought of losing her father terrified Kate.

She thanked Toby, excused him; ran to Noble's room, and knocked on the door.

"What is it, Miz Nettie? I'm nappin'!" he grumbled.

"Sorry, Daddy, I'll come back later." She replied sweetly.

"Kate! Sugar! Come in, please!"

Kate peeped in to find her father propped up with pillows in the middle of his bed, in a robe, unkempt and unshaven, reading materials strewn all about. He slid over to one side, as she hurried in to give him a hug, a kiss on the forehead.

"I heard the dogs fussin', wondered who it was. What brings you home so early, Sweetheart? Nothin' bad, I hope?"

"No, I'm fine. But what's this I hear you've been sick, Daddy? That's not like you."

"I'm just tired, Kate, to the bone."

"I see. But what about that fellow, Stokes, who came around?"

"Darn! Meant to tell Miz Nettie not to mention that!"

Noble looked askance, brow puckered, clearly wrestling with his thoughts. Then he swung his legs over the edge of the bed, and gestured toward a chair in the corner:

"Pull up a seat, Kate. You're goin' to need it!"

He waited till she complied, exhaled with a groan, and began:

"Stokes is a private investigator. Will and I hired him to look into Anderson's death. So much about the police reports – conflictin', missin' information, made us suspicious.

"Well, Stokes didn't come up with anythin' solid at first. So, we paid him off, and forgot about it. But then he got another idea, couple of months ago, and called me. I had him follow up on it... Kate..."

He looked her solemnly in the eyes. She nodded.

"He found Mike Anderson, alive and well, in Texas, workin' for Gulf Oil!"

Kate stood up abruptly, horror-struck, then slumped back to her seat.

"No! Dear Lord!" she cried despairingly, holding her head, as if to protect it from further injury. "How could you, **Mike**? How could you do such a thing?"

"He was desperate, Kate," Noble responded, "his business failed; a mother and sister to support."

Kate began to sob, bowed her head.

Noble plucked a handkerchief from his nightstand drawer, tossed it into her lap, and carried on:

"He was in love with you, Kate. You knew that. His life here was a mess."

Kate looked up. "His family knew?"

Noble nodded. "Evidently. They're in Texas with him."

"But why, Daddy? Why would he fake his death?"

"Stokes thinks it was Hagar's idea. Figured he'd scare the rest of us, kill the Association... He figured right."

"Hagar? What would Mike be doin' with him?"

"I don't know, Kate. But Stokes said they met up, more than once. Stokes' theory is that when Mike realized that the hemp-oil deals were dead, he was willin' to do anythin' to get back in business."

"So, there were deals?"

"Apparently, everythin' he told you initially was true. It wasn't till all else failed, with respect to hemp, that he turned to Hagar, and stopped callin' us."

"And there was no accident?"

"His car went off the cliff, all right, he just wasn't in it."

Kate ran her hands through her hair, and down the back of her neck, massaging her neck and shoulders, trying to ease the tension. "I'm worn out, too, Daddy," she said, "think I'll spend the week in my sanctuary, clear my head."

She kissed him on the cheek, and walked slowly toward the door.

"I'm glad you're home, daughter," he said thoughtfully. "I feel better already."

She turned and blew him a kiss, albeit with the saddest eyes.

The next few weeks were the gloomiest Kate had known since her first split with Will. The would-be welcomed rains came, in torrents, to the cropless farm; and the frightful headlines from Europe culminated in the disastrous: GERMANY INVADES FRANCE.

Kate wrote to Will often, mostly at his office in England, and now and then at the Paris office. She opened with a few lines of upbeat news, from family or friends; the newest Davey story, an insight from Nettie; and closed with the same loving theme:

I hope you've returned safely to England, my Darling, and received my letters. In case you or the letters have been waylaid, however, I want you to know how sorry I am that we quarreled, and that I miss you more than words can say. I've made up my mind, Will, Lord as my witness, to change. I promise to let you speak your piece from now on, and 'to respond to you kindly, always' (Aunt Nettie's latest cure-all for spats), so that we never again leave each other angry, and suffering with regret.

The rain lightened up, finally, one morning, as the Burnetts' permit arrived from Washington. Noble, Joe, and Kate were in the barn with the doors open. The men were sharpening tools; Kate, in britches and boots, was grooming her horse. They saw Nettie come jogging back from the mailbox, all smiles. She was holding an umbrella in one hand, waving a piece of mail excitedly in the other.

Noble scowled, and took off for the house.

"Mister B!" Nettie shouted after him, "looks like you got your permit, just in time!"

Noble entered the house, and closed the door without looking back.

Kate joined Nettie under the umbrella. They gave each other a 'chin up' gesture, and followed him in.

He was sitting stiffly in his reading chair, in the living room.

He held up his palm toward them as they entered, as if to say, 'keep your distance!'

"I wouldn't get too excited, ladies," he spoke in a gruff, sarcastic manner; totally out of character, and making the 'ladies' cringe. "We've got no use for a permit."

Kate opened the envelope, which was addressed to both her and Noble, and skimmed the notice inside. "Well, we've got a permit, Daddy, right here. Good for the entire year; and I think we should put it to use."

Noble ignored her, directing his further comments to Nettie:

"Government can't be trusted, Miz Nettie. No tellin' what they'll do next. Revoke the permit, fast as they gave it, confiscate our crop, throw us in jail! No tellin'. They've got a madman runnin' the Bureau of Narcotics! What can ya expect? I'm not growin' till he's gone; just not worth it."

"Sorry to hear it, Mr. B," Nettie replied sadly. "My Joe's gonna be so down. He's been waitin' on this permit, just itchin' to grow some hemp.

"Specially now, whole world needs it. Joe's been readin' up on it; new bulletin. Says Germans are growin' hemp in their backyards, keepin' their navy in rope and such. Shame we can't do that for our side, awful shame!"

Both Kate and Noble were shocked at Nettie's comment. It was so unlike her to utter a negative word, let alone take a political stance. Indeed, Kate had asked Nettie on more than one occasion why she rarely read the newspaper, or took an interest in current events; and Nettie had replied that the news of the day was mostly bad, and that she already had enough praying to do.

Noble's heart went out to Nettie. She and Joe were such good souls; he couldn't bear to disappoint them. He refrained from saying he was sorry, however, for fear of crying.

Nettie read his mind, and eased it: "Don't worry, Mr. B, Joe'll be fine in no time; he gets over the blues faster 'n I do!" She laughed a bit.

Noble didn't laugh either – again, for fear of crying.

Kate took hold of Nettie's hand and gave it a squeeze. Then she turned to her father. She was about to hand him the permit, but recalling the incident in which he'd ripped up a licensing petition, decided against it. She placed the permit next to the lamp on his reading table, and crouched down to his eye level.

"Please reconsider, Daddy," she said kindly. "I'm itchin' to grow some hemp, just like Joe – I came home early to give you a hand. Remember?"

Noble looked away from her. "I'm not signin' that permit, Kate. You're wastin' your time."

Kate stood up.

"Well," she said decidedly, "if you don't mind, Daddy, I am goin' to sign it. Just in case you change your mind. Or someone in Washington comes to their senses – been known to happen under FDR, as you know."

"You'll do no such thing!"

"Daddy, I..."

"I won't have it, Kate," he interrupted. "I will not be their puppet! All of a sudden they need us? So we just forget what they've done? The schemin'? The lies? The endless greed? No! I won't forget!"

"This isn't about us, Daddy. Or them. It's about our country, and a world at war against evil, a cancerous evil, that's threatenin' the freedom of all. America has taken sides, and so must we!"

Nettie slipped quietly into the kitchen at this point. She could feel another storm brewing, indoors and out.

As if on cue, the thunder began to roll again as Noble rose from his seat, red-faced, and stomped toward the front door.

"Wait! Daddy, please!" Kate shouted after him. "You've lost your objectivity! You must put your bitterness aside; it's warpin' your judgment!"

He turned around, and came stomping back. "I've lost my objectivity? Have I? Well, I beg to differ, Kate. Seems to me I've gained my objectivity, finally.

"I was the one who trusted these politicians," he went on in a raised voice. "I was the one who took them at their lyin' word. Remember? It was me gave them the benefit of the doubt.

"I've learned my lesson. I'm done with politicians, all of 'em, and their business pals, n' puppets, n' pawns. Won't be usin' me again!"

"So help me, God!" he shouted, and swept the permit off the table with his hand, sending the lamp crashing to the floor, broken glass and sparks flying.

He slumped into his chair, and watched through the window, as the rains came down.

Kate was dumbstruck, but her expression spoke of her anguish.

"I'm a farmer, Kate," he tried to explain, "a farmer. They've taken my crop. Destroyed my livelihood."

"You're also an American, Daddy, proud, and honorable. No one can take that away from you."

There was a lengthy silence in the room. Nettie peeped in, having heard the crash. She saw Kate and Noble sitting quietly, locked in a stare; and she slipped out again.

"I love you, Daddy; and you're my hero," Kate affirmed, with great affection. "I know you know that. But sometimes a little reminder helps."

Noble's eyes welled up with tears. He covered his face, and began to sob.

Kate rushed to give him comfort, but he was too embarrassed for it. He held her off, composed himself somewhat, stood up, and walked hurriedly out of the house and into the downpour.

Grabbing an umbrella from the stand, Kate followed him at a distance, across the rain-soaked yard, around the house, to the fence surrounding the fields.

He began to heave and sob again at the sight of his barren land. Letting out a plaintive wail, he turned his back to the fence, leaned against it, and crumbled to the ground.

Kate dropped the umbrella and ran to him. He was ready now. She sat in the mud beside him, wrapped her arm around him, and cried with him in the rain.

He calmed down momentarily, and managed a faint smile.

"Mind if I get somethin' off my chest?"

"Please," she replied, right there in the mud. He seemed to lack the wherewithal to get up out of it.

"They came to me first, Kate," he murmured sadly. "I met them in Richmond, the night before the hearin'."

She knew what he was referring to.

"Anderson and Mead; they came to me first."

"I figured they would've."

"I lost my nerve, Kate. ...Ashamed to say it, but it's true."

"No, Daddy! You stood by your principles."

He shook his head. "It was fear, Kate. We had the bastards against the wall, but I couldn't do it. Couldn't take 'em down. I wanted to, but I couldn't. Couldn't say 'no' either; 'fraid of goin' either way.

"So I left it to you..." He started to weep again. "my little girl."

Kate dried his eyes with her sleeve, and responded in her most maternal voice:

"And your 'little girl' did exactly what you expected her to. She stood by your principles. And let me tell you what Aunt Net told me when I cried to her about it: 'That sorry story's *over*, Honey! No need to be fussin' 'bout it. Plenty of things to be happy for here and now.'"

Noble nodded in agreement. "She's always right, that Nettie," he said, straight-faced, "it's gettin' to be annoyin'!"

Kate laughed out loud; and so did he.

They realized suddenly that the rain had stopped, and that they were still sopping wet, and sitting in the mud. They laughed about that too, as they leapt to their feet, shook themselves off, as best they could, and headed to the house. After just a few paces, though, Noble stopped abruptly, and back-tracked to the fence. She joined him, without a word; and they gazed upon the emptiness in silence for a long while.

"What's on your mind, Daddy?" she asked him finally, although she knew full well.

"What do you say we grow some hemp, partner, while we've got the chance?"

"I say yes! I say hallelujah! Oh, happy day, we're growin' hemp!" She whistled, then, boisterously and obnoxiously, like a rough-neck at a ball game. Her brother had taught her how to do it. It had always embarrassed her mother, but 'the boys' found it hilarious.

The entire seven hundred ninety acres of Katelyn's plough-lands were sown and sprouting within the month. It was a joyful, satisfying labor of love for the hemp folk. At the same time, it was their most worrisome period, ever. Will had yet to return from Europe. No one had heard from him, and the situation abroad was worsening by all accounts.

On the first day of summer, Kate returned to the countryside from a short stay in Richmond. Four hounds, her two black labs, and two puppies; gifts from Nettie and Joe, grand-fathered by the ol' boys, and fathered by mutts unknown; ran to greet her. She got out of the car, smiling, and sat down on a tree stomp to pet and ruffle the animals.

HEMP

Noble approached on horseback, with Kate's horse, Georgie, in tow.

She smiled and waved at him. He waved back, and moved in close.

Kate stroked and sweet-talked with the horse a bit.

"Well, go get into your britches, partner, and hop on," Noble gestured toward Georgie. "We'll take a ride; fill me in on the gossip from the city."

"I can't," Kate sighed, half-grinning.

"You can't fill me in?"

"I can't get on a horse, Daddy, or a ladder!"

Noble jumped down, and embraced her delicately.

"We've got to get your husband out of that war zone," he stressed.

"I'm afraid to tell Will," Kate moaned, "after what happened last time. I'm terrified to even mention it. Think I'll wait till the baby's much bigger, or until Will's home safe and sound."

"Good idea," said Noble, and gave her another supportive hug.

Kate received a phone call from James the next day. She was out near the fence, chatting with Joe, when Nettie shouted for her from the French doors:

"Hurry, Missy! It's Mr. James, long distance."

Kate made it to the house, fast as she could, without running. She thanked Nettie, took the receiver from her, and dropped to the sofa, breathless.

"Callin' from a hotel in New York," Nettie filled her in.

"Hello, James, how are you, Dear Heart? How was your flight?"

"I'm fine, Kate. Flight was amazin'. You know, a bit scary, but absolutely worth it to get home so quickly.

"And how are you, Kate? Just spoke to my parents; heard the good news. Congratulations! Will's goin' to be over the moon!"

241

Kate breathed a heavy sigh. "I'll be fine, James, soon as he's home. I thought you had stayed behind to wait for word?"

"I did. Waited long as I could, Kate. Sorry to say, no word as of yesterday. Tess' ship gets in tomorrow, she and the girls. We'll be comin' in on the train from New York Wednesday; see ya'll by the weekend."

"Thank God ya'll 're safe... My prayers are answered. One more to go. What's keepin' him, James? Tell me what you know... Give me somethin' to picture, to pray for."

"There's every reason to believe he's safe, too, Kate, I swear to you. He's probably on his way to Switzerland by now, or there, watin' for a plane, or whatever, to get out. Must be chaos there, you know? Nazis all over France!?"

"But what held him up, James? Why would he stay, even one day, after the invasion?"

"Things got complicated, Kate. He was waitin' for some documents we bought. Forgeries, actually. American passports. Thirty thousand dollars worth!"

"Good Lord! Why?"

"You remember the Goldmans? Albert and Ana? He headed up our German division?"

"I do, of course! Lovely couple – Jewish." Kate smiled as she recalled her last meeting with the Goldmans. She and Will had dined with them at a restaurant in Munich. Ana was with child, well along; and she let Kate feel the baby kick – so sweet!

"Yeah. Well, Albert's been workin' our Paris office since we closed in Germany. Probably saved their lives, Kate, gettin' them out of there. It's horrible what's happenin' to these people. You have no idea.

"Their friends and families are literally disappearin'; hauled off to work camps, middle of the night, everything they own confiscated. No one ever hears from them again! For no reason; no crime, apart from bein' Jewish; which *is* a crime there, incredibly! Ana and Albert are frantic. His parents are missin', one of her brothers and his wife, and their boy, ten years old, gone! The stories comin' out of those camps are too ghoulish to believe, Kate, even for the Nazis! It sickens me to even think they might be true.

"Anyway, Albert spent his life's savin's on fake passports, for himself, Ana, and the two children. All he got was his... Contact made off with the rest of the money."

"No! Dear Lord," Kate moaned despairingly.

"Yeah, desperate times these... It was hell tryin' to find another forger. I followed leads all over England for two weeks. Will did the same in France – nothin'. He finally got lucky, though, right after the invasion; a 'legitimate' forger, if you can imagine! The last I heard, they were expectin' the papers any day, then gettin' out via Switzerland. Will said he'd call or wire me as soon as they were safe.

"We had to come home, though, Kate. It's not safe in England anymore either."

He started to cry, "I'm so sorry, Kate. I wanted to stay..."

"You did what you had to, James," said Kate, her voice breaking up too. "No one can fault you for lookin' after your family.

"And I want you to know, James, there is no doubt in my mind that Will is alive and well. If somethin' terrible had happened to him, I would've known it; I'm certain of it!"

"Thank you," he replied tearfully. "I feel the same way, like I would 'know' somehow. Still, it's a relief to hear it from you, Kate. I appreciate your straight-talkin'; always have. You're a good woman; I'm so glad you and my brother found each other."

"Me too," she murmured.

"By the way," he added, "you're not angry at Will, are you? For stayin' behind? Helpin' the Goldmans?"

She smiled through her tears. "Of course not, James. I'm proud of him. I'm just cryin' because I miss him so."

"He knew it!" James sounded almost gleeful. "He said you'd be proud of him!"

And they closed on that happy note.

As fall approached, Kate was entering her third trimester of pregnancy, her 'condition' was evident, and she was, as she put it in her diary, "basking in the clichéd 'maternal glow.'" Ironically, for one who had been described as 'beautiful' all of her life, she suddenly felt beautiful, for the first time.

She had yet to hear from Will, but she remained confident that he was safe, and making his way back home, albeit painstakingly slow. She understood, as she followed news of the war closely, that traveling in and around an occupied zone was complicated, at best, and that detours, delays, and detainments were routine. With Nettie's coaching, she had also given up worrying about Will.

"Seems to me you have a choice, Missy," Nettie would say. "You can spend your time worryin' 'bout Mr. Will; or, you can spend your time prayin' for him, and sendin' him love."

One of the ways Kate 'sent him love' was by nurturing a totally new attitude about her 'condition.' She began to think of it as a 'delicate' state, which needed special attention and tenderness, both of which she was naturally inclined to provide. Her behavior changed accordingly. She stopped all running, rough and tumbling, and accepted her in-laws' offer to loan her Toby, as a chauffeur, for the duration of her pregnancy.

Kate quite liked Toby, and found him courteous and competent as a driver, but it wasn't easy for her to call on him at first. She'd been driving herself around, in her own car for more than a decade, and took pride in it. It also made her feel guilty, regardless of her 'condition,' to have a paid chauffeur at her beck and call, especially in these hardest of times, when millions of people weren't getting enough to eat.

Lucy put it all into perspective, however, with humor, the first time Kate came to pick Lucy up in the chauffeured car. They were heading to Alan House, a special meeting with Mrs.

Alan. "My, my, how the world turns!" said Lucy with a laugh. "From 'Miss Independence' to 'Miz Uppity,' overnight!"

Kate laughed slightly, then pretended to pout and complain. "It's only temporary, Luce. I'm just doin' it to please Will... And extra protection for the baby."

"Just teasin' you, Kate; can't help myself. But you know I know you're doin' the right thing. Wouldn't expect less for my little niece or nephew!"

She leaned over to Kate's belly, and spoke softly to the baby: "Auntie loves ya, Darlin', don't mind her jokes."

The women heard Toby chuckling, barely, in the front seat, and they started giggling again. And that's the way it was, all the way to the soup kitchen.

Kate hadn't worked at Alan House since her pregnancy began to show. After she'd missed two Wednesdays in a row, Mrs. Alan asked Lucy if Kate had gone back to Europe with her husband. Lucy replied that she had not, and neither was she 'ill,' as such, but that it would be at least six months before she returned to Alan House.

Mrs. Alan's face turned pink, as she put two and two together.

"Well, give her my regards, please, Lucy," she stated guardedly, "and tell her I look forward to her return."

Lucy reported the exchange to Kate en route to the special meeting, adding emphatically, "I hope you're not lettin' her get away with that!"

Kate replied halfheartedly, "I suppose it's time to say somethin'."

Kate had arranged the meeting to notify Mrs. Alan that she was 'visibly' pregnant, and that, to avoid a fuss, she'd be volunteering at the Red Cross for the duration.

"Suppose?! You suppose?!" Lucy nearly shouted. "Your husband's supportin' her charity, Kate. And I know she knows it; she's just pretendin' not to!"

"My husband's supportin' her charity?"

"Yes! Anonymously! Which is why you're unaware of it! ...And hereby sworn to secrecy!"

Kate raised her right hand, and nodded. "Miz Alan's broke? She needs support?"

"Well, not 'broke,' in any real sense; she won't be dinin' at the soup kitchen! She's got enough to be 'old-people rich' for the rest of her days. And her heirs are set for life... But her philanthropic career is definitely over, Kate. If it weren't for my mama, and your 'Mister Anonymous,' Alan House would have been boarded up; was fallin' apart, you know, two, three years ago. That would've been the end for Miz Alan. Whatever her shortcomin's, the woman lives to serve the poor. It's what keeps her goin'. And that is why it peeves me so when she's disrespectful to Will!"

"I see," said Kate. "and I agree. But, tell me, Lucy Ledger, what else do you know about my husband that I don't know? ... And before you answer, let me remind you," she leaned her face towards Lucy's and tried not to laugh, "there's another advantage of havin' a driver. I can look you straight in the eye, point my finger at you, and tell if you're lyin'!"

Lucy cracked up. "Nothin'! That's it, I swear! And I would never lie to you, Sweet-pea; you know me better than..."

"Yes," Kate interrupted, "I do. Nevertheless, a lie of omission..." Lucy chimed in, "is still a lie!" and they laughed; and Toby chuckled, ever so lightly.

Mrs. Alan was genuinely thrilled to see Kate, and pretended not to notice the bulge under Kate's cloak, until it was removed. "Gained a bit of weight?" she said to her favorite volunteer, with a totally out-of-character smirk.

"I have, indeed, Miz Alan," Kate responded with a smile, taking hold of the elder's arm, leading her to a private nook in the lunch-room, gesturing for Lucy to follow.

"I am with child," she clarified, in a whispered tone, as the three took window-seats. "And that is why I've come to have a word with you. I'd very much like to continue volunteerin' here, at least for another month. But not if it requires denyin' my husband, with whom I am very much in love, and of whom I am extremely proud."

Kate went on to explain why she found Will so admirable: his humor, brilliance, kindness and generosity. It wasn't till after they were married, she said, that she learned from several persons in the know, that the Fairfields, Will, his brother and parents, were not just 'generous' with the locals, they were major American philanthropists. During the 1920's and '30's, they had given away more money, goods and services, most of it anonymously, than any of the famous philanthropic families in the nation. From the time Will was a boy, moreover, both he and his mother enjoyed participating in the giving, hands on, and did so, on a regular basis.

"As you may recall, Miz Alan," Kate offered an example, "Will was here dolin' out bread and blankets with his driver, and wound up with a black eye for his efforts?!"

Mrs. Alan nodded. "I can understand why you're proud of your husband, Kate," she spoke defensively, "but my concern, as a temperance leader, is the *source* of his money. I believe that tobacco is a destructive substance, and as such, is evil. I cannot help but conclude, then, that tobacco peddlers are doin' the devil's work!"

Kate responded confidently: "In this world, Miz Alan, the only certainty is change! What appears to be 'evil' today, appears to be a gift from God tomorrow. And vice-versa. There was a time when Christians received wine as a sacrament, the holy blood of Christ. And then came Prohibition, with millions of Christians denouncin' wine as Satan's brew. The same is happenin', as we speak, with my own precious hemp crop. Known for centuries as the plant of a thousand uses; touted yesterday as 'the road to recovery.' Today, despite its revival for the war, the official word from Washington is that hemp is the new 'evil weed'!

"People are smokin' it, gettin' drunk on it; and sellin' reefers of it to children... God help us!"

"And your point, Kate?"

"My point, Miz Alan, is that there's no point, or 'right,' in judgin'. Whatever you think you know about a person or thing is subject to change. If you keep that in mind as you go about your business, I think you'll find, as I have, that it makes your life, and the lives of those around you, a lot easier."

Mrs. Alan's eyes had gone from narrow, blue slits to big blue marbles. Her jaw finally dropped, and she looked as though she'd been told off.

Lucy had all she could do to keep a straight face; but Kate carried on intently:

"Some very intelligent people I know take great pleasure in smokin' tobacco, albeit in moderation, and therefore feel that it enhances their life. Who's to say they're wrong? Certainly not me! I've learned my lesson!

"Nor will I be judgin' you, Miz Alan. I ask that you allow me to speak the truth about my husband, should the subject come up, while I'm at work here. I'll give you a while to think it over. If you say no, I'll do my volunteerin' at the Red Cross."

"As will I," Lucy put in, "though my mama will carry on here."

"There'll be no hard feelin's, Miz Alan, I assure you," Kate continued. "We'll respect you, and appreciate your good works, as always. And pray that God continues to bless you..." She stood up, and smiled, as she noticed the crowd gathering outside the window. "And keep you... We leave you now," she nodded to Lucy, "as your 'children' are linin' up already."

Mrs. Alan's eyes, back to blue slits again, were watering profusely. She stood and held out her arms to Kate, and then Lucy.

"Please stay, My Dears," she beseeched them humbly. "I've learned my lesson too!"

The women rushed to huddle with her, and the three cried joyfully together.

"You were amazin', Kate!" Lucy remarked, straightaway, on their way home. "Absolutely amazin'! You're beginnin' to sound as wise as your 'Aunt' Nettie."

"Thanks, Luce. I'm prayin' almost as much as she does. It's exhaustin'!"

They laughed.

"You havin' fun?" Lucy asked.

"I am, always, with you!"

"Missin' Will?"

"Madly!"

"Worried 'bout him?"

"Not much. Sendin' him love instead."

"Good idea."

Kate stayed overnight with June and Lucy in Richmond, as she had an appointment with Dr. Linden the next morning, to be followed by a visit with Will's parents, at the Fairfield office building.

Kate's relationship with her in-laws was mutually loving and gratifying from the day they met. The Fairfield seniors saw in Kate what Will saw, immediately; kindness, intelligence, integrity, a sense of humor, and a boundless, natural beauty that emanated from inside and out. Kate found them to be delightful in every respect as well. But what impressed her most about the Fairfields, and was obvious to her from the beginning, was their brilliant parenting; born of great love and devotion, and firmly founded on a set of principles akin to the one she'd been raised by.

Oddly enough, prior to their introduction, the Fairfields had been wary of Kate. They had never seen their son so dazzled by a woman, and they feared, because of Kate's renowned beauty and the fact that her family was not "quite" rich, that she might be a 'gold-digger.' They put off meeting her, hoping that Will would get tired of her, like he did with all the others. And they told him so.

Will shook his head at them and chuckled. "Not rich enough, hmm? ...Since when did we get all snooty?

"All I can tell ya'll, is wait till you meet her; then we'll talk! She's a dream come true, this Kate Burnett! You'll be prayin' she never gets tired of *me*! And don't worry, I promise not to tell her we had this conversation!"

He was right; his parents admitted it. And *they* told Kate about the conversation; had a good laugh with her.

Joan, Jack, and son, James Fairfield, were catching up on a backlog of work, in the head office, on the top, fourth floor, of the Fairfield Building, on the morning Kate came calling. Their receptionist buzzed them from the lobby to say that Kate was in the elevator. The three looked at each other anxiously. James jumped to his feet, and headed toward the rear exit.

"I've got to go, he said. "She reads me like a book."

"Thanks, Son!" Joan complained. "What about us?"

"You warm her up, talk about the baby, gettin' together with the girls. I'll pop back in, though, I promise. I'll tell her... I still haven't figured out how... See ya'll."

He was gone, and a second later, they heard their secretary in the front room exchanging pleasantries with Kate.

Joan heaved a sigh.

"Perk up!" her husband advised.

She shook her head 'no.'

"That's an order!" he kidded with her.

She smiled at him.

"It'll be fine, Joan," he said assuringly. "I love you."

"I love you, too."

Kate knocked, opened the door, and peeped her happy face inside. "Hello, Dear Hearts," she said brightly, "I come with wonderful news!"

The Fairfields rose to greet her.

"Come in, Darlin'," said Joan, holding her arms out for a hug. "Tell us all about it."

Kate hugged her at length, and then Jack.

"We could use some good news," he let slip as they embraced.

Joan glared at him in disbelief behind Kate's back.

He mouthed a silent, "Sorry!"

Kate sensed the tension, and quickly pulled away. Head tilted, she eyed her in-laws curiously.

"Where's James?" she asked them. "Eileen said he was up here with you."

"Ah, he… Ah… He had something to do… But, ah… He'll be back shortly." Joan answered.

"Good! Can't wait to see him."

Kate's smile faded.

"Nothin' from Will, then? …Mom? …Dad?" She looked from one to the other.

They shook their heads sadly.

"Soon, though, Darlin', we're sure of it," Joan offered, and changed the subject:

"So, what about this good news, Sweetheart? …How's our baby comin' along?"

"Doctor Linden says all is well with 'our' baby!" Kate replied, beaming again at the thought of it. "He's strong, healthy, and in perfect position… And should arrive in seven or eight weeks, give or take."

Jack clapped his hands, and nearly shouted, "Bravo, Kate! Wonderful news!

"All we need in the meantime," he added pensively, "is for the daddy to come home."

"Please, God," Joan prayed aloud.

"And thank God," Kate affirmed, as if it were done.

Joan buzzed James, and he answered.

"It's Mom, here, Darlin'. Are you still busy? Kate's waitin' to see you."

"Hello, Kate!" he responded excitedly. "I'll be right there!"

Kate's face lit up.

"I declare, I love him like a brother!" she voiced her mind.

"He loves you too, Kate," Joan replied tearfully. "We all do."

James was there in a flash, as promised.

Kate ran to him, and they hugged, and said how good it was to see each other. (James and family had spent a couple weeks with Tess' parents, in Florida, upon their return, and had yet to visit with Kate). He asked about the baby; she asked about Tess and the girls; and then they came to the hard part:

"Can you honestly tell me you haven't heard a word about Will since you left, James? It's been nearly four weeks."

James pulled up a chair for her at the desk, and took his. He looked briefly across to his parents for help, but they were useless for it.

"All I can tell you honestly Kate, is that we believe that Will is fine; and we have no information to the contrary. However, the Goldmans wired England from Switzerland – they're safe, all four of them. Albert and the older boy got there first, we don't know why – a week or two ago; Ana and the young one were supposed to come the next day, but had just arrived – again, no idea why."

"And Will?" Kate whimpered, her eyes flooding with tears.

James sighed.

"No details yet, Kate. We got the main words, and filled in the blanks. Apparently the 'safe house' they were stayin' in; may have been the Fairfield warehouse near the Swiss border, 'bout 30 kilometers, was 'stormed' by Nazis; and the inhabitants, no one knows how many, or their nationalities, were placed under 'house arrest.'

"For what, James? On what charge?"

James shook his head, threw his hands out in despair. "Sorry, Kate, they didn't say. I've been talkin' to people I thought might have a clue. 'Harborin' fugitives?' 'Conspirin' with the Resistance?' Everyone said it depended on who was in the house, and from where."

Kate buried her face in her hands and moaned. James was sorry he had answered her question.

"Anyway," he carried on glumly, "after some time, they released the women and children. Thank God! But no further word about the men, includin' Will."

"The American consul is on it, Kate," Jack put in. "We know that for certain. Will may be on his way home as we speak. That's why we hesitated to tell you, to put you through the worry, especially now..." he gestured toward her belly.

Kate took a deep breath, sniveled a bit, and stood up. "I understand," she said calmly. "And I'm fine, truly. Thanks for bein' upfront with me, James... Mom... Dad," she gave them each a bit of a smile. "...I need to go home, now, and pray."

The dogs, as usual, announced Kate's arrival, and Nettie was out on the porch of the farmhouse waiting for her. They hugged and rocked for a long while. Nettie listened to her stories; the good news about the baby, the worrisome about Will; and then they prayed together in silence.

Noble was gone; off to Richmond that morning to spend a few days with June. Nettie decided to stay overnight with Kate, let her 'boys' fend for themselves. "Appreciate me more tomorrow!" said Nettie, with a laugh.

Kate was delighted. She had tried earlier to conjure up a vision in her mind's eye, of Will, his arms raised in exultation, standing in the light of God's love. That vision had given her comfort in the past, when Will was abroad; and whenever she mentioned it to Will, he'd say in his inimitable, half-jesting way, that he'd "seen the light and felt the power!" She was unable to hold the vision on that day, however, and spoke of her frustration to Nettie.

"No need to 'try' with seein', Missy," was Nettie's response. "You either see it, or you don't. It'll come when you're ready, and he is."

It came, in the midnight hour, and woke Kate out of a deep sleep!

"Yes!" she shouted, and bolted upright. She rushed into the sitting area, where Nettie was asleep on the couch, and sat down on the floor beside her.

"Aunt Net," she whispered.

Nettie opened her eyes, and smiled ethereally. "I saw Mr. Will," she said softly, "did you?"

"Yes," said Kate, with great relief.

"In the light?"

"Yes, Aunt Net, in the light!"

While Kate was looking for Will in the light earlier that evening, he was, in fact, struggling with the darkness. It was pre-dawn his time, the sky was pitch black, and the rain was pouring down. He was in his car, on his way to the Swiss border, low on gas, short one headlight, and unfamiliar with the road. Having just snuck out of the bathroom window of the company warehouse the Germans had seized, he was also scared – terrified. He'd taken nothing with him but the clothes on his back, his passport, a few francs, and the key to his car. He was due to be released by the Germans at nine a.m. that morning, but a voice in his head woke him at five, screaming, "Get Out Now!"

The rain let up finally as he came to the '30 k to Border' sign, but the road began to wind there and the hills grew steeper. Suddenly there were headlights in his rear-view mirror, approaching at high speed. "Damn!" he cursed, as he hit the pedal, to no avail; the car behind him was on his tail in seconds, and stayed there.

After what seemed like miles, he saw a homestead lit up ahead on the right. He signaled with his arm, floored the car, gained a little distance, slowed down to negotiate the turn, and skidded to a tumultuous halt. The car tailing him zoomed on by, as if to say good riddance! He cursed it again, turned off the engine, and sat there, panting, and sweating profusely, despite the chill in the morning air.

He thought about the Goldmans; wondered if Ana and the boy had made it safely across the border. He'd given her almost all of the money he had, and had tried to give her the key to the car as well. She refused the latter; said she was a 'terrible driver.' She and the boy would walk, she insisted, or hitch a ride. A young mother and a five-year-old, with American passports. Surely they could hitch a ride.

Kate wandered into his mind then, again. Every thought, it seemed, led back or forward to her. Her radiant face and the sound of her laughter were always there, in the wings, waiting to flood his consciousness. He needed to get home to her, make it up to her. He was determined never to fight with her again, *if* she promised to stop being so difficult! He chuckled at his own wisecrack. She would have too. Kate did not take herself too seriously; one of the million things he loved about her.

"I'm comin' home, Kate, Darlin'!" he shouted to the lady in the wings, and started the car.

He was no sooner back on track, however, when he spotted what appeared to be a road-block up ahead. He pulled over immediately, and turned off his beam. His heart started to pound at the thought that the Germans might be combing the countryside for him, but in the next thought, he reminded himself that he wasn't all that important.

He'd have to find a way around the checkpoint, nevertheless, or leave the car and walk the rest of the twenty-plus kilometers. There was a road map in his glove box, but he'd left the flashlight behind, and the dawning light was still too dim to read by. He decided to wait for the sun, give it a half-hour or so to brighten. If not, he'd hoof it.

In the meantime, he'd rest, try to ease the tension; it was draining him. He sat there for a while, rolling his neck and shoulders, and then laid his head back, and closed his eyes.

Drifting into slumber-land as the sun came up, he was abruptly awakened to the ghastly realities of war! A vehicle pulled up behind him, four car doors slammed shut, four pairs of boots came marching toward his automobile. He jolted upright, turned on the ignition, but it was too late. Four German soldiers were already in the car. They dragged him out, beat him to the ground with sticks and gun-buts; ignoring his pleas of innocence, in German; shouting over him, also in German, "American swine!" "Trouble-making, Jew-loving bastard!"

They continued to beat him until he fell silent, stole his papers and valuables from his pockets, kicked him into the ditch alongside the road, and took off, two in his car, two in their own.

Will lay there in agony, knowing he would die if he stayed in the ditch, but unable to lift himself out. To avoid losing consciousness, he kept his mind busy counting cars as they whizzed by. All of them, from what he gathered, were on his side of the road; the mad rush to get *out* of the war zone.

Kate's commentary on war, after they'd spoken with a woman who had lost her husband to the 'War to End All Wars,' but then lost her son to the current conflict, ran through his mind:

"It's a hideous thing, this killin' in the name of God or country. A pity human beings are still at it; war after bloody war, eon after eon... Not all that bright, or Christ-like, are we?" she asked more of God than of him; and in the next breath had the answer: "We must pray harder, Will! We must find a way to break the cycle!"

He remembered the passion in her eyes, the conviction in her voice at the end...

And then came the light, the glorious light; a shimmering, white, funnel-shaped luminosity, beaming down upon him from the heavens. It was inexpressibly beautiful and uplifting. He managed to crawl out of the trench, and close enough to the road to be seen.

Within seconds, another car pulled up. Two doors slammed shut; and the last words he heard before slipping out of consciousness were in English – heavenly, American English; spoken by two female good Samaritans:

"My God! That's Will Fairfield; from the safe house."

"Is he alive?"

They bent down, felt for his pulse.

"Yes!" said one, elatedly.

"We must stop the bleeding," said the other, "get him to the doctor, at once!"

Katelyn Farm, three weeks later:

Noble, out in the field just behind the house, inspecting his crop, was in the best of moods. It was a picture-perfect day – sunny, dry, and breezy, with deep blue skies, and scattered, fluffy, white clouds. The entire season had been ideal for growing hemp; just enough rain, mostly in the evenings, plenty of sunshine, but no scorchers; and the Katelyn yield reflected it.

As luck would have it, this back-from-the-dead, Depression-era crop would reap the Burnetts a healthy profit. Their new wholesaler already had the lot of it sold at a good price. The bulk of the fiber would be used, much to the farmers' delight, for the manufacturing of basics – rope, sacs, canvas and such; needed by the navy and merchant marine for the transfer of arms and supplies to the war-torn world.

The return of hemp to Katelyn had also affected the farmers in a personal way, inspiring them to make sweeping life-changes. They had always valued Nettie's counsel, and heeded her advice in problem-solving. But once a specific problem was resolved, they'd carry on with their old ways, which included a good deal of judging and worrying; the sort of behavior, Nettie advised, which disrupted their peace of mind, and got them into trouble in the first place.

As the reprieve of hemp became reality, however, it dawned on Kate and Noble, quite simultaneously, that they'd been wasting a lot of time "feelin' bad;" resenting what had happened before, dreading what might happen next, and passing judgment on those they believed were to blame. It was time, they determined, to break the cycle, to make Nettie's way – peace, joy and non-judgment – their way; and to set the example for others, as she had for them.

The event of Will's disappearance, and the confirmation of Kate's pregnancy strengthened their resolve. They sat down with Nettie, round the dining-room table, and plotted a new life-course. Kate, and to a lesser extent, Noble, had practiced the basic steps of the course from time to time; the idea now was to make each step second nature. They put the keywords of their plan to notepaper, and posted them as reminders throughout the Katelyn homes.

Step one was to 'keep to the "here n' now,"' as Nettie called it. "Now's where life is," the healer pointed out, "where we find God, love, and all that is real. The rest – what's gone, or yet to come?" She answered with a wave of her hand, "just a lot of thoughts in people's minds!"

The next step was to 'keep mindful of the joys of the present.' "Sad things happen here n' now," Nettie acknowledged, "There's a time to be sad. Don't want to get to stuck in it, though. Easy way out is to 'count your blessin's'. Write 'em down, when you're feelin' down; think about 'em. Little things sometimes bring great joy: the kind words spoken by a teacher, or a neighbor, the smell of night-jasmine in summer," she looked to Noble, caught a smile, "the sound of your best friend's 'hello' on the telephone, and her giggle when she hears it's you," she shared a giggle with Kate, as they thought of Lucy. "It's easy, folks!" she promised. "Make a list, before you go to sleep: 'Blessin's of the day.' Wake up in the mornin' with a happy heart! ...That was Mrs. B's secret, remember? ...She taught me so much!'"

Kate and Noble acknowledged; and the three reflected for a moment on the joyful, inspirational soul Kate's mother was. How one so blissful could have died so young had long been a mystery to the Burnetts. Nettie's explanation, Mrs. B hadn't *died*, just left her body, was making sense to them only now, as they, too, began to follow their bliss.

The final step, which wrapped it all up, was to 'go within,' to pray, meditate, and otherwise lose the 'self' in the oneness of All Being. The last came easiest for Kate and Noble. The Burnetts were a prayerful people, and as farmers, communed with nature daily. They were confident, thus, that maintaining a continual sense of oneness, and a prevailing peace of mind, was well within their reach.

Nettie tapped her heart. "The peace you seek lies here," she encouraged them. "The more you go within, the more peaceful you become, the more peace n' happiness you spread all around you. It's catchy, too," she emphasized. "You'll see! Your friends'll be doin' it. Children, big n' small. Mine were so high," she held her hand out just above the table, "already meditatin'! Before we know it," she gave them a wink, "whole wide world'll be goin' within! Might even find Mr. Anslinger talkin' peace instead of trouble on the radio!" She chuckled heartily.

Kate, and then Noble, joined in. They were already feeling uplifted, full of hope, certain that the course they were taking was guided; and that their actions would thus make a positive difference, not just in their own little world, but beyond.

At the same time, they held no illusions about the future of farming hemp. Indeed, they suspected that the war on hemp would be resumed the moment the war of the world was ended. Even if Anslinger somehow came to his senses, his new Prohibition seemed to have taken on a life-force of its own. The happy difference for the 'new thought' farmers was that it no longer worried them! They were too busy counting their blessings, including the current hemp revival, and eagerly anticipating the arrival of a new baby, the return of the baby's daddy, and the wedding of the baby's granddaddy.

Noble and June had made arrangements to wed at last. The affair would be small, family and close friends only. The ceremony; lunch, with their Temperance pals; and dinner, with the champagne crowd; were to be held at June's country estate. The date, set with love and prayers: two Saturdays after Will's homecoming.

Noble looked up, and hurried to meet Kate, as she walked out of the farmhouse toward the fence. She was glowing, holding her great belly tenderly between her hands, and practically singing "good mornin'" to her father.

"Good-mornin', Sugar," he returned, "How're you on this gorgeous day?"

"Ecstatically, over-the-moon happy!" she proclaimed, as she propped her elbows on the top rail of the fence. "And you, Daddy?"

"Likewise," he affirmed, with a nod. "Life is grand!"

They had reason to gush! Kate had received a letter from Will the day before. Penned in France, posted from Switzerland, the dispatch was more of a note, actually, single page, very brief. But Kate had kissed and savored every word:

Alive...Safe... Well... On my way home by the time you receive this... I love you, Always... P.S.: Saw the light, felt the power! Saved my life – no joke!

Noble observed the position of the sun in the sky. "Bit late for your walk today, hmm, Sweetheart?"

Kate said yes, without an explanation.

She trekked the quarter mile from the farmhouse to the new house and back every morning, weather permitting, at about 8:00. She was nearly an hour late on this day, however, having made up for lost sleep. A certain bark from her dogs had awakened her in the pre-dawn hour. She got up, threw on a robe, and rushed out onto her balcony, heart pounding, expecting to see Will's car pull up any second. Some time later, as the dogs had gone silent, and Will had failed to appear, she accepted that she had been dreaming. She was deeply disappointed, but determined not to let it spoil her mood. Will was coming home, she was certain of it, if not on that day, then on the next. She went back to sleep, picturing him running toward her, in the sunshine, feeling the warmth of his embrace!

"Where's Aunt Net?" she queried Noble, "Couldn't find her in the house?"

"She n' Joe drove over to Franklin farm, get some chickens. It's a bit far, but Franklin's are the best, Miz Nettie says; she wants to make gumbo."

"Gumbo? You sure?" Kate asked doubtfully. "That's Will's favorite… What if he doesn't turn up for days?"

"Well, she said if he didn't show up today, she'd roast the birds, n' buy a couple more when he gets here, which is sure to be soon."

Kate hesitated, mulled it over. "I suppose that's a good sign," she said. "Aunt Net usually knows before I do when Will's comin' home." She laughed then, waved good-bye to her father, and started down the road. "We're off to 'go within,' baby and me!"

"Ya'll be careful, now!" Noble shouted after her. She turned, nodded, and waved again.

On the way to the meadow, Kate decided to be *extra* careful, and make a change in her routine. Instead of treading directly into the wildflowers, where the bees had been overly abundant of late, she'd carry on to the picnic table by the lake. There was a panoramic view of the meadow from atop that table, and there she'd sit and 'chat' with the flowers. After that, she'd proceed as usual: up the hill to the house, and into the nursery, plop into the rocking chair, rock, and sing to the baby. Over to the piano, in the living-room, play a bit of "Katelyn," perhaps complete the bittersweet piece she'd been composing, her first, in Will's absence. Finally, to mommy and daddy's' room, picture Will asleep on the big bed, waking up with a smile at the sight of her...

"He's comin', my Baby," she'd coo to her unborn, "your daddy's homeward bound!"

Her plans changed again, however, as she approached the meadow, and looked up toward the house. Just above the hedge along the circular driveway, she saw what appeared to be the roof-top of a car parked under the portico. Her heart beating wildly for the second time that morn, she hurried, without running, to the foot of the drive.

It was Will's car! Or one exactly like it! She heard a door slam. "Must be him," she thought; "who else would be in our house?" She made out the top of his head, then, behind the vehicle. It was his hair, no mistake! It was him, coming down the hill, round the bend, the sun on his smiling face, as she had pictured it again and again! Will was home!

He'd been waiting for her at the new house, to surprise her, peeking out every few minutes. They told him she'd be coming right around eight. He was about to get in the car to go fetch her, when he felt her presence, and started down the hill.

"Kate, My Darlin', Kate!" he shouted, at the sight of her. And then fell silent, as he noticed her gait; it was different... And the loose smock she was wearing; not like her. And the cardigan that didn't quite close over her belly...

She saw the shock and joy on his face as he realized that she was with child, late term; the baby they'd been dreaming of! Clearly, no one had told him!

He signaled with his hand for her to wait; and she did. He came running, tears streaming, straight into her open arms. There were no words, only sighs, tender looks and caresses, as they wiped away each other's tears; and kisses in between, the sweetest kisses.

He bent down then, and softly held and kissed her belly, and put an ear to it, smiling, crying harder, as he heard the heartbeat. "Daddy's home," he whispered to the baby, "Your daddy's home!"

THE END

Afterword

Although this story is fictional, its depiction of the criminalization of the hemp-plant, as implemented by Harry J. Anslinger, a real person; on behalf of the barons of Big Oil and their anti-hemp allies; most notably, Andrew Mellon, a real oil baron, who also happened to be Secretary of the Treasury, 1921-32; is based on historical record, including actual Congressional testimony, from actual witnesses. Perhaps the most mind-boggling fact interspersed in the fiction is that Anslinger managed the war on hemp from the Federal Bureau of Narcotics, a division of the U.S. Treasury; to which Anslinger was appointed chief, by his uncle (through marriage), none other than oil-man/Treasury Secretary, Andrew Mellon!!!

When World War II ended, and with it the pressing need for hemp rope and canvas, Mr. Anslinger resumed his anti-hemp crusade with a vengeance. He eventually secured the outright prohibition of industrial hemp, which remains in effect in the United Sates to this day, to the unending benefit of the petro-chemical and logging industries, and the untold detriment of the rest of the world!

Given the virtues of hemp, Mr. Anslinger's quarter-century-campaign to outlaw the plant, world-wide, was incredibly successful, though incomplete, when he was finally persuaded to retire, under the Kennedy Administration, in 1962.

"History tells us that history is not to be ignored!"
Nini Martino, Zack DiLiberto, 9/29/09

265

About the Authors

Nini Martino has been an instructor/practitioner of yoga, meditative and natural healing for thirty years, and has written on these subjects throughout. Her first novel, "THE MYTH," (2005), co-written with members of Netti's Circle, a meditation group she founded, was also published with iUniverse.

Zack DiLiberto is an actor, musician and freelance writer, living and working in Los Angeles, CA. He and Nini Martino partnered previously to write the screenplay, "The Hemp-Man's Daughter," on which this book is based.

To contact the authors, go to: zackd9@hotmail.com or www.zackdiliberto.com